A Drowning at the Maze

A Spotlight Sleuth Mystery
Book Three

Rene Averett

Pynhavyn Press

Copyrights

Dedication

For everyone who has encouraged and supported my writing throughout my journey. I deeply appreciate you all.

Author's Note:

My main character is Isla Reed. The name is pronounced I-la with a silent "s" as in island.

Bat Corn Maze

A Drowning at the Maze

Principal Cast

Isla Reed – Theatre Owner and Amateur Sleuth
Henry Higgins – Theatre Cat
Daphne Chase – Isla's Great-Great Aunt, Ghost
Rob Fenmore – Real Estate Developer
Isolde Thornewood – Owner of Mystic Moon Apothecary
Andie Langley – PR Person and Office Manager
Glen Harper – Local contractor and handyman
Tara Laughton – Event organizer
Rolf Swensen – Carpenter
Katie Beldon – Sweet Shop and Glitz Lady Salesperson
Kevan Conklin – Sheriff's Office Detective
Giovanni Marcello (Gianni) – Town Historian, unofficial
Gary Denton - Set Crew Lead
Tony Kohn – Lights and Sound Technician
Steve Jones – Lights and Sound Technician
Melissa (Missy) Evans – Wardrobe Mistress
Louise – Director
Hallie Connor – Drowning victim ghost
Ryan Connor – Hallie's father
Bridget Connor – Hallie's mother

Other Players: Barbara Stevens, Carter Hamilton, Ellen Saspoura, Grace Allison, Cindy Babcock, Jeri Paige, Deputy Aaron Wilson, Betsy Fitzgerald, Sherie Kowalski, Deputy Diane Walsh

TABLE OF CONTENTS

Chapter One
A Haunting Proposal

AS I CLIMBED OUT of my Volkswagen Rabbit in front of Fairbourne Mansion, a brisk autumn wind sent gold and crimson leaves swirling across the gravel drive. Before I could shut the door, Rob Fenmore came striding down the front steps like he owned the place.

Which, apparently, he did.

"Isla Reed!" he called, flashing a wide grin and stretching both hands toward me. "Thanks for coming."

I met him halfway along the path, ignoring the handshake and slipping my hands into my jacket pockets instead. "Your note was cryptic. What's this about?"

"Oh, just an incredible opportunity for you and the Playhouse crew." He gestured grandly toward the sprawling house behind him. "I want you to turn this beauty into Arbordale's biggest haunted house attraction. The whole thing. Costumes, scares, the works."

That stopped me cold. I glanced past him toward the mansion's three turrets and crumbling Gothic balustrades. The place looked like something out of a Victorian fever dream—massive, ornate, and visibly neglected.

"And you want to do this… now?"

He beamed. "Closing went through this week. She's mine. Halloween's only a few weeks off, and I've already started the promo blitz—radio, TV, a billboard on Route 7. I'm telling you, Isla, this could be legendary."

The way he said it—*legendary*—made my neck prickle.

"Why us?" I asked. "Why the Playhouse?"

"Because you know how to create atmosphere. You've got the actors, the tech, the vision. And let's be honest—your theatre's shut down for plumbing repairs anyway. This is perfect timing."

He wasn't wrong. Our Halloween production had been scrapped while the bathrooms were being torn out and replaced. A remodel that was long overdue. I'd hoped to delay it, but when the toilets gave up the ghost for good, my hand was forced.

I took a slow breath, then glanced at the grand, crumbling house again. "Show me around and we'll discuss it."

"No harm in looking," I added under my breath as he gestured toward the wide steps.

Rob offered his arm gallantly. I breezed right past him.

The heavy front door creaked as I pushed it open—and a sudden draft met me head-on, a chill that rolled through like a curtain of icy mist. I flinched. Not from the temperature, but from the *wrongness* in the air. A moment later, Rob stepped in behind me and gave a visible shiver.

"Geez," he muttered. "Doesn't feel this cold outside."

"Old houses," I said, though the words didn't even convince me. The sensation lingered along my arms, crawling up the back of my neck. "They tend to hold onto things."

The grand hallway unfolded before us, dimly lit by streaks of late-afternoon sun slanting through dust-flecked windows. Straight ahead, a staircase loomed—broad, ornate, and worn with age—flanked by heavy double doors on either side.

Despite the stillness, something prickled at the edge of my senses.

The carved redwood walls, dark with time, seemed to lean inward slightly, as if they'd been holding their breath for too long. I didn't expect to feel anything unusual, but the air had *texture*—not just cold, but dense with a kind of hush. An imprint, maybe. Something left behind.

Then came the shimmer.

Faint, nearly imperceptible, but definitely there: a soft drift of lavender and gray brushing the corners of my vision. It wasn't strong, not like Aunt Daphne's presence sometimes was—but the sadness in it was undeniable. A sense of waiting.

A woman's face flickered in my mind—delicate features, a veil of sorrow in her eyes, peering from a shadowed window above.

Just an impression, gone almost as quickly as it came.

I blinked and exhaled. Rob had continued on, oblivious, pushing open the doors to the right.

"You've got to see this drawing room," he called over his shoulder. "You won't believe how perfect it is already."

I followed, one hand brushing the wall beside me—more for balance than comfort.

Although the lingering energy unsettled me, I shook it off. If there *was* a spirit here, how would they feel about the house being turned into a Halloween attraction?

As I stepped inside the drawing room, I gasped. It was equal parts faded grandeur and eerie decay—like a haunted house pre-decorated by time itself.

Deep blue wallpaper with silver flourishes clung to the upper walls, while dark oak wainscoting wrapped the lower half like a forgotten tuxedo. Near the corners, carved gargoyle faces peered from the molding, European in style, and definitely handmade.

At the far end, a marble fireplace dominated the room, its chipped edge hinting at either age or vandalism. Tall, shuttered windows stared blankly onto the weed-choked garden.

Dust veiled the velvet settees, while the chandelier overhead drooped with grimy crystals and layers of spiderwebs too thick to be fake. Honestly, we might have to remove a few for safety—but if the stage crew could preserve them with a little sticky spray, they'd be perfect.

Excitement flared in my chest. The realism was unbeatable. With a little effort—and maybe some ghostly cooperation—this could be the most authentic haunted house Arbordale had ever seen.

"What do you think?" Rob asked, watching me.

"It has potential," I said, reining in my enthusiasm. "But this is just one room. Show me the rest."

We crossed the grand hall to the dining room on the opposite side. I peeked in briefly—-a wide space, vaulted ceiling, faded elegance clinging to its edges like the last breath of a forgotten ball. Rob gestured toward the back. "Kitchen's through there. We can check it later."

Instead, he steered me toward the study, just off the drawing room. This one felt different—tighter, darker, cloaked in shadows that didn't quite match the lighting. Bookshelves lined every wall. An oversized oak desk dominated the far corner beneath a dusty window, and layers of dust smothered the scattered papers on a side table.

Even with daylight filtering in, the place looked like a scene already staged for a fright night. I could practically see a skeleton bursting out from between the shelves.

We climbed to the second floor. The carved banisters caught my attention—each gothic face along the railing unique, like small wooden watchers from a forgotten time. My fingertips skimmed them as I ascended, a mix of admiration and foreboding crawling up my spine.

The second floor held a sitting room, bedrooms, and two baths. I only peeked into a few, enough to get the vibe: abandoned, drafty, and layered in time. Still, something made the fine hairs on my neck rise. I squinted into the hallway. A blue-white shimmer hovered—faint, more suggestion than presence. But I didn't imagine it.

At the hall's end, a glass door led to a once-stately balcony. The other end opened into a conservatory filled with skeletal plants and broken pots, the scent of mildew trailing behind us.

Back on the front steps, Rob turned to me, beaming. "Well? Can you see it? The best haunted house Arbordale's ever had?"

I studied the mansion again—its jagged roofline, brooding charm, and eerie energy humming beneath the dust. A fright night for the locals... and maybe the spirits, too.

"I see potential. But for just a week? What's the plan after Halloween?"

He grinned like a man with aces up his sleeve. "Let's just say this is phase one. A little theatrical haunting gets attention. Then? Who knows. Restoration. Partnerships. Investors. Publicity, Isla— priceless."

"Mm-hmm." My arms folded. "And what cut does my team get for transforming your ghost palace?"

"Fifty percent of the gate, full reimbursement for setup costs, and I'll pay every crew member who signs on. Plus, twenty percent to a kids' charity—my choice."

I stared at him. That was... generous. Suspiciously so. "I'll run it by my crew. No promises yet."

"Fair enough." He fished a brass key from his pocket and held it out to me. "Take another look whenever you want."

As I reached for the key, a flicker of movement drew my eye upward. Perched on the highest turret, a massive black bird—either a raven or the world's largest crow—watched us silently.

An unbidden shiver danced down my spine.

Was it curiosity I felt from the house?

Or a warning?

Chapter Two
Maze of Intentions

I LINGERED A FEW minutes longer at the mansion, taking several photos with my phone to show the theatre crew. I'd snapped several inside as well, but they didn't capture the overall magnificence of Fairbourne Mansion,

Still, while I drove the short distance down the road to the Alford farm, apprehension tugged at me. I hoped Daphne could provide some information about the house and its former residents.

A big painted sign bedecked with cornstalks and pumpkins announced the Alford Farm's Annual Corn Maze, coming on October 15th. The maze would run until Halloween, which meant I had my work cut out for me if I took on the mansion project as well. Although I admitted, the maze wasn't as big a project from my perspective.

The Alford family did most of the work, leaving the design, theme, and decorating to the committee, which Meryle Alford chaired with enthusiasm and openness to all suggestions.

As I pulled into the parking area, a paved section of the farm's frontage area, I spotted Rob already chatting with a small-statured woman I didn't recognize. His hand gestures kept returning to the beginning of the maze, which was about twenty feet behind him. I strolled up to the group of committee volunteers with barely so much as a nod at the man.

"Isla, hello." Isolde Thornewood, the owner of Mystic Moon Apothecary, an herb, crystals, and potions shop, greeted me with a warm smile. Rumors suggested she practiced witchcraft and led a local coven.

So far, I'd not explored the supernatural in that area, but sometimes, she appeared to know more about me than others did. Now and then, she squinted at me, making me wonder if she could see my aura, and did she know I could see them also? She reached her hand to take mine in hers, and I half-expected her to flip it over to read my palm. Another talent of hers, palm reader and, oh yes, Tarot cards stood out as her specialty, especially at fairs and mystic gatherings, like our corn maze.

"We're just getting started, dear," she stated as she released my hand. "It appears we already have a problem." She tilted her head toward the woman talking so animatedly with Rob.

"Who is that?"

"Her name's Andie Langley. She's apparently Mr. Fenmore's office manager and does some PR work for him. Looks like she's got a bee buzzing her butt now."

I watched for a few moments as the Langley woman waved her arms around and pointed to the maze. Near the lead-in path to the newly cut corn, Raymond Alford stood with his arms crossed, a frown on his face. I turned back to Isolde. "What happened?"

A breeze grabbed the end of her lavender-colored scarf, flipping it in her face. She caught it and tied it back around her neck where it sat like a lump on the neckline of her fluttering green maxi-dress. "Tumbling moonrocks, the woman is making a fuss about a missed curly cue on the maze design. Can you believe it?" She shook her head in disapproval.

So that was why Alford was frowning. He'd spent the last three days cutting the intricate bat design into the field only to have the lack of gratitude manifest in the woman's complaints. I observed Rob's face turning a radish color at her tantrum. He frowned and his cheek tightened as he said something to her that shut her up instantly. Would I have to work with this woman if I accepted the mansion haunting job?

"Was it important to the design?" I couldn't see how a small circle might be a big issue in the overall design. It wasn't like anyone could see the bat's wings unless you were in the air above it.

Isolde shrugged. "Must be to her, but I don't think it's enough to warrant her reaction. Let's join the others, shall we?"

"Of course," I agreed and followed her to the group of three other committee members who had the plans out, studying the design.

Glenn Harper greeted me with a big smile and a murmured, "Hi, Isla," A local contractor and handyman, he'd done a little remodeling at the theatre two years earlier when I'd needed to replace some wooden trim around the statue recesses. I had loved his splendid work in blending the new with the old.

After I greeted him, I turned to Tara Laughton, the event organizer, who was handling this maze. In turn, she spoke quietly to Meryl. All I heard of the conversation was "nothing to worry about ..." a muffled sound, then "… rearrange."

Meryl lifted a hand to wave to me, then Tara turned around, her tan cardigan swinging in my direction. "Good, you're here, Isla. Now, if we can get Mr. Fenmore over, we can get this walk-through underway." Her head swiveled from person to person, while her short dark hair in a layered bob, flew free and resettled perfectly into place. Kate Spade eyeglasses completed her business look.

She waved a beckoning hand to Fenmore, who caught the movement and set a quick pace to join us. Then, she turned to count heads and added, "Has anyone seen Mr. Swensen?"

I knew the name, but it was attached to a Norse god-like man I'd met at the Vineyard Pub while I was investigating in September. Could it be the same man? I knew he was a carpenter, and I'd hoped he would come by the theatre, but he didn't. No one spoke up, so we prepared to begin the survey of the maze.

Tara held up the map. and I noticed an inked red circle marked surrounding the missing swirl.

"Now, I've marked each location where our sponsoring vendors will have a goodie station. This will vary by day since some of them only agreed to one week and not the entire run. Each vendor is responsible for decorating their area and providing handouts." Tara paused to catch her breath before addressing me. "However, we have six locations that are spook stations where we will set up creepy scenes that move or we have actors scaring them. Is that correct, Isla?"

"Yes, I have a dozen volunteers who are sharing the duty, and the tech crew will handle the decorating and special effects." I hoped the techs wouldn't be needed the whole time, or it would make doing the mansion more difficult.

As I'd responded, Rob Fenmore shot a quizzical look my way. I shrugged my shoulders. I guessed he was thinking similar thoughts.

Raymond Alford opened the gate to the maze path and ushered us through. Andie shoved her way to the front of our small group and set her pace with Tara's.

I was a little farther back and as I came up, Glenn stepped beside me, a big smile on his face and muttered, *"Come the light of day, the ghosts will fly away."*

I glanced at him, "Spouting poetry, Glenn? Did you just make that up?"

He winked at me and said, "Byron."

I nodded and moved ahead, slipping in behind Andie and Tara, close enough to hear Tara's comments when we came to each station. I had my phone out, ready to make verbal notes as needed, so I had a clear idea of what the tech crew and the actors would need to do.

Stepping onto the initial path, we strolled along the firmly packed soil that had not been planted since the first maze was constructed. Raymond chose to keep it open and clear, so the four-foot-wide path was easy to navigate into the cornfield. The workers had picked almost all the ears along the pathway, but a few stragglers remained on the stalks. The maze would officially open next week, allowing enough time to complete the harvest.

Once past the entry prelude, we turned into an arcing path at the tip of the bat's left wing. Tara held up the drawing to point out the entry on it, so we had a clear idea of where we were heading. The first station came up within the initial curve.

"This will be the welcome station," Tara announced. "The Chamber of Commerce will have autumnal signs and welcome candies, like they did last year. They might have a 'magic' potion or spell to protect the adventurers. That's all being coordinated by their point person."

Who was not in this meeting, I concluded. Typical of the chamber to skip informative meetings.

"Do they know where they will be in the maze yet?" Isolde asked.

"Not yet. We haven't distributed the map to any of the vendors. They all have a general idea of the points and what they can expect, but I haven't sent the detailed map with their assigned locations yet. I wanted to go through them all today, so all of us agree with the layout and spook station locations."

"When will the vendors be setting up? Some of us may need more time than others." Andie studied the ten-foot opening in the corn as she spoke. "This is kind of a small area."

"It's the size we always make, and it was detailed on the application," Tara answered through gritted teeth. "The vendors can set up the afternoon before the maze opens or between eight a.m, and noon on opening day. The maze will open at one p.m."

"I suppose that will work." Andie scrunched up her nose and mumbled something under her breath that I couldn't hear.

"Let's move on." Tara strode forward like a tour guide, and we followed, tripping a little now and then over crushed corn stalks.

The next two stations were assigned to the Garden Center and 35 Ice Cream. Easy, so far, each of those had their own plans for the space and would be doing something spooky, but undisclosed.

The next stop was one called Spiral Misdirection, where my tech team would install the special effects to create an optical illusion or rotating mirror setup. One of the *spook stations*, featuring flickering lights and a sudden reveal—a costumed "mirror twin" stepping out from the shadows,

"Oh, that will be exciting!" Andie clapped her hands. "You mean the twin will look exactly like a mirror image of the person, right? That is so clever. How can we work that into the advertisements?"

Tara frowned. "We're not going to give away the spooky aspects in advertising. We can hint but not show anything."

"Same old droll stuff. Honestly, last year's promotions were adorable—but we need real sophistication this time. Something actually effective."

Tara's lips pressed together tightly, and her eyes narrowed. "We've always had an excellent turnout, Andie. Our traditions matter."

Andie's smile faltered for a beat before hardening into something sharper. "I'm just trying to keep things from looking like a junior high harvest fair, Tara. If we're not evolving, we're dying— especially in public events."

Her tone was sweetened with condescension, like a poisoned truffle. I winced inwardly. Tara's jaw clenched.

I turned my gaze to the ground, toeing another wayward corn stalk. Andie played with fire now. A sharp breath from Tara informed me that she was under control as her tight voice called out, "Let's continue to the next station."

And so it went, one by one, we reviewed the stations, each defined by whoever would be decorating. We'd covered almost half of them when Rolf Swensen caught up with us.

"So sorry, I'm late. I had an emergency call." His face was flushed from the run through the start of the maze to find us.

"Well, I'm glad you finally made it. To those who haven't met him, this is Mister Swensen." She waved a hand at him. "He's a carpenter and has volunteered to help us out with signage."

"Splendid," Andie spoke up, her petite frame forcing her to look up at the tall man. "We can use some clever signs through this maze. So far, it's had more dead ends than a road in Mississippi."

Tara shot a glare at her. "Mazes are supposed to have false trails."

"Well, they can get truly lost in this one." Andie huffed.

"I think it looks about right," Rolf cut in. "I only got onto a dead end one time while catching up. But I can certainly craft some signs. We could even do an Irish Sign in old Norse."

"Huh?" Glenn said it before any of the rest of us.

Rolf smiled, the edges of his eyes crinkling. "It's a novelty thing. Irish signs often point to paths that don't exist where the sign is placed, but if you go down the road a way, you find the road. The old lettering will make it tricky to decipher and be interesting."

"That sounds terrific." I threw in my two cents, and Rolf turned his gorgeous smile on me.

"Isla, isn't it? I had planned to stop by the theatre, but the timing hasn't worked out."

Tara took control again. "Okay, we will work the signs out, so let's get going again." And she strode off on the path once more. We came to point seven and that was another spook station, this one with an animated scarecrow. Again, I made notes, but I noticed Andie also scribbled something into a day minder she'd brought along. Why? I wondered.

"I can help build the frame for the stuffed scarecrow to stand on," Rolf volunteered as he came up next to me, close enough to whisper.

"Great." I nodded my head and continued to the next spot, then the pond came into view. We didn't include the pond for several years, not after a tragic accident a few years earlier when a young girl had fallen in and died, unable to get to the small dock.

The theatre's sponsored station, we planned to light up the pond and create an eerie fog drifting over it. My tech team overworked their brains figuring out spooky prospects for this.

I walked along the pond's edge. The Alfords installed fencing around the pond after the accident, but it remained somewhat murky. A dock toward the northern end jutted into the water a few feet, enough to reach the rowboat tied to it. Cattails, lady fern, and other water-loving plants surrounded the edges in most places. Once we got underwater lights and firefly effects on the little lake, it would be enchanting.

For our maze event, the sponsors would provide dozens of plastic ducks with numbers painted on them, which would float in the water, waiting to be scooped up in a net. Each guest who catches one wins a prize based on the number with only three ducks having grand prize numbers.

I strolled down to the water's edge where the rushes mingled with the ferns. A bit of movement caught my eye, and at first, I thought it was a fish. Then it bobbed up—a mottled flash of yellow drifted back into the plants before emerging again.

A rubber duck, its colors faded and covered with pond slime, floated forward like it had a purpose. Almost in reach, I edged closer, trying to avoid stepping into the soft shoreline. Bending low, I stretched my arm to grab it. As my fingers touched the duck's grimy surface, a sudden chill brushed my neck.

The air changed. Still. Heavy.

Somewhere behind me, the softest *plop* broke the silence, like another toy shifting through water. I froze. For just a heartbeat, it felt as if something unseen had been watching from beneath the surface.

I shook it off. "Don't be ridiculous," I muttered. But my foot slipped in the mud, and I emitted a startled squeak as I lost my balance—just as a strong arm snatched me backward.

"Gotcha," Rolf said, holding me steady while I tried not to drip duck pond on his boots.

He held onto me a few more moments, allowing me to steady myself on dry land with water filling my thrift store running shoes.

"Ew," I muttered and turned to face my rescuer. "Thanks, Rolf. I misjudged that stretch."

"Yeah, you did. Good thing I was watching you, huh? What were you after?"

I held up my prize. "This."

"An old rubber duck?" The expression on his face was priceless, like I'd lost my mind to go fishing for it.

I nodded. "Yeah, it looked like it needed rescuing."

Rolf's eyes squinted with a puzzled look in them. Or he really thought I was crazy.

"Well, it's unusual. Um, we haven't had the duck grab from the pond in several years, so I was surprised to find this little guy here." What I didn't say was that holding it now felt eerie, like something was amiss in this little lake. Like the duck really did want me to rescue it. The teenager who'd died a dozen years ago wasn't the first to drown here. Could it have a lingering spirit?

Rolf shrugged it off, but retained his doubtful face.

I squinted to observe the water for a few moments, not detecting anything with an aura, but something didn't feel right. Another question for Aunt Daphne.

Rolf and I rejoined the group, and we continued to the next two spots until we came to the thirteenth station, which was on one of the bat's spines and Tara announced this station was co-sponsored by Beldon's Candy Shop and Glitz Lady Cosmetics. Katie's businesses— both of them! She didn't tell me about that. What was she going to do at her booth?

We turned to move to the next station when an unexpected fellow joined us. "Gianni, what are you doing here?" I said in reaction to seeing the town's unofficial historian.

Curly dark brown hair peeked out from under Gianni's straw hat when he tipped it to me and offered a big smile. In his mid-fifties, he'd spent years digging through old papers and documents to piece together the story of Arbordale. Aunt Daphne had adored his enthusiasm and sense of humor, which often tended to offbeat. "I heard through the corn whispers that the first walkthrough of the maze was happening now, so I hurried over to get a first look. I do it every year, if you recall."

"Of course you do," Isolde chortled, stepping into the conversation.

"You're all wet." Gianni noted the state of my shoes and jeans.

"I slipped into the pond, but luckily Mr. Swensen caught me before I slid all the way in."

"It's Rolf," the big man answered, holding out a hand.

"Giovanni Marcello, but everyone calls me Gianni." He took Rolf's hand for a moment, then shook his head in a disapproving way. "Do be careful around that little lake. Some bad things have happened there."

"A couple of drownings," Ray Alford sputtered. "Careless girl six years ago decided to jump in and got caught on a branch near the bottom. The other? A questionable one long ago. Could have been murder or suicide."

"Yes, I know about those. The first victim was Emily Fairbourne Grant, a niece of the mansion owners," Gianni replied. "But there are other reported incidents with the lake. I believe Ray put the fence around it for good reasons."

"Incidents?" Andie spoke up. "What kind of incidents? Isn't this a safe place? We're going to have people with children going through the maze." She turned to glare at Tara. "Maybe you shouldn't have included it in the maze design!" Her voice rose at the end until it reached a shrill C.

Tara's lips twitched. "Nothing has happened since the girl's accident and the CofC received many comments from people wanting it back in the maze. At night, the view is spectacular with lights and torches."

"Truly magical," Isolde sighed and gazed into the distance.

"Well, welcome, Gianni. Let's move along now to get this done." Tara turned her back on Andie and strolled along the path, expecting us all to follow—which we did.

"I regret not getting here sooner, but I'll walk along the design alone to see if I can determine what it is without seeing the sketch." He seemed as amused by the maze as the children did.

"I'll go back through it with you, Gianni." Isolde volunteered and her eyes held a bit of sparkle at the prospect.

"Delighted." His brown eyes twinkled as he dipped his head to her.

Did I detect a budding romance or was he just playing along with the witch?

I noticed Andie and Rob had lingered behind us and now Glenn joined them. They appeared to chat about something intensely with a few hand gestures helping the conversation along. Perhaps Glenn was going to do some work for Rob, possibly at the mansion. Whatever it was, Andie wasn't left out of the conversation.

When we came to the last station, Andie pointed at the tip of the batwing and loudly stated, "That's where the extra curl was omitted. We were going to use it in conjunction with our display!"

"It's a moot point, Andrea," Rob spoke up. 'We can work around it, so let's just move on."

Her face reddened. "Fine. All the work I put in—"

"Can still be done, but in a different way." Rob glared at her, and she backed down, although like a terrier tugging at her leash and wanting to rip into someone.

All this building tension slipped into my awareness and crept up my spine, threatening a headache.

Tara turned with a bright smile and declared the walk through a success. "I will send out details to our vendors in the morning. Isla, let me know what your techs will need to build the special effects. Rolf, same on the signage; just send me a list. Glenn , we can talk about your construction ideas at the office."

"Can I show you my marketing ideas?" Andie stepped forward to ask although her expression read "don't' say no."

Tara took a moment, then smiled. "Of course, you can, Andie. I look forward to seeing them."

Walking back to my car, I glanced over my shoulder at Andie Langley, still vigorously talking to a clearly irritated Tara. A shiver ran down my spine—one that had nothing to do with the cool autumn air. For a fleeting moment, I wondered just how deep those tensions ran, and how dangerous they could become.

Chapter Three
Plan for the Maze and ...

"SO, THE MAIN CHALLENGE for the maze is the lights in the water, right?" Gary asked, lounging on the stage floor and propping himself up on one elbow.

"Well, that and the fog generator, and the ghost rising out of the water," I said.

We were circled up like campers at a bonfire—minus the fire, of course—on the theatre stage. I'd called the meeting to go over the haunted maze's tech stations. Gary, Steve, Tony, and the rest of my crew had already worked out the scare designs, but I wanted clarity before we committed.

"Power dem with solar. Less risk," Tony offered in his thick Brooklyn accent. He stood as usual, jittery with energy, hands tucked behind his back like a coach waiting for halftime.

Steve nodded. "I'll test it. Safer if no one's fiddling with water lines and electricity in the same breath. How are we lighting the water horse?"

"You guys came up with that bit." I raised a brow. "Don't you have a plan?"

Tony snorted. "Just bustin' ya, boss. 'Course we got it. Da mirror twin's easy. Right, Gary?"

"Yup. Basic haunted-mansion trickery. Like the Disneyland ghost ride." Gary scribbled something in a spiral notebook, old-school style. I liked that about him.

I took in the circle of familiar faces. Besides the tech team, I'd invited a few actors, our accountant Barbara, and Louise, the latest director to join our fold. If we were going to take on Fairbourne Mansion for a haunted house, everyone needed to be looped in.

From the open lobby doors came the echo of construction work—plastic drapes, tools, and clanging sounds. Our bathrooms were getting a full remodel. The only working one was in my upstairs apartment, which made this meeting feel a bit like a countdown.

I drew a breath. "So, here's the scoop. The theatre's not usable right now, but we've got an opportunity. Rob Fenmore offered us Fairbourne Mansion for a Halloween haunted house event. We'd get fifty percent of the profits."

"Only fifty?" Barbara's eyebrow arched.

"Fenmore's donating twenty percent to a children's charity—he says we can help pick which one. The remaining thirty is for promo and advertising. But we'd be reimbursed for materials."

"Still sounds like we do the work, he gets the glory," Missy muttered.

"I'm negotiating. Maybe we push for sixty. But even at fifty, it's a big payout—and it keeps us active while the theatre's shut."

"Fairbourne, huh?" Carter Hamilton rubbed his jaw. "Isn't that place haunted?"

"Allegedly," I said. "But that's part of the charm, right?"

Everyone started talking at once—some excited, some skeptical. I held up my hands.

"We'll check it out tomorrow—Gary, Tony, Steve, and Ellen are coming with me. If the house looks workable, we'll go forward."

Missy tilted her head. "Will *she* be involved?"

She didn't have to clarify. Everyone knew who she meant. I'd told them about the maze tensions.

"No," I said. "Fenmore promised full creative control. And I won't be deferring to Andie Langley."

Murmurs of approval rippled through the room.

Barbara finally spoke. "It's risky, sure. But we've always pulled off miracles. And if Isla believes we can do it, I'll change my vote."

Carter grinned. "Then I call dibs on the vampire costume."

Laughter broke the tension.

"Great," I said. "We'll scout the house in the morning."

Missy wagged a finger. "If we're doing this, I'll need help with costumes."

"Noted," I said. "Maybe Katie can help with Halloween makeup through Glitz Lady."

"Hey!" Grace piped up, her voice uncertain. "Can I be a banshee?"

"You'll make a darling one," Missy cooed. "We'll work on your wail, sweetheart."

LATER, I CLIMBED THE stairs to my apartment just as Katie arrived with a blue-bordered bag from Dimitri's Deli.

"I brought lunch." She held it up. "Gyros. Jimmy added something special for you."

"Baklava?"

She grinned. "Let's eat upstairs. Still too much construction up front?"

"Yup. Patio okay?"

"Perfect."

Higgins met us at the door, purring up a storm. Katie gave him a chin scratch and followed me through the kitchen.

We settled in with sodas and the scent of lamb and spices. A peaceful moment. Until I brought it up.

"Why didn't you tell me about your booth at the corn maze?"

She looked up, chewing. "I haven't seen you. Did I need to?"

"No," I said. "I was just surprised when I saw Glitz Lady on the sign. And Beldon's."

Katie blinked. "You seemed too busy lately to talk. I figured you'd find out when you did."

I hesitated, emotions I hadn't sorted prickling. "I guess it just... caught me off guard."

Her voice stiffened. "I don't need your approval to run my businesses, Isla."

"That's not what I meant."

"Then what *did* you mean?"

I stood too fast, the scrape of my chair loud on the patio floor. "Forget it. This is stupid."

I moved to the railing, staring out at Arbordale's rooftops. The bite in her tone stung more than I wanted to admit.

Behind me, Katie was silent.

I turned back. She sat rigid, picking at her pita.

"I'm sorry," I said. "I think I took it personally when I shouldn't have. I've been so buried in all this maze and mansion stuff, and I miss hanging out like we used to."

Katie looked at me for a long moment, her guard slowly lowering. "I've missed you too, Pix."

"Truce?" I held out my pinky.

She hooked hers around mine. "Truce."

We finished lunch, the tension thawing like ice in the sun.

Then she pulled out the Glitz Lady bag.

"Now," she said, waggling her brows, "wait until you see the glitter rot."

LATER, AFTER FEEDING HIGGINS and closing my laptop, I stepped out
onto the patio with a crocheted throw draped over my shoulders. The autumn wind carried a crisp bite, but the view over Arbordale glowed with soft amber lights—porch lanterns, flickering window candles, and the faint glint of Halloween décor already showing up around town.

I closed my eyes and let the chill settle into my skin.

Then I called out softly, "Aunt Daphne? If you're around, I could use your advice."

Sometimes she answered immediately. Other times, she didn't show up for days. Ghostly aunt or not, she had her own schedule.

I waited, watching Higgins paw lazily at a wind-blown leaf near the flowerpots. Then, all at once, he froze—tail bristled, ears pinned, eyes wide. He gave a low, grumbling meow and bolted for the sliding door, disappearing into the apartment like something had lit his whiskers on fire.

I didn't have to wait long after that.

The air above the patio shimmered faintly. Like heat waves off pavement—only chilled, laced with lavender and cedar. A moment later, Aunt Daphne appeared, already mid-sentence as she often was.

"—a pity, really. The theater district in San Francisco has lost so much charm."

She took shape gradually—ethereal and elegant in her gauzy wrap and silver-streaked curls. Death hadn't dimmed her flair for drama.

"I take it you were eavesdropping on my call?" I asked with a tired smile.

"I prefer to call it *keeping an ear out,*" she said, gliding over to perch on the air just above the patio table.

"I'm thinking of saying yes to the haunted house project at Fairbourne Mansion," I told her. "But I need to know if it's... safe. Or even wise."

Daphne's expression darkened, just slightly. "That house remembers pain, dearest. It clings like layers of old wallpaper—-faded grief and splintered joy. I've always suspected Mrs. Fairbourne never left."

"She died there?" I asked, though part of me already sensed the answer.

"In childbirth. A tragedy. The kind that etches itself into the woodgrain. You'd be wise to proceed gently."

"I felt something when I toured the house. A presence. Not malicious... just watching."

Daphne nodded. "Spirits often stir when people return to places they loved—-or feared. And you're unusually receptive, Isla."

"Which brings me to the duck."

I led her inside and pointed to the dresser. The rubber duck sat innocently among a cluster of framed photos, its eyes dull, its torn seam barely noticeable now that it had dried.

Daphne floated closer. Her face twisted into a grimace the moment she neared it.

"Oh dear. That thing hums."

"Hums?"

"Not audibly. But energetically. You can't feel it?" she asked, turning to me. "It's faint, but it's there. As if it's soaked up emotion ... or memory."

I shivered, suddenly regretting putting the duck in my pocket. "It was floating near the edge of the pond at the Alford farm. Practically swam into my hand."

Daphne drifted backward. "Be cautious. Sometimes small things are tied to big energy. Toys are especially good at holding on—-children's laughter, or worse ... fear."

Just then, Higgins reappeared from the hallway. His hackles rose the moment he entered the bedroom. He leapt onto the dresser, sniffed the duck once, and gave a low growl—then hopped down, darting from the room.

Daphne's eyebrows arched. "Even *he* doesn't like it."

"So, what should I do?"

"Leave it out, somewhere you can watch it. Just in case it's tied to something... residual. But don't discard it yet. If it's part of a story, it may find a way to tell it."

Aunt Daphne floated toward the window, the edge of her gown catching the breeze like silk caught in a current.

"Will you come to the mansion tomorrow?" I asked.

Daphne's eyebrows rose to a new level. "Well, I suppose I could. Higgins might be helpful also."

"Higgins?"

"Uh-hmm, he can detect supernatural things, you know, as well as vermin. Very well, I will do it. I will meet you at the mansion. Just call for me."

I stood alone in the soft glow of the bedroom lamp, staring at the duck. Higgins eyed it from the hallway, clearly debating whether it was worth the trouble.

"Fine," I muttered. "But I'm keeping the Claddagh necklace on."

Then I picked up the duck and placed it in the center of my dresser—right under Aunt Daphne's favorite photograph.

Chapter Four
The Haunting Begins

AS SOON AS I lifted the cat carrier off the front seat of Vee-dub, my vintage Volkswagen Rabbit, Higgins released a demonic howl, sounding like all the furies of the world were about to eat him. Tony, already at the front gate of the mansion, flinched so hard he nearly dropped the latch.

"Wat da hell?"

"That would be Higgins. He hates car rides. Thinks he's being exiled every time." I admitted the cat had produced a rather disconcerting wail.

"Higgins senses the unrest surrounding the property." My aunt's familiar voice spoke from behind me. I resisted the urge to look, knowing the attention of the rest of my crew was on Higgins and me.

I lifted the carrier, accompanied by a continuous low-throated growl, then strode through the gate, motioning to the others to follow me. Ellen fell into step, followed by Steve, who looked like he'd wandered in straight from the beach, then Gary and Tony bringing up the rear. Daphne, of course, was suddenly floating at the top of the staircase. Ghosts and their entrances.

I slid the key into the lock and turned it. As I pushed the door open, it ripped from my hand with an abrupt jolt, swinging inward as if wrenched by invisible fingers. A wave of frigid air surged past me—not just cold, but very old, laced with the biting sting of something long buried. It grazed my skin like frostbite.

Behind me, Ellen recoiled, hugging herself tightly. "Okay— what was *that*?"

"Whoa. Central air from the crypt?" Steve offered, eyebrows raised.

Gary frowned and stepped forward, his expression folding into a deep crease. "Man, who turned on the dead man's A/C?"

"That was … weird," I offered lamely and shrugged while Higgins continued to growl.

"Why'd you bring the cat?" Ellen asked as we entered.

"To look for vermin." Technically true. Just not the kind she meant.

"It's an old, abandoned house, Isla. It's a given they're in there." She cocked an eyebrow at me.

The drawing room was the first stop. I opened the door and let the group take in the scene. Cobwebs, ancient wallpaper peeling like tree bark, and the sort of eerie silence that pressed on your ears.

"This is magnificent," Ellen declared. "We could stage a ghost ball in here."

"Not every night," I objected. Was she talking about fake ghosts or a real people ball?

She laughed. "No, of course not, but maybe on the thirty-first, we could wind it up with a costume ball. That would be lots of fun, and we could get someone to cater it with refreshments and maybe a cash bar."

"Hmm, we might do it."

"Let Higgins out," Daphne whispered near my ear. "He can't sense anything stuck in a box."

I opened the carrier. Higgins shot out like a bullet and made a beeline for the fireplace. He crouched and sniffed along the baseboards, tail twitching.

The tech guys were already measuring walls and discussing light rigging like it was just another stage setup. I caught Gary scribbling in his notebook rather than using his phone.

Steve gazed at the ceiling, likely looking for potential placements for lights and special effects.

Higgins continued to investigate the fireplace and the molding along it, staring intently and sniffing like a dog. Maybe he'd detected a nest of mice behind it. As old as this place was, I could well imagine any number of pests within the walls. I shuddered. Still, we needed to ensure the place was safe.

After twenty minutes, I urged everyone to the den next door. When we passed the staircase, Higgins hissed and stared at the upper level. Taking his cue, I squinted, applying my aura vision to the area. The open space appeared foggy, yet I didn't sense the vibe of a living person.

Tony and Steve huddled together discussing a possible mirror twin set-up in the room, while Ellen waved me to the front.

"We can construct a fake wall over here…" She pointed to the open corner at the front of the room where about five feet of wall space was empty.

'What for?" I prompted, not following her idea here.

"Actually, it would be a fake small cell—no door on it, only a barred window. Behind it would be the Cask of Amontillado with a ghostly actor guarding it."

"Oh, I get it now! That's brilliant. I bet Tony could rig spooky sounds for it." I projected my voice enough that he caught the last part and ambled over, moving like one of the Jets from Grease.

"I hears ya'," he said, with a smirk. "That's cake. I make spooky soundtracks in my sleep. Trigger, loop—done."

Gary sauntered in so he and Tony riffed on wiring setups, tossing around tech jargon like it was beach volleyball. It boosted my spirit to see their enthusiasm.

They were still at it when I pressed them toward the dining room and kitchen area where Steve was already pacing off the floor. Ellen studied it for a few minutes, then said, "Let's rig the dishes to fly—plates, silverware, the whole shebang. Lights dim to near blackout, then snap back to half-power. Instant goosebumps."

"Gary, do we have enough tech to make the dishes fly?"

He paused, eyes looking upward. "Yeah, I think we can. Not many though We can duplicate the theatre fly system, but it could get gnarly."

"It will send chills through the guests," she chortled. "But leave the kitchen alone. We'll need it for snacks. Scaring folks works up an appetite."

Steve ambled to the pantry, muttering, "Wouldn't surprise me if somethin' weird was tucked in here." He opened it halfway—and let out a startled bark.

We froze in place and my heart leaped for my throat where it pounded against my vocal cords, freezing them so I couldn't sputter out anything.

But Tony yelled, "What da fook, man?"

Steve flung the pantry door open and laughed like a maniac while he pointed to the monster in the pantry—a head form holding a long black wig with a fake spider in the hair.

"You jerk!" Ellen shouted, bending over with her hand on her knees as she, too, recovered from the shock. A dirty trick, but keeping with the spooky house agenda.

I waved a hand. "You caught us on that, Steve. That would give anyone a shock, but if it had been dark –"

"Dude, with a purple light? That'd freak people out in the best way." Gary grinned while he strolled over to get a better look.

"I think Steve's yelp did most of the work." I forced a laugh to lighten the tension. I leaned against the wall, breath hitching as my heart settled back into place. Steve's prank was dirty, sure—but it fit the vibe. And honestly? A pantry with a pop-up head, eerie lighting, and a scream track? That had potential.

"Keep it in mind," I said and pointed everyone to the stairs. I ascended to the second floor with trepidation and a reluctant cat.

Ellen came behind me, her steps slow while the guys passed me as they charged upstairs, eager to see the other possibilities.

My aura vision didn't reveal the fog that had hovered at the top earlier so the ghost must have moved elsewhere, yet my skin crawled, my body sensing spirits while Higgins stalked, crouching beside me on each step.

Ahead of us, the guys turned to the right, heading for the master bedroom.

"This place is really creepy—even in daylight." Ellen's voice was barely above a whisper. "Do you think it's haunted, Isla?"

"Absolutely. So does Higgins, and I trust his judgment." While I couldn't tell her I detected spirits, the cat's actions were enough to alert anyone who paid attention. Even his whiskers twitched as we reached the top. He took a short run to the left, then sprang straight up like he pounced on a mouse, except his fur resembled a bottlebrush and his body arched as an unearthly yowl accompanied his sudden action.

I tensed, grabbing the railing along the hallway and squinting toward him. The cat landed on all fours, facing back toward the stairs. Claws scraping, he scrambled behind me.

A gray man shape stood facing us, watching.

Aunt Daphne? I called in my mind. *Help!*

"Do you see that kind of fog down this hall?" Ellen whispered, her voice scratchy, and her head just behind my shoulder.

"Uh-huh. I think it could be ..." My voice trailed off. What could I tell her? But she saw it also, so she was somewhat attuned to the supernatural.

"A ghost?" Ellen completed my speculation.

"Um, hello … Do you hear me?" I asked, not sure if the ghost had auditory access. "I'm Isla from the local theatre. We are-uh-considering doing …"

The gray shape moved closer.

"Are you Mr. Fairbourne?" My voice trembled a little.

Ellen stepped back a few paces, edging her way to the stairs. I considered joining her, but I didn't sense aggression from the ghost. "Can you hear me? Maybe you can make a noise or something …?"

I waited, holding my breath.

A soft thump sounded, like someone had tapped the wooden floor.

"Was that you? Tap once for yes, twice for no." I hoped he understood.

Another thump. To test it out, I needed a negative answer. "Are you the only spirit here?"

A thump, followed in a heartbeat by a second one.

"So, there are more spirits here? Two?" I asked.

A single tap. Encouraged, I continued. "Do you know about haunted house attractions, Mister Fairbourne?"

Two thumps.

"Oh, okay. Let me explain." I spewed out a shortened version of what we were doing and asked if he understood.

After a lengthy pause, I heard a single thump.

"Great. Would you be okay with us transforming the house into a scary house where people walk through, scream a little, and leave feeling frightened and happy?"

The pause extended longer and I feared I'd lost my connection with him.

"Are you trying to talk to it?" Ellen asked. She'd retreated to the top of the stairs where Higgins sat, waiting for my response.

"Yeah … I think he hears me, and I'm trying to tell him what we're doing, but I'm not sure he understands. I guess haunted house attractions weren't around in his time."

A single thump punctuated the sentence.

"Are you sure?

A thump.

"I think he agreed to it," I told Ellen.

"Do you think it's a good idea to have an actual haunted house for a fake one?" Ellen raised a skeptical eyebrow and waved a hand toward the hall.

"Well, we could say it's authentic?" I suggested. "But I didn't know you could see ghosts."

"I saw a gray shape, and I've seen some a few times before now. I don't see much detail though. Like I couldn't tell if that one was a man. Obviously, you saw more than I did." Ellen's eyes locked with mine.

'I can sometimes hear spirit voices. But keep this between us. No one else knows," I told her.

Ellen's lips tightened as her eyes grew rounder. "I would hate to see the theatre lose the opportunity to do this and make some decent money, but if something went wrong and a real ghost showed up—it could be a nightmare."

"I get it, Ellen. And I agree. But yes, I believe he's agreeing."

She nodded and turned back to the stairs. "I'm going down. I think I could use some fresh air."

My gaze went to the feline sitting on the top step, his eyes focused on the foggy figure. "Right. Keep an eye on Higgins. He's jittery with the vibes in this place."

Ellen called him and he responded, seemingly eager to leave this floor.

I glimpsed the golden haze that was Daphne manifesting close to Fairbourne. It lingered for a few moments before they floated to the middle bedroom door and went through it.

Mustering my courage, I strolled to the bedroom door and lightly knocked on it. I didn't expect a response but thought I should alert the ghosts I was entering. A chill permeated the room, and I spotted Daphne at once where she sat on a green, brocade-covered love seat talking to the gray haze next to her.

"I hope I'm not intruding. Since you can communicate with him, Auntie, I'd like for you to relay a message for me." My voice sounded terse.

"You don't need me to talk to him, dearie. He can hear everything you say ... but you need me to give him the ability to speak to you." She placed her hand on his, and in a blink, Fairbourne was visible.

He cocked his head to one side when I gazed at him for a moment or two. Where he was once handsome, sorrow had etched a worn looking face—one that no longer smiled. When he spoke his voice sounded gravelly, like it wasn't used much. "I heard your explanation of the haunted house affair, but I'm not sure I quite understand what that means."

"It's a form of entertainment. It seems people enjoy the rush of being frightened by unknown and unexpected things while going through a house decorated in a ghoulish manner. We don't normally use actual ghosts."

I explained Rob Fenmore's plan to him, telling him Rob wanted the theatre company to bring it to life for one week at Halloween. "Of course, he doesn't know you still reside here. I only sensed you yesterday. So, if you don't want us to do it, just tell me and I will decline the offer, suggesting Rob not proceed with his plan."

Fairbourne's dower expression grew even darker. "You are proposing to bring numerous people into the mansion to scare them. Do I understand correctly?"

"Yes, that is exactly it." I laughed a bit. "But if it's an intrusion, then we—"

"No, I think it would be quite amusing." His lips pulled into an almost smile. "Nothing has happened here for many years. But I will warn you ... I am not the only spirit here."

"I thought that might be the case. Your wife is also around, isn't she?"

'She is. And another—a young woman often haunts the premises—searching for … something. I do not know what or who. Unless you fear the spirits, then I have no objection to seeing your entertainment this fall."

Relief washed through me. "Thank you. I assure you we'll not do any permanent damage to the place. Although, I must tell you that Mr. Fenmore has plans to restore and sell the mansion after Halloween."

A dry-sounding chuckle slipped through Fairbourne's thin lips. "He does, eh? Perhaps you can dissuade him."

"Maybe …" I didn't hold out much hope for it. "It was a pleasure to meet you, sir." I caught Daphne's eyes and rolled mine toward the door, encouraging her to follow me out.

"The pleasure is mine," he replied before Daphne lifted her hand, and I couldn't see him any longer.

Once outside the room, Daphne leaned close and said, "Fairbourne is a sad, but gentle spirit and his wife is mostly unseen. She still suffers the tragedy of her death and relives it now and then. But she won't harm anyone."

"What about the other one?"

She shrugged.

"Will she be a problem? I can still decline Fenmore's offer." A ghostly wild card. Not something I'd like to contend with.

"I think we can handle her, luv. The town needs a good haunt, don't they?" She blew a kiss to me and for a moment, a sweet, strawberry scent wafted toward me before Daphne left.

When she said "we" could handle the wayward ghost, who did she mean?

EVERYONE, EXCEPT ME AND the cat, left after they finished the inspection of the first two levels. The third floor, attic, and tower were off the table so far as using them, although I told Steve we could illuminate the tower with its beautiful stained-glass window. My brief negotiations with Fairbourne included an agreement to only use the first two floors.

I sat in the drawing room, waiting for Rob to arrive. I'd called and told him I wanted to discuss the offer, so he said he'd be over by one-thirty. My thoughts drifted to the third ghost. Who was she and why did she come here?

Although the house seemed quiet, an underlying throb of energy ran through it, setting my teeth on edge. Clearly, Higgins detected it also. He circled the room, eyes darting in all directions, like he suspected an ambush.

Soon, Rob arrived with a smile, polished loafers, and that air of casual confidence that always made me want to double-check the fine print. I rose to greet him.

"Isla," he said, extending a hand. "You've got that I-mean-business look today."

"That's because I do." I smiled sweetly as he leaned against the wall. "Your offer—very generous, very polished. The crew appreciated the charity element especially."

"But…" He arched a brow.

"They're asking for sixty percent to the theatre instead of fifty."

He sat back. "Sixty? That leaves me with what… twenty for promo?"

"And a write-off. Plus, local media coverage for being the hero who backed Arbordale's spookiest Halloween yet." I held his gaze. "You said yourself you want this place to shine."

He let the silence stretch, then chuckled. "I should've known you'd circle back for more."

"Only because I know the value of what we bring—and I'm protecting the interests of my people."

"Sixty it is. But I want signage—Sponsored by Fenmore Properties—at the front gate."

"Done." I offered my hand.

"You always were a handful, Reed."

I crossed my arms and sat in the armchair, Higgins settling on the arm by my side. "My theatre crew looked it over and we are confident we can do it. But I have a few things to discuss. First, what kind of budget are you looking at for the transformation so far as supplies, tools, special effects, and set pieces?"

"Set pieces?" His mouth quirked to one side, and his eyes asked a question.

"Yeah, false walls, painted illusions, and things to add scarier ambiance than spider webs."

"Oh, right. I get it. Say a top of ten thousand?"

"Ten thousand!" My voice shot up a level. With what we could repurpose from the theatre and new supplies, that should be more than enough. But Rob misread my surprised voice.

"All right, fifteen. I can go as high as fifteen."

"That's fine," I replied, keeping my voice level. "We can make it work. Now, let's discuss the deal and the dates. Then I want it in writing."

"Sure, of course …" he answered, pulling out his phone to make a note. "A schedule. I can write it down for you."

I cleared my throat. "I'm talking about a contract, Rob. If the theatre is going to work on this, I need a contract that states the terms, the expected work, and the monetary arrangements."

His whole demeanor shifted, his shoulders lowering as his head tilted to one side. "I thought we could just do a handshake deal. I tell you what I'll pay for all of it, and we shake on it. No paperwork, you know." He offered a coaxing smile.

"I can't do it on just your word, Rob. I need backup paperwork and the guarantee of payment. This is business. I'm sure you're covering your expenses along with the renovation with accurate accounting and agreements with other contractors. In this sense, my theatre is one also. For my accounting purposes, I need a contract with all the details spelled out."

He gaped at me, his mouth open but saying nothing, then he sputtered, "I … can't … believe this."

With a heartfelt sigh, I said, "No offense, Rob, but if I'm putting my people in here, I need guarantees."

He lowered his phone hand and did a one-eighty turn, gazing at the room. For a few moments, I thought he might just drop the whole deal and leave, then he peered at me with a calculating expression as he accepted the terms. "All right I will get the contract drawn up this afternoon. Okay if I bring it by the theatre later?"

"Sure. But I need to check in at the Maze at four, so I won't be back to the theatre until after six."

"Fine. I'll make it later then. Now tell me about the ideas your crew has for this place."

So, over the next thirty minutes, I recounted what the tech team planned to do, and he loved it. Especially, the ghostly mirror trick, the head in the pantry, and Amontillado wall. When I told him we were only using two floors, he bristled a bit.

"Why not use the third floor and the tower? They have smaller rooms and could be really scary."

More than you know, I thought, but answered. "We have plenty to build and decorate in the two main floors. We don't have time to transform the whole house. The staircase is a little shaky going up another level and the pull-down ladder to the attic isn't safe to allow people and kids in costumes to go climbing up. But we will install a light behind the stained-glass window at the top of the cupula."

"Okay. I see your point. I guess it would be a lot more work. And you're using the solarium, right?"

I stroked Higgin's head, feeling the cat's tense body. "Absolutely. Wait until you see it. It will be a showstopper."

Rob grinned, pleased with the plans and turned to leave. "I'll see you later. But I have to ask … Is the cat part of the deal?"

"Uh, no. This is Higgins, my theatre cat. He's just helping me out today, looking for mice or other pests in the place." *And ghosts,* I added silently.

FIFTEEN MINUTES LATER, I coaxed Higgins back into his carrier, an easier chore than I expected, but the cat wanted to leave the mansion. I drove the short distance to the maze site.

Earlier Tara sent me a text saying she would be there making a few adjustments to the setup, so I figured it would be a great time to negotiate a better spot for Katie. I lowered the window on Higgin's side of the seat, so he had plenty of fresh, cool air, then I hurried to the maze entrance.

I found Tara at the third station, talking to Rolf, the Viking. He lifted his head from the paper she was showing him, and his eyes seemed to sparkle when he saw me. Probably a trick of the lighting, but the smile was genuine.

"Good afternoon, Isla."

Tara pivoted in my direction. "I didn't think you were coming by today."

I held up my phone. "Need to get some more photos around the lake for my techs. They're adding the effects and special motions this weekend."

"Super good." Tara's voice didn't sound particularly enthused.

"Is something wrong?"

She sighed and lowered her gaze to the clipboard. "Not really. I just need to rearrange a couple of vendors to move Fenmore's spot to a better position before Andie has a cow."

"Oh, she's not happy with the final slot." I expected that. "Sorry, but while you're rearranging, can I ask a favor?"

She pinned me with her gaze, ready to challenge. Then I explained about Katie's booth being in a bad spot. "So, if you could move her closer to the front, it would be more logical."

"I didn't realize she was painting children's faces. I just thought she was demo-ing cosmetics and handing out candy. Yeah, I can juggle a better space for her." Her eyes were already running down the vendor list to see who she could move.

"Thanks. I'll go on over to the lake. If you have any questions, just text me." I winked at Rolf as I stepped past him. He grinned back at me.

A short time later, I came to the lake and pulled out my phone to get the photos. I'd taken about six different angles and noted the pier position for the guys, then I heard a quack. Not a real quack, but a squeaky one. Like from a rubber duck. It didn't come from the water but closer. Like in my sweater.

It couldn't be. I'd put the duck on my dresser. Slowly, I slid my hand into the pocket until my fingers touched the rough feel of the old duck. In disbelief, I pulled it out and stared at it in consternation. How had it gotten back into my sweater? Did Higgins do it?

As I stared at it, the reflected light from the lake glistened on the crescent-shaped gouge in the dull yellow rubber.

Chapter Five
The Duck and the Doubts

AFTER CHECKING IN WITH the crew still demolishing the lobby bathrooms, I consoled myself with the thought that the facilities would look brand new once they finished.

I'd released Higgins as soon as we entered, and he shot off like a jet toward the upstairs storage area. Now he sat in front of the apartment door, waiting for me to let him in—calmer now, recovering from the ordeal of the mansion.

I shrugged off my sweater, slipping my hand in the pocket to remove the curious duck. I stared at it for a moment, then stepped into my bedroom, casting a searching glance at the dresser where I'd left it the previous night. Yep, it was empty except for a little glass jewelry box Katie gave me last Christmas.

Still holding the duck, I returned to the kitchen, grabbed a cold soda, and sat down at the round bistro-sized table. "Did you somehow put this in my pocket, Higgins?" I addressed the cat, who lingered over his food dish.

He blinked at me, twitched his whiskers, and a low rumble of a growl answered before he darted off toward the living room and tucked himself into his "secret" hiding place behind the curtain. He didn't like the duck. No question about it. But I didn't think he would even deign to put his mouth on the old rubber.

The rip caught my attention again, prompting me to look closer. Getting up, I rummaged through the catch-all kitchen drawer for a magnifying glass, found it after a minute and sat down to examine the cut more closely.

The slash curved, not quite half an inch long. A red stain coated one edge. I used my fingernail to pull it back slightly. The rubber cracked—too brittle now to push further. What might have caused the gash?

A sudden noise of scrambling claws and a sharp thud interrupted my thoughts. Startled, I jerked, my attention pulled to the sudden movement. Higgins had darted out from the curtains and leapt onto the sofa where he sat staring at the empty space between it and the door.

A spontaneous chill sent shivers down my back. A ghost? "Aunt Daphne. Are you here?" Her appearance hadn't brought this uneasiness before, so I doubted it was her. Higgins continued to stare, and a low rumble came from his body. I called my aunt again and I narrowed my eyes. The duck slipped from my fingers onto the table when I rose and stepped closer to the nervous cat. A moment later, he jumped down and darted into the bedroom.

The atmosphere in the room seemed to change, shifting back to normal. My aunt didn't appear, yet I felt someone, or something, in the room.

I returned to the kitchen, pulled out a plastic bag, and slid the rubber duck into it. I needed to find out more about the incident six years ago.

At that point, my phone chirped, alerting me to a text message. I picked it up, thinking it could be Rob with the contract, but it was Katie.

Meet me tomorrow for coffee and scones?

I messaged back agreeing. The bakery at McKenzie Square was our go-to scone place. Deciding I could use a treat right now, I returned to the kitchen, opened the freezer to pull out a pint of Rocky Road ice cream, and grabbed a spoon.

While I ate, I made a few notes about the maze set up, then sent them and the photos to Gary, who would coordinate the various builds there. Most of the preliminary work was done and ready to move into position. He'd estimated that with ten volunteers working on it, they would get most of it done this weekend. They'd finish up in the evening on Monday and Tuesday, then start in on the work at the mansion if he could get the supplies by Wednesday. The mansion rework was now dependent on the contract.

By eight in the evening, I figured Rob wasn't coming tonight. Maybe the contract took longer than expected or he changed his mind. As for the bagged duck, I put it in the drawer under the bulletin board—and my *sometimes* murder board— near the door. "Let's see you get out of this," I murmured.

I retreated to the living room with my laptop computer and searched for information on the drowning six years earlier. For an accidental death at a popular Halloween attraction, it garnered little coverage in the news media.

I found one mention in an online site, but no details to speak of. Not even the victim's name, just that she was nineteen and appeared to have fallen into the Alfords' pond. Preliminary reports showed she must have banged her head underwater or on the pier. Subsequent tests showed she'd been drinking before the accident.

The local online news site didn't reveal much more except the approximate time the accident had occurred–1:20 a.m.—and the time her body was found. Her name was withheld while the sheriff investigated, but it seemed a follow up article was never published. Maybe it was ruled accidental, and her family asked to keep her name private.

Maybe Gianni knew more about the accident. I decided to contact him in the morning. After looking up information on the Fairbourne family, I marked a ditto in my note to ask Gianni. The basics of their lives were recorded on various pages and a dozen conjured ghost stories with conflicting accounts.

The basic information hadn't changed. Thomas passed away in the house at 62, his wife died giving birth to their child when she was 29, and the son was killed in the first World War. Tragic, but nothing helpful.

When I made my usual rounds of the theatre before going to bed, I found a legal-sized envelope lying on the floor in front of the mail slot at the entrance. Inside was a two-page agreement between Rob Fenmore of Fenmore Development Company and me for the Playhouse Theatre. So, he dropped it off without bothering to tell me.

I took it to my office to be reviewed in the morning. After I confirmed all the locks were set, I turned off the house lights, leaving the ghost light in the middle of the stage providing the only illumination, which left the auditorium dimly lit with many shadowed areas. I never stayed down here long after the lights were out.

I hurried to the elevator and pressed the up button, then waited. It should have been on the ground floor, not either of the upper levels. Maybe the door was stuck, but when I tried it, it opened easily. The elevator wasn't behind the door. I looked up. It was descending—slowly. That was enough to spook me. I slammed the door shut and scrambled up both flights of stairs to the top floor.

Safely inside my apartment, I closed, locked, and bolted my door, then checked the patio sliders. Higgins followed me over, watching as I made sure the pole was in place to prevent the panel from moving. His head tilted to a quizzical angle.

"I don't know what's going on, Higgins. But something weird is happening." I spoke softly, but he seemed to understand as he put a paw on my arm and patted it.

Or maybe he wanted a treat.

My dreams were peppered with foggy scenes.

A partial moon with clouds drifting past and a misty-looking lake. Fog clung to the lake's edge. A shadowy figure raised a flask, his voice drowned in the mist. My hand reached for his — or maybe for the drink — and the whispering around us grew louder, like reeds brushing each other in the dark.

Repeated variations occurred as I turned and tossed.

"YOU LOOK TIRED," KATIE said as I slid into the booth across from her. I'd made it to the bakery shop only a few minutes late. The bicycle ride over woke me up a little more and stimulated my appetite. A pot of coffee, two cups, two glasses with water, and two plates loaded with pairs of deliciously plump scones sat on the table. "I ordered one each of their seasonal specials, apple and pumpkin."

"They look amazing." I reached for the coffee and added a bit of cream. "I didn't sleep too well last night. I had some odd dream snippets."

"Snippets?" She spread some clotted cream over the pumpkin scone. "What about?"

"Kind of like flashes of a story, little bits and pieces, but they didn't seem to weave the tale together." I wasn't sure how to explain the black and white mystery teasers that had disturbed my sleep.

"I think I may be reacting to an old story about the pond at Alford's farm. Someone died there six years ago in a drowning accident, but I couldn't find any details on it."

Katie took a bite and chewed it. "I kinda remember something like that. A girl fell in and couldn't get out. I think she was a little younger than us. But that's all I recall. Why is this bothering you?"

I sipped my coffee, relishing the warmth and the caffeine. The aroma alone could sharpen my wits. "Remember that rubber duck I found a couple of days ago?"

She nodded, washing down her scone with a gulp of coffee. I broke off a piece of my apple scone and slathered the clotted cream over it while the scent of cinnamon and warm apples made my stomach rumble. Still holding it on the way to my mouth, I said, "Well, the duck seems to have a story to tell." I bit into the treat, chewed slowly to savor the flavors, then swallowed before I told her about the adventures of the duck yesterday.

"That's a little out there, isn't it? I mean, the duck can't actually move on its own, so you're probably right that Higgins moved it."

"What about the squeak? It can't do that without squishing it. Besides, there's a tear in it and it's hard to get the sound out of it."

Katie smiled, a little laugh slipping out. "Come on. You probably bumped against something, and it was just enough to make the noise."

"I thought that, too. But nothing I brushed against around me would have hit it hard enough. This is going to sound really strange but bear with me. I think it might be trying to send me a message," I said, though even I wasn't sure what kind.

Katie's mouth dropped open. "What? Have you lost it, girl? An old, barely functional rubber duck can't do that." She popped another bite.

"I told you it was strange. Of course, the duck isn't actually doing it, but a spirit stuck in this realm might." I waited for her reaction. Skeptical, she wasn't entirely convinced of paranormal events. I'd never confided to her or anyone else, save for my aunt, about my aura vision gift.

She swallowed, almost choking and grabbing for the water glass to wash it down, apparently not trusting the coffee to do the job. "Are you saying a ghost is talking through the duck?"

"Not exactly, but I think it's connected somehow."

I let that sit with her for a bit, while I ate two more bites and finished my first cup of coffee. As I refilled it, Katie slid hers over.

"So, does this tie into your dream fragments?"

"It might. The rip is crescent-shaped like a fingernail dug into it. I think it's possible the drowning victim grabbed it. It's even got a red stain on it. Could be nail polish or blood."

Katie gazed at me, eyes unblinking for about six seconds. "Nail polish wouldn't leave a stain unless it was wet. And wouldn't blood wash off?"

"Well, what else could the red stain be?"

"Pond scum? Rust. I don't know. It just seems unlikely." She shook her head. "It's a stretch, Isla. Maybe all this Halloween prep has you seeing ghosts where there aren't any."

"You know I see Aunt Daphne." I countered, biting into the pumpkin scone and savoring the spices. I decided to take home a half dozen of each they were so delightful. "We have ghosts around us, and the whole Christmas chorus last winter was performed by ghosts."

"I know that's what you said. But this is downright spooky." Her eyes drifted toward the table, and her frown told me she meant it. She wasn't comfortable with the supernatural world.

"I get that. But I honestly think there's something more to this duck. "Sometimes objects hold echoes. I've seen it before."

"Kevan might be able to help," Katie said. "He could look into the drowning—and maybe even check out the duck."

Katie was dating the sheriff's detective, Kevan Conklin, while he and I had a friendly connection through my freestyle investigations.

"You think he'd hear me out and not fall off his chair laughing?"

"I didn't say that! But he'd listen. And if anyone can dig up something, it's him."

"You're right," I agreed. "Oh, I almost forgot. I persuaded Tara to move your booth closer to the start of the maze, so you should get more business there."

Katie's eyes lit up, a big smile conveying her joy. "Thanks. That's wonderful."

We polished off the rest of the scones, and I placed my order for a dozen to go while she scurried out the door to get back to the candy shop. I, on the other hand, would visit the sheriff's office once I procured my pastries.

Time to see if Conklin could shed some light on the pond drowning story.

Chapter Six
Sometimes a Quack is Just a Quack

WITH THE DUCK STILL In my sweater pocket, I locked my bike to the rack near the sheriff's office and strolled inside, feeling somewhat foolish about bringing this to Conklin's attention. I fidgeted, rubbing at my fingernails, while I waited for Deputy Ochoa, the front desk officer, to contact him.

"What can I do for you today, Isla?" Conklin asked when he came out and motioned for me to follow. He shared one quarter of a block of cubby desks with the other deputies, but his was neat and organized.

"It's nothing really important, but I hope to find some information on a woman who drowned in the Alford farm's pond six years ago." I sank into the chair across from him, feeling the weight of my own doubt.

"What kind of information?" He turned to his computer.

"Well, to begin, I'd like to know her name since I can't even find that out. The articles didn't report it, so it's difficult to narrow it down."

His eyebrows lowered with a hint of a frown. "That's odd. What day was it?"

"Uh, I'm not exactly sure whether it was October 30th or the 31st. The reports weren't clear when she drowned, but she wasn't found until the 31st."

"Okay, let's start there and see what I can find. Why is this of interest to you?"

I knew he would ask, so I took a breath and dove in. "This is going to sound strange, but I found an old rubber duck in the pond. I think it might be connected with the victim."

His gaze sharpened. "A rubber duck? And you think it's somehow connected to this woman's death."

I nodded.

He turned his attention to the computer, paging through the logs while looking for a match. "Okay, we have a report on the 30th of a missing girl, but no follow up case notes. On the 31st, I see a case marked 'accidental drowning.' Let's see if that's it."

He tapped two more keys, and I leaned closer, waiting to see if this was it. He gazed at the screen for about thirty seconds, his eyes scanning the report. "This sounds like it. The sheriff went on the call with Deputy Bilhurst. The victim was Hallie Connor, nineteen years old. The tox report showed she'd been drinking and had MDMA in her system –"

"What's that?" I interrupted.

"Ecstasy … a popular drug with the college crowd."

"Oh, yeah. I heard the name at school. I just didn't know the other."

A curious look entered his eyes as he studied me for a moment, then he turned back to the computer. "The sheriff's team found no evidence of foul play and there's no mention of a rubber duck."

I entered Hallie's name into my phone, so I had a starting place to learn more. I hesitated, wetting my lips, then I slid the duck from my pocket. I set it on Conklin's desk. "This floated to me three days ago when I was at the pond, checking it out for the maze event."

He stared at the plastic baggie with the toy. He tried to stifle a laugh, but a sharp chortle escaped. "And this is connected how?" he asked when he'd got his subsequent chuckles under control.

Taking a deep breath, I related the whole story to him, except about the ghostly activity. But I pointed out the cut in the duck and the red stain. To his credit, he maintained his professionalism and picked the duck up to examine it.

"A fingernail could have done this, but there are other possibilities. As to the red stain, I don't know if it's blood or not. I would think blood would have washed off if the … object was in water the whole time."

"Can you test it?" I knew it was a longshot, but I had to take it.

He set the duck down. "Maybe. But what would it prove? What do you think happened?"

"I think it's possible the girl had the duck in her hand when she died, and she clenched it hard enough that her fingernail cut it. It must have caused the nail to lift enough to bleed." I struggled to express what I felt. "I just… get the feeling there's more to it than an accident."

He didn't laugh again. Instead, he studied the duck a moment longer before setting it down.

Conklin turned his eyes to the far wall as he leaned back in his chair, absorbing my words. He inhaled deeply, then shifted his gaze to me. "I respect your intuition, Isla. But I think it might be pushing it to tie this toy to the girl's death. The sheriff found no indication of foul play at the scene. The Connor woman, under the influence of drugs and alcohol, likely stepped wrong, and fell into the water. She had bruises, and a contusion on her skull suggested she hit her head as she fell, or she encountered a boulder on entering the water." He paused. "It's tragic but not murder."

Then why is the duck haunting me? I thought, but I couldn't tell Conklin that part of the story. "You're right. The duck is just an oddity." I picked it up, slid it into the baggie, and put it back in my pocket. "Thanks for your help. At least, I know who the victim was."

Conklin had dispelled any hope of a different outcome. I left feeling deflated, the duck heavier in my pocket than before.

I glanced at my phone, checking the time, and decided I had time to stop by Isolde's shop for a quick chat. Sometimes her readings were accurate—or so I was told—but other times, they seemed out of this universe.

TWO BLOCKS OFF MAIN Street, Mystic Moon Apothecary stood out in an older neighborhood of town. Several homes in this area had been transformed into businesses and Isolde's shop occupied a cottage about the same size as the one Aunt Daphne had rented for us when I moved in with her. The exterior featured aqua blue paint with a darker marine trim. A repeating pattern of pale-pearlescent moon phases stood out across the front trim. Hand painted, I suspected since they weren't identical.

Above the door, a half-circle wooden sign, with a carved and painted, glowing full moon partially obscured by silver-streaked clouds, drew my attention and a thrill of anticipation ran through me. *Well done, Isolde*, I thought, appreciating the finesse she'd put into the signage.

When I opened the door, a chime attached to it signaled my entry. It felt like I'd stepped into another world—one scented with dried lavender, sandalwood, and a hint of salt air, like a breeze off the coast. Deep twilight purple walls somehow instilled a sense of peace within the room. Within this cave-like setting, shelves lined with crystals, candles, spell jars, potions, and moon-phase wind chimes, like the one on the front door, invited more inspection.

I'd not visited Isolde's shop before although I'd met and talked to her at fairs and events like the maze. Aunt Daphne knew her quite well and told me she was the real deal. The place fascinated me. From behind a tall, full-sized bookcase dominating the right side of the shop, a voice called out.

"Isla, welcome. What brings you to my shop today?" Isolde stepped out of the shadows and glided toward me. With her long dress and deep purple wrap, she appeared ethereal, floating rather than walking.

"I have something odd to talk to you about. It has to do with the Alford's pond and the maze." Now that I was here, I found I was unsure of where to begin.

The self-proclaimed seer focused her full attention on me, drawing my eyes to her probing dark ones. Instinctively, I squinted at her, catching the full view of her aura. Silver streaks cut through with varying shades of blue and rose highlights. Compassion. Insight. A shimmer of the supernatural. I may have underestimated Isolde. I read good-hearted and blessed with insight into those colors.

"You have a gift, don't you?" she asked, a gentle smile spreading her lips. "You can see mine."

I blinked. "Yes. It comes when I squint."

"Ah, a kindred spirit." She reached for my hand and held it palm up in hers, studying the lines crossing it. "So, come tell me what troubles you over a cup of tea." She lowered my hand, leading me through the back door into a small kitchen with a cozy round table to the right.

A moon and stars tablecloth covered the top, draping off the sides. Two blue velvet-covered padded chairs faced one another on each side. She released my hand, and pointed to one, saying, "Please sit."

I did, sliding into the seat and feeling the tension in my body ease. The fragrance of mint, rosemary, thyme, and other herbs freshened the air, adding to the sense of calm.

Isolde had a kettle of water boiling already and poured some over the tea leaves in two cups. I cleared my throat. "I didn't come for a reading,"

"I know. It's just tea, my dear." She set the cups on the table and pushed a pot of honey toward me, its golden surface catching the light.

"Thank you. I haven't had a proper tea since Aunt Daphne passed." The gesture moved me to a touch of melancholy. I missed this. But Isolde's warmth made it easier, so I told her about the incident at the pond and how I found the duck.

"I remember that day. The poor girl, so young and such a dumb accident ... if it was one." She traced a finger in a spiral on the tablecloth.

"Do you have doubts?" I asked.

"Don't you? Isn't that what you've insinuated here?" She tapped the middle of the spiral three times.

Was she casting a spell? For my ability to read auras and see my aunt's ghost, I'd never considered spells—or witchcraft in general—as anything more than metaphor. But now, unease crept in.

"May I see the duck?" She extended her hand, palm up.

I hesitated for a breath, then pulled the bag out of my pocket again, placing it in her hand.

With care, she opened it and removed the rubber toy. I felt a flicker of self-consciousness, but she regarded the duck with solemn intent. Her eyes half closed, and she hummed a little tune in a minor key. I watched, unmoving and silent, not wanting to disturb whatever she was doing.

After a few minutes, Isolde closed her eyes for a few seconds, then she set the duck on the table as she opened them. "I detect someone there, but it's not clear who is attached to the toy. A girl, I think. But she won't talk to me."

"Can you encourage her?"

Isolde shook her head. "No, I believe she has chosen you."

"What do you mean?"

'To be her champion."

The words chilled me. Champion? I wasn't ready for that. But then Daphne's whisper cut through my doubt.

She is awake. Be on your guard, luv.

Chapter Seven
Painted Faces and Hidden Truths

THE CORN MAZE OPENED on the second Friday of October. I left home early so I could check on the crew working at the mansion. I'd signed the contract with Fenmore after Barb had given it the green light, so the first phase of the haunted house was underway.

As I walked inside, a creaky floorboard made me jump. I didn't recall one in front of the drawing room door and when I looked, I didn't see anything that appeared loose or uneven.

Gary laughed, brushing dust off his jeans. "Diggin' the vibe, Isla? Or is it Elvira" he said with a wink, remarking on my spicy costume that Missy had whipped together in a burst of brilliance. "I dropped a sensor—makes the plank creak when someone steps on it. Adds a spooky vibe, yeah?"

"Clever. So long as no one has a heart attack." I crouched to check the sensor, spotting it tucked low on the door jamb like a secret. Then I stood and took in the room, stunned by how much Gary and the tech crew had already pulled off.

They'd added more cobwebs to confuse the spiders, then touched them up with a glo-in-the-dark spray paint, giving the webs an eerie shimmer that didn't damage the real cobwebs ... much. Gary jabbed a thumb at the wall. "Tell me that Gene Simmons painting doesn't look like he's the one who invited the spiders."

Following instructions, I strolled to look at the KISS star's portrait where someone had created a great likeness. But when I got to within two feet of it, the paint melted off his face and only a skull remained. I stepped back, unsettled. Clever—and creepy.

""How'd you pull that off?" I turned to Gary just in time to catch the smug little grin spreading across his face.

"Wait—don't tell me," I added quickly. "I don't wanna know. It's magic, and I'd rather keep the illusion alive."

"It's actually just—" Steve started, eager to explain.

"Nope. Seriously. Don't ruin it. You guys are straight-up wizards." I waved him off like I was swatting away facts.

Gary laughed. "You always knew that, boss. This place? Total playground for us."

"That, and you've got the budget to make it sing." Rob had come through with the full amount, and the crew was determined to spend every penny with flair.

I wandered toward the fireplace at the back wall, drawn by a flicker I couldn't quite place. The air grew warmer as I approached, dry heat brushing my skin like a whisper from the desert. A log shifted, flames danced—and there it was. A demon's face, horns and all, grinning from the fire.

"Pretty neat, huh?" Tony said from the side, fiddling with the flame controls. "We ain't runnin' it full-time—just a few minutes per group. We're riggin' up a wicked sound to go with it. Think we can get any real ghosts to volunteer?"

I snapped my gaze to him, heart thudding. Did he know?

But Tony just grinned, all teeth and mischief.

"Da guys was sayin' this place's got ghosts," he added with a shrug.

I nodded slowly. "Yeah, I've heard the stories too. But nah—probably no ghostly help on the payroll. You've knocked out a ton today," I called to the room. "Whoever's still working on the maze—wrap it up and get over there."

I turned to Gary. "Rob around?"

Gary shook his head. "Haven't seen him. Glenn Harper's floating around, though. I spotted him maybe ten minutes ago—might've ducked into the study."

I frowned. What was Glenn doing here?

I strolled to the den's door and laid my hand on it, just as Glenn's voice drifted through.

"Well, just how much is all this costing?"

No reply. He must've been on the phone. After a pause, he spoke again.

"Are you crazy? With the restoration, it's gonna run the price way up." Another beat. "Trust you? Just don't blow the budget."

Silence. Then footsteps—soft, deliberate—but they didn't come toward the door. The air felt heavier.

I took a breath, knocked, and pushed it open. "Oh, hi, Glenn. Gary said you were here. Everything okay?"

"What? Oh, yeah. All fine. Just checking in with Andie on the plan."

His eyes flicked over my spicy Elvira costume. "You're definitely in the spirit."

"Of course. I'm heading to the maze in a few minutes. You coming?"

"I didn't realize it was that time already. Good thing you stopped by, Isla."

"I didn't know you were involved in this haunted project."

"Yeah, I've got a little money in the remodel—more than the spooky stuff." He chuckled. "Rob's got some grandiose ideas, but sometimes they pay off."

"Only sometimes?"

"Most of the time. But hey, everyone hits a dud now and then."

His laugh rang hollow. My eyes narrowed. A flicker threaded through his aura—dark, evasive. My stomach tightened. "I've gotta go, Glenn. See you at the maze."

"I'll be along soon," he said, waving me off.

But my gut told me he was relieved I'd left. Something was off.

I paused at the drawing room door. Half the team had already cleared out; the other three were wrapping up.

"Great job, guys. This is gonna be the GOAT.

AS I DROVE TOWARD the Alford farm with only fifteen minutes before the opening time, I encountered a wave of fog rolling in from the coast.

While it would enhance the atmosphere in the maze and add an extra challenge layer for the guests trying to navigate through it, it made driving more hazardous. Anyone who lived along the coast knew how thick it could get and were used to dealing with it. I just hoped the inland visitors were driving cautiously.

When I pulled in, I found the parking area filled with cars already and had to tuck Vee-dub into a tight spot at the end of a row. Laughter and chatter from people of all ages filled the air and I smiled, absorbing the joy in the voices.

Dozens of people milled around, hot ciders in hand from the welcome booth, chatting as they waited for the ribbon-cutting to open the maze. I wore a pumpkin-colored, screen-printed vest that marked me as a volunteer, though I recognized plenty of familiar faces from the theatre.

"Is this going to be the best maze ever?" Cindy Babcock asked, thrusting a microphone toward me with practiced enthusiasm. She was our local evening news roving reporter, born and raised in Arbordale and always ready with a smile.

"Absolutely," I said, flashing a grin. "Just wait until you see it—it'll make your hair stand on end and leave you wondering, 'How'd they do that?'" I added a wink for good measure, leaning into my best local-celebrity voice.

"Can you give us a sneak peek?" she asked, quick on the follow-up.

I dropped into a mock-serious frown. "Sorry, no can do. It's top secret. Spoiling the surprises would ruin the fun."

We both knew the spook stations wouldn't stay secret for long once the crowds poured in, but for now, mystery was part of the magic.

Cindy looked mildly disappointed, but I pressed on. "Come on down, folks. You're gonna love it. Proceeds go to charity, and don't forget to bring a can of food for the food bank."

Cindy turned back to the camera, her smile bright and practiced. "The maze is opening in just a short time, and we'll bring you a glimpse or two of what's waiting inside."

A ripple of excitement moved through the crowd. Someone cheered, a few clapped, and several raised their cider cups in salute.

I gave a wave, trying to look confident and not too flushed from the adrenaline. The pumpkin-colored vest caught the light, making me feel official—even if my heart was thudding like a drumline. Still greeting folks and dodging cider cups, I made my way to the ribbon where Tara stood in her ghostly hooded robe, volunteer vest layered over the gauzy fabric. She held up her phone, the countdown ticking in bold numbers as the crowd pressed in, buzzing with anticipation.

Jeri Paige, Arbordale's ever-poised mayor, stood beside the glowing pumpkin-colored ribbon, oversized scissors gleaming in the twilight. She smiled for the cameras, her hand steady, waiting for the cue.

I slid in next to Tara, and we locked eyes as the final seconds flashed. Together, we counted down—"Three... two... one!"

Jeri snipped the ribbon with a dramatic flourish, and the crowd erupted like it was New Year's Eve—cheers, whistles, cider cups raised high.

But just as the sound peaked, a sharp caw sliced through the air.

A big black crow swooped overhead, wings outstretched like shadows against the twilight sky. It circled once, then vanished beyond the trees.

I froze, heart skipping. The timing was too perfect. Too theatrical.

My nerves prickled, but I forced a smile and waved to the crowd, hoping no one noticed the chill that had stiffened my spine.

To their credit, the attendees lined up and entered the maze in small groups with enough time between the starts for them to be spread out along the walkway. The fog continued to thicken, obscuring a group within minutes of them walking onto the path.

The theatre volunteers had already taken their stations, some of them doing double duty as they'd worked at the mansion earlier in the day.

Once the big crowd had progressed, I slipped into the maze to do a status check. I tucked the map into my pocket, just in case I got disoriented. For lighting, hundreds of solar candles cast low light, enough to see the pathway, and provide a guide. Eerie music and spooky sounds emitted from several speakers placed within the stalks. Overall, the sounds and light created an eerie experience.

When I rounded a bend in the path, a splash of purple and glitter drew my eye to a booth tucked just off the edge of the maze. Katie had transformed the space into a witch's salon—complete with cobwebbed mirrors, dangling crystals, and enough sparkle to be seen from orbit.

Perched regally on a tall stool, Katie wore a deep violet velvet gown stitched with silver sigils and crescent moons. Her makeup was full glam-ghoul: smoky eyes, ghost-pale skin, and dramatic black lips.

At her feet, a little girl sat wide-eyed on a lower stool while Katie deftly painted a delicate butterfly across her cheek.

Three more children lined up behind her, bouncing with excitement, while two moms browsed Katie's eerie-fabulous display of Glitz Lady products. The shelves brimmed with shimmering palettes and iridescent lipsticks nestled between rubber rats and strategically placed plastic spiders. One of the women clutched two jars of highlighter like she'd struck cosmetic gold.

I smiled at the scene and waved. "Looks like you're painting the town—literally."

The girl in the seat burst into giggles, just as Katie was adding the antennae. One black curl landed smack in the middle of her nose.

Katie sighed dramatically, whipping out a baby wipe. "You're sabotaging my masterpiece, darling," she said with mock severity. "Butterflies don't giggle during makeup."

The child nodded solemnly, still grinning, and Katie expertly fixed the design.

"It's going great, Pix," Katie whispered as she rang up the mom at the display. "Thanks so much for the killer location. I'm telling you, this spot is haunted … by commerce!"

The sparkle, the laughter, the painted faces—it felt like magic. The kind that heals.

Delighted her business thrived there, I snatched a candy off Katie's platter of Beldon's chocolate balls. Each one was wrapped in glimmering foil with the Glitz Lady logo—charm and calories all in one bite.

A voice behind me purred, "Careful with those. One taste and you'll be emotionally bonded to cocoa for life."

I turned to find Missy smirking, resplendent in gothic princess glam. She looked like she'd stepped out of a haunted couture runway. Midnight tulle cascaded from her shoulders like a storm cloud, and her bodice shimmered with black sequins that caught every flicker of light. A tiny crown perched atop a teased bouffant of violet-streaked curls.

"You've outdone yourself," I said. "You look like Maleficent went clubbing."

Missy struck a pose, one gloved hand on her hip. "This old thing? Just wait until you see what I'm unleashing for the Mansion Ball. It'll make this look like I dressed in the dark."

"I can't wait." I lifted my phone and took a picture of Missy with the fog hanging behind her. Amazing.

We walked along the maze together for another two stops before Missy moved ahead, not as inclined to stop and chat with the vendors as I needed to do.

A few stops later brought me to the pond's edge, not quite to the theatre's station but at the shallow end where several children splashed in the water, laughing at the cluster of plastic ducks floating more toward the landing pier than this end. Over the next few days, they would disperse more in the water so it would be easier for visitors to capture a prize duck.

For now, I was concerned about the children getting into deeper water as the fog grew thicker. But I saw the four adults with them were keeping a close eye on the kids and already began herding them out of the water. Relieved, I moved closer toward the edge to enjoy the mystical glow emanating from the middle of the pond. The lights the tech team had placed in the water shimmered like pools of fairies or evil creatures with glowing white, blue, or orange lights to create an underwater masterpiece.

As I watched, a creature seemed to emerge from a point near the landing, its head breaking through the water and rising into a full white horse with gleaming red eyes. Even from here, I heard the eerie sound of a demonic horse's neigh. My tech guys had created a pooka! Brilliant! The image reared up in the air and the cry grew louder, echoing across the water like a warning, then it vanished below the surface.

A single plastic duck floated close to the edge, bumping against a rock along the shoreline. I hadn't expected one to drift in so soon, but I reached down and retrieved it. My phone light caught the number stamped on the side.

Nineteen.

Icy fingers slid down my spine. Hallie's age when she died.

"Hallie?" The name slipped out on a breath I hadn't meant to release.

I wanted to step back from the water but couldn't—not with the fog thickening above the pond, curling like smoke. Shapes stirred in it. I could almost make out a figure—long, wet hair clinging to a pale face, lips tinged blue, eyes dark and bottomless.

Was this another illusion from the tech team? Or was I seeing Hallie's ghost?

I squinted, calling on my aura vision. No shimmer. Just a faint, unnatural purple halo—like a bruise in the mist. It pulsed. It pointed at the duck in my hand.

I looked down. The bill was red. Not orange. Red.

A chill gripped me as a vision flickered behind my eyes— Hallie's fingers digging into the rubber duck, tearing it in desperation before it slipped from her grasp.

I lifted my head. The figure was gone. Vanished, like the pooka that had dropped beneath the water.

Then came the caw.

Sharp. Echoing. Too close.

I snapped my gaze upward. A black crow sliced through the mist overhead, wings wide and silent but for that single cry. It vanished into the trees, but the sound lingered—like a warning.

Third time.

First at the mansion. Then during the walk-through. Now, opening night.

My breath hitched. The duck still clutched in my hand felt heavier than plastic. Something was circling. Watching.

And I wasn't sure it was just the guests.

I almost threw the duck back, but decided if it was a message from Hallie, then I should keep it and put it with the rubber duck. Regaining control of my body, I backed away from the water's edge, turned, and hurried toward the landing.

Before I reached it, shouting cut through the fog. Andie's voice, sharp and unmistakable.

"You switched things around again! Why is my booth shoved into some side-stop spot half the people won't even find?"

I paused, just a few feet from Tara and Andie, hidden by the maze's twists and the thickening dark.

"Most will get to it, Andie," Tara replied, her voice tight, like she was speaking through clenched teeth. "The signpost's near the bend, and it's marked well enough. Maybe go back to it—just in case someone does come your way."

In my mind's eye, I saw Tara's fists balled, shoulders squared, fighting every urge to slap her.

"Fine! But you haven't heard the end of this. I'll talk to Rob and we'll settle it tomorrow. My station is unacceptable. And that sign? It's a joke. No one can read it!"

Heavy footsteps thudded toward me. I stepped forward, trying to look like I'd just arrived.

Andie clipped my shoulder as she passed, glaring. Her eyes dropped to the duck in my hand.

"What's with the creepy duck? Maybe it's trying to tell you something. Like the prize ducks are for paying customers—not volunteers."

I bit back a retort. No use feeding her drama.

She stomped off, feet pounding on the dirt path, raising puffs.

Stunned, I stared after her. Did she know anything about the other duck? Or was she just being her usual venomous self?

I continued down the path and found Tara standing in the dirt, arms wrapped around herself, visibly shaking.

"It's all right, Tara," I said, pulling her into a hug. "Don't let that toady woman get to you."

She leaned her head against my shoulder and gave a brittle laugh. "I wish I could turn her into a toad. She has the most abominable personality. How does she pass herself off as a marketing expert?"

"It's only in her mind. She's here because Rob Fenmore's a sponsor. We can evict her."

"Not soon enough." Tara lifted her head and stepped back. "Thanks, kiddo. You lift my spirits."

"Anytime. Go find some happy people, Tara."

Resuming my journey, I reached the landing where the tech team was tucked into their hidey hole behind the corn stalks, wires snaking through the dirt like roots.

"Everything okay?" I called out as the last group of visitors cleared the path.

"All good!" Gary shouted back. "Did you see the pooka?"

"It was freaking amazing! I'll give you all an extra cookie in your pay packet."

Laughter rippled through the stalks, warm and easy. I smiled, but the promise of cookies wasn't just a joke. I'd bake them. They'd earned it.

I waved goodbye and turned to continue my rounds, but Hallie's face kept surfacing in my mind—wet hair, blue lips, that purple halo. Not imagined. Not tech.

I was sure it was her.

And somewhere in the maze, something else had shifted. I could feel it. Like a thread pulled too tight, waiting to snap.

A FEW HOURS LATER, the last of the visitors trickled out and we closed the maze for the night. One night down. Only twenty more to go.

Katie passed me on her way to the parking lot, cider cup long gone, exhaustion etched into her face.

"Boy, this is more work than I thought it would be."

"Tell me about it. I've done a few nights each year, but with the theatre dark, I signed up for more this time. Starting to regret that decision—but it was fun. Mostly."

"Yeah, it was. Although I may have second thoughts about ever having kids." She frowned, keeping pace beside me.

"Rough time?"

"Trying to keep a five-year-old sitting still is impossible. I went through an entire pack of baby wipes."

I laughed—soft, surprised. Katie was usually the calm one. Seeing her rattled by toddlers was a novelty.

"But I bet you kept that smile and professional façade the whole time."

"Barely. At least it's just weekends. I couldn't do this full-time."

We reached her car and hugged goodnight. I continued down the gravel line to Vee-Dub, now sitting alone in a shallow puddle of fading light, the solar panel dimming with the last breath of day.

As I unlocked the door, a blackbird landed on the hood. It perched on the edge, still as stone, and stared at me with those glossy, beady eyes.

Was it the same one from the mansion?

From the walk-through?

From the pond?

Three times.

I stood there, keys in hand, heart ticking louder than it should.

The bird tilted its head, watching me.

Judging.

My breath caught. The night wasn't done with me.

And the night didn't feel quite finished.

With a piercing caw that echoed in the night, the bird lifted its wings and flew into the heavy mist toward the mansion. I watched until it disappeared, uneasiness settling deep in my bones.

BACK HOME, I FED Higgins, who had a great deal to say about being left alone all night without sufficient food. Never mind the bowl was full when I left. I set the new duck on the floor next to him, and he hissed. His reaction to it was the same as it was to the rubber duck.

Picking it up, I carried it into my bedroom and set it next to the rubber duck. I blinked. Somehow, the rip in the rubber one seemed a darker red, not as faded, and it looked like it matched the shading on the plastic one's beak. A sensation akin to spiders crawling over my skin. Creepy. Primal.

I sat on my bed's edge, hands folded and held between my knees, and whispered, "What really happened to you, Hallie?"

Chapter
Eight
Whispers in the Fog

THE CALL CAME AT 7:18 a.m. with Tara's name on the screen. Her voice trembled like a ghost's whisper in the morning light.

"Isla," she said, voice cracking, "It's Andie... she's dead. They found her by the pond. Alford did, just before dawn. Oh god, I can't—"

I sat straight up in bed, heart pounding, Higgins opening one sleepy eye from where he snoozed at the edge of my pillow. "Dead! What happened?"

"They don't know yet. Two sheriff's deputies are here with Detective Conklin. He won't let anyone near the area. But I saw—she was in the water. Her face..."

Tara dissolved into sobs, and I promised I'd be there in ten minutes. I sprang out of bed, adrenaline already surging, threw on my jeans and sweater, pulling my long hair into a ponytail, and grabbed my keys before running out the door and down the stairs.

By the time I arrived, the crime scene tape fluttered like a warning across the edge of the pond. Yellow against gray fog. The deputies guarded the corners, one near the duck station, where the unreleased plastic critters floated in containment. Conklin stood at the landing, arms folded, and shoulders bunched as he leaned on the railing next to the boat launch, his attention directed to the mist-shrouded pond. He heard my footsteps when I approached.

"Isla …" he said as he turned to face me, then added quietly, "You didn't need to come."

"I did."

He nodded, exhaling through his nose. "You're not going to like this."

"I already don't."

He glanced around, then motioned me off the path, out of earshot.

"We're treating this as suspicious. Cause of death isn't official, but there's bruising. Head wound, possibly before she went in. I've got forensics on their way from Santa Rosa, so we'll know more once they finish their sweep. For now, Wilson is looking at everything he can without disturbing it. The main issue is keeping everyone away from the scene."

I tried to make sense of it—of Andie, sharp-tongued and self-important, now silent beneath a sheet.

"I saw her last night," I said quietly. "Just after she argued with Tara."

Conklin's gaze sharpened. "When exactly?"

"Around eight-thirty. Maybe a few minutes after. I was on my way to the theatre's tech station here. I talked to Gary for a bit, then continued my rounds, checking on vendors."

"Do you recall what time you talked to each vendor?" His tone shifted, more focused now.

"Not exactly. No. I know it took a few minutes to get from one to the next. This is a big, sprawling maze." I paused, trying to recall the order, but the night blurred. Still, I pieced together what I could.

"I saw the 35 Ice Cream booth—they sold the space ice cream that comes in packets, and they had a small freezer unit. They were busy, barely having time to talk to me. I went by Andie's booth, but she wasn't there, and I talked to Isolde Thornwood for a few minutes.

Peter Pumpkin Eater, the Pie Party's booth, was also busy with lots of people buying slices."

"Wait. You said Ms. Langley wasn't at her booth. Can you estimate the time on that?" Conklin's eyes reflected the calculations he was making.

I thought for a minute, seeing the vendor stations in my mind and gauging the time from one to another. "I'd say about nine-fifteen."

"What time did the maze close and get everyone out?"

"We closed the entry at nine, but stragglers still wandered the maze for at least another fifteen to twenty minutes."

"So, all the vendors would be packing up to leave by about nine-thirty. Is that right?"

"Yes, that sounds right."

"What about the volunteers?" He glanced at his tablet, probably noting the names he had on it.

"Gone as soon as the last visitors left. One or two might have remained behind to clean up the welcome booth, but most of the maze tidying up will take place today…" I read the negative expression on his face. "… if we can get in to do it."

"Probably not. At least, not until we've gotten every clue we can get of what happened here." His voice softened. "I know it's hard to accept. What time did you leave?"

"About nine-forty. Katie and I talked on the way out."

He made a note on his phone, but his voice stayed even. "That helps. We'll want to verify alibis, check if anyone saw the victim between that moment and—"

"You think I'm a suspect?"

His brow twitched. "I think you were near the victim shortly before she died, and that's the job, Isla. Doesn't mean I'm booking you."

I blew out my breath. "Fine. Who else?"

"About five hundred people were here last night. That's the problem. Anyone could have killed her, or it might have been an accident."

But you don't think so. I left my thoughts unspoken.

He paused. "You hear anything about Glenn Harper being in the maze?"

I blinked. "Someone saw him here? He was at the Fairbourne Mansion earlier when I stopped by before coming here."

"Not sure. But his name came up. And Rob Fenmore—though no one remembers seeing him at all, which is its own kind of suspicious." He looked at me. "Don't repeat that."

Glenn's name again. And Rob—missing entirely. My gut stirred, but I kept my face neutral.

"You said you talked to Isolde Thornwood after you passed Langley's booth?" His lips tightened at Isolde's name. I didn't know what that meant—but I filed it away.

"Uh huh." I watched his lips tighten a bit, making me curious. "Penny for 'em."

"Just trying to place everyone where they were so if someone wasn't where they were supposed to be ..."

"Then you have a suspect. But I did see Isolde. Not that she didn't leave after I talked to her. Am I free to go?"

I wasn't sure if I wanted to leave—or dig deeper.

LATER, I SAT ON the steps of the welcome booth, nursing a cup of leftover cider, under a cloudy morning sky, threatening rain. Not that the mist wasn't damp enough already—I could smell it in the air. I kept running through the events of the previous evening, looking for clues within my actions and what I saw. Katie found me.

"You okay?" she asked, perching beside me.

"I don't know. I keep thinking about that duck I found last night. Andie saw it in my hand. She made a crack about it, right before she left. And now—"

Katie lowered her voice. "You didn't hear this from me. But Kevan thinks Andie might have left her station for a while, but no one noticed. Someone thought they saw Glenn, but they weren't sure."

"Sounds like a magician's trick—now you see them, now you don't."

She gave a humorless laugh. "Except the assistant didn't disappear. She turned up dead."

Katie's phone jingled a merry tune, jarring against the morning's somber quiet. She snatched it up, listened a moment, then replied, "I know. I'm on my way." She gathered her things before she turned to me. "I gotta run. Mom's at the shop and needs help. Call me if you need anything."

I watched her retreat, wondering if I needed to stay much longer or if I should check in at the mansion. I'd already been here almost two hours, so the guys should be arriving to work there soon.

Before I decided, a van bearing a Sonoma County sheriff's emblem pulled into the parking lot, and two casually dressed men hopped out, opened the van door, and pulled out two cases and a camera. The crime scene forensics team, I deduced.

When they approached me, I intercepted them. "Looking for Inspector Conklin?"

The lead one, a balding guy with a generous paunch, nodded. "Yep. Do you know where he is?"

"I do. Come on, I'll lead you to him. He's in the maze."

"Good thing we have a guide then," the second man answered. "I'm Bill and that's Jeff." Bill, a thin man with a scruffy beard, carried the camera and one of the cases.

"I'm Isla," I told them. "I'm on the corn maze committee." I led them onto the path, setting a brisk pace toward the landing. As we passed Rolf's Irish signpost, I got my first good look at it and thought it looked amazing. Norse-looking lettering, but still readable and arrows pointing in five different directions. We took the path marked swamp which branched about twenty feet from the sign.

Behind me, I heard Jeff's heavier breathing and slowed a little so the guys could keep up. "It's only a little farther."

A few minutes later, we arrived at the landing. At the end of the boards, Conklin talked with the deputy stationed at the cordoned area but shifted his attention our way when he heard us approach.

"I've brought the Santa Rosa team," I announced and stepped aside to let the two men pass me.

"You saved me a trip to the entrance," Conklin answered, coming forward to greet the new arrivals. "Thanks, Isla. I'll take it from here."

It was a dismissal, yet I lingered, hoping to get a glimpse of what the men might find. But Conklin flicked his hand like he was brushing a fly away, making it clear he wanted me to leave. With reluctance, I headed back to the path, choosing to go to the exit point so I could go by Andie's booth.

I found Tara sitting on a stool in the booth, her eyes red-rimmed from tears and a downcast expression on her face. The tragedy had hit her hard.

"Are you okay, Tara," I asked and stepped close to her.

She looked up, eyes squinting like the reflected sunlight through the fog bothered her. "I think so. Just feel so ... so helpless. How did this happen? I argued with her, Isla. Did I say something to send her to the lake ...?"

"Don't even consider that thought." I pulled up another stool, and sat beside her, dropping my hand on her shoulder. "Andie wasn't the kind of personality to let a little argument, especially one where she felt she had the upper hand, lead her to do anything foolish."

Tara's eyebrows twitched and her eyes caught mine. "So, you don't think she purposefully—"

"Absolutely not. She might have tripped and fallen in, but she didn't commit suicide."

"Oh god, we shouldn't have included the pond in the maze this year. It's like six years ago all over again." She pulled a tissue from her pants pocket and blew her nose. From the red skin tone around it, I surmised she'd done a lot of wiping.

She sniffled a few times before she spoke again. "Conklin asked for a list of everyone who had booths and what I knew about them. He's checking to see if each was in their station or if they heard anything. I expect he'll contact all of them. He asked me if I knew if Andie had any enemies … I almost blurted out everyone."

I cracked a smile. "Good thing you didn't, even if it is true. She rubbed people the wrong way."

"Did she ever. Conklin said he'd heard Glenn was in the maze around nine, but I didn't see him. I was at the front the whole time and I would have seen him come in."

"Unless he entered the maze at a different point. He could have come through the exit or any of the loops. But why would he?"

I ran my eyes around Andie's booth, a bit surprised at the lack of Halloween atmosphere in it. Plastic pumpkins with candles sat on a table to one side covered with black cloth. A bowl of candy corn sat in the middle and an animated witch hovered behind it.

The main table offered information on Rob Fenmore's real estate development business and flyers promoting the Fairbourne Mansion haunted house. Clearly, she and Rob had a single-minded objective. I took a flyer, folded it and stuffed it in my jeans pocket to look at in detail later.

A paperweight caught my eye, nothing fancy, but unusual. A spiral-shaped paperweight made from a fossilized nautilus shell, it was polished to a pearly sheen but with strange, iridescent veins, shimmering faintly in the foggy light. Embedded in the center sat a petite, cloudy opal. When I moved my head, the coloring changed, yet it appeared to watch me. The urge to touch it was strong, almost magnetic. But something in me recoiled. I took photos instead, resisting the pull.

Stepping back, I used my aura vision to look at it, not expecting anything from a dead fish's shell encased in glass, yet I observed a luminous muddled-looking green aura surrounding the object. A prickle of caution shot through me; the paperweight held an energy source.

Don't touch it! Warn the detective.

The words whispered in my mind. I jerked my head, like a fly had flown into my ear canal.

"Is something wrong?" Tara asked.

Was that actually from Daphne—or was I channeling her? I only wished I could speak to my aunt directly, not just hear warnings in my head at times like this.

To Tara, I replied, "Just a bug flew in my ear. No problem."

"Not at all what she pitched to the committee, is it?" Tara said, waving a hand at the sparse decorations.

"Maybe it vanished with her … magically."

Tara snorted. "Let's get out of here. Conklin doesn't need us hanging around and I have a stack of paperwork to address at the office. I'll need to notify our insurance company about the death."

As we strolled to the exit, a duck quacked—sharp, sudden. I spun around, heart thudding. Nothing in the sky. Nothing in the maze. "Did you hear that?" I asked.

"What?"

"I heard a duck quack." First rubber, then plastic, now an invisible quack. What was going on?

"No, I didn't hear it. And it sure wasn't one of the floaters. They're silent birds." Tara chuckled, her amusement breaking through the somber mood.

After Tara drove away, I strolled back toward the entrance, my thoughts drifting back to the ducks. Was Hallie reaching out—or was my mind chasing shadows? I turned to revisit the crime scene, when I spotted Conklin coming around the batwing curve toward me.

"I was just coming to –" I said, at the same time as he spoke.

"I wanted to ask you—"

We both stopped and laughed, then he said, "The lady first. What's up?"

I almost shrugged it off, but Daphne's words hung in my mind. "Uh, I noticed a paperweight on the table at Andie's vendor spot that you might want to check out. It's unusual and could have fingerprints on it." I paused and called the photos up from my phone.

Conklin took my phone and pinched the image larger, his eyebrows pulling together some as he studied it. "Do you think it's important?"

"I don't know, but there's something weird about it and my intuition is telling me to be careful around it. Don't touch it with your bare hands. It might be …" I paused. Might be what? What could I tell him? Cursed? Haunted? Evil? I had no idea. "… connected to what happened."

"Okay. I'll check it out. This is about the victim, right?"

"I think so. Or it might be connected to whoever killed her."

"I didn't say anyone killed her." He handed my phone back. "Do you suspect someone?"

"Not really, but I think it's a possibility. Do you have any clues?" I pressed for a little information. Had the forensics guys turned up anything yet? Their van still sat in the parking area.

"Actually, I wanted to ask you if you heard the argument Ms. Laughton had with Ms. Langley?"

"Only a little. Andie was upset about her booth placement and threatened Tara by telling her she would take it to Rob Fenmore, who is one of the sponsors this year."

"How did Laughton take it?"

"When I came to her, she was handling it okay. She and Andie had clashed a few times already. Andie is … was … kinda pushy.

Wanted things her way. It's strange there's another drowning at the same place Hallie died."

Conklin tilted his head a little to the left and gazed at me with the interest of a cat stalking a mouse before he cautioned. "Don't chase ghosts, Isla. Right now, we're looking at the people who argued with Andie, the ones who weren't seen at their booths ... and maybe even those who saw her last."

I swallowed involuntarily as a lump formed in my throat. "That might be me," I said, voice low. "Andie bumped into me right before she died."

I paused. "But someone else must have seen her leave the booth. Right?"

Chapter Nine
Echoes in Glass

CONVINCED THE TWO DEATHS at the pond had too many connections, I hurried to my apartment to resurrect my murder board. I quickly pulled down the notes on it, tucked them in the drawer and pulled out a new pad of sticky notes. *One of these days, I'm going to get a white board for this*, I promised myself. *One day I'll be a grown-up investigator with a real board.*

I wrote Hallie's name on a note and stuck it on the left and did the same for Andie on the right, then drew two chalk lines down, leaving a shallow gap between them for overlapping items. I stared at the two names—Hallie and Andie—like ghosts pinned to the wall.

On Hallie's side, I tagged the date of her death, the location and cause—drowning—which were in the shared zone, and people known to be around. Isolde, Glenn, the Alfords, and anyone else on the committee that year. The pond was another common element for both deaths. Then there was the rubber duck; everything I'd experienced since finding it connected it to Hallie. What little I knew about the investigation suggested an unclear timeline of her death, no witnesses, and it occurred inside the maze layout.

I shifted to Andie's side, writing down yesterday's date and pointing an arrow to the pond's sticky. Time of death was still unknown, but estimated at around nine-thirty, after the close of the maze. Cause of death was drowning, but she had possible head trauma. Location within the maze at the pond and the suspect list included anyone on the committee who was there last night, the Alfords, and the entire vendor list.

Who had a recent clash with Andie? Or better yet, who hadn't? Who was at both events? I looked at Hallie's list and noted Isolde, possibly Glenn—although unconfirmed for both but hints he might have been at each— and the Alfords. Was Tara on the committee then? I needed to see the vendor list from the maze six years earlier.

In the overlap area was the maze, the pond, and uncertain time of death. I knew being in water could affect the accuracy of the TOD and both women died at night and weren't found until the next morning.

Where should I put the plastic duck? Was it connected to Hallie or was it a warning about Andie? Nineteen was Hallie's age when she died, so I put the plastic duck under Hallie.

Two similar deaths in the same location at the same time of year and by drowning. They had to be connected. If they were both murdered, then it might be the same person.

In my mind, I heard the duck's quack again, the memory sending a tingle through my system. Coincidence? With no visible source? I couldn't dismiss it. Then there was the strange aura around the paperweight.

A spell? An enchantment? I wasn't sure I believed in either— but I'd seen enough to keep an open mind.

A jingle from my phone interrupted my contemplating. I picked it up and displayed the text message from Isolde. It said:

I'm at the front door, but I can't get in. I need to talk to you.

Perfect timing. I hurried downstairs to let Isolde in through the far-left theatre door and picked up the mail at the same time. My visitor stepped into the lobby, spotted the plastic tarps near the auditorium entrance and the various tools, removed broken toilets and other debris littering the theatre.

"What happened?" she gasped.

"I'm renovating the bathrooms, and it's turned into a major repair on plumbing as well. The workers are off today and tomorrow, so it's quiet down here now. Let's go to my office."

I led the way to the hall that accessed the ticket office, my office, and a small storage area before it took theatregoers to the balcony. I invited her to sit and threw in a prefilled coffee filter to make a pot for us.

I sat at the desk and leaned across part way, detecting the nervousness in her eyes as they darted toward me and dropped. "What can I help you with, Isolde? "

"I heard about Andie Langley when I got up to my shop this morning. Conklin was at my door, wanting to ask me a few questions. He wanted to know if I left my booth last night between eight-thirty and nine-thirty."

She paused to draw a breath, but when she didn't continue, I prompted. "Did you?"

Her eyes dropped to her hands where she folded and unfolded a tissue, worrying it like it held a secret she wasn't ready to share. "I did. I went to the privy thing. I told Carlotta at the next station that I was going, and I'd be back shortly if anyone asked. But when I told Conklin, he said Carlotta didn't mention it."

"Well, that doesn't mean you didn't do it. It just means Carlotta didn't remember or didn't understand you." I poured a cup of coffee for her. "Cream or sugar?"

"Cream, please. I usually drink tea, so the cream makes it more palatable. I appreciate it, dear."

After I handed it to her, I fixed mine and took a sip.

"You saw me at my booth last night, didn't you?" Her voice carried a frantic note.

"Yes, of course, I did. We talked for a few minutes. After I left you, I noticed that Andie's station was empty. I'm not sure of the exact time, but it was around nine-fifteen. With the vendor stations spaced the way they are, it's difficult to say if someone was in their booth at any given time. It's not like a person was right next to you unless you had a team."

"Glenn was supposed to help me last night, but he called and begged off," she said, her anxiety lessening some.

"Glenn wasn't there?" So much for someone seeing him.

"No, he told me he was working late and couldn't get away. All apologetic. Moon phases."

I blinked. Was that code for something?

"But I saw Glenn at the mansion shortly before I came to the maze," I told her. "He told you he was at the office?"

Her eyes lifted, rounder and wider. "He lied to me."

"Unless he considers the Fairbourne mansion's den his office, yes, he did."

"And I was going to pay him for helping out." Now, her voice took on a deep fury. "Wait until I see that wayward turd again!"

I raised an eyebrow but didn't argue. Glenn had earned the title. "Look, Conklin's questioning everyone. Don't worry about it. It's his job."

"But why is he doing it? I thought it was an accident."

"Maybe it was. Listen, since you're here, I have something to show you and maybe you can help me out." I opened my phone paging through to the paperweight photos.

I held it out to Isolde. "Have you seen an object like this before?"

She took the phone and studied the photo, holding it close to her eyes.

"I took two more from different angles. Look at them." She did, examining them as closely.

"Most unusual," she murmured. "Where did you see it?"

"In Andie's booth. That's not all. I detected a muddled green aura around it."

"An aura? That's unusual. It's not a living thing, so it's an energy haze. Green is usually a positive or good indicator, but muddled? In what way?"

"It varied in shades from light to dark with brownish streaks in it. I didn't touch it, but it seemed ominous to me."

Isolde's lips flattened and her eyes narrowed. "I would like to try a reading on it. Is it still there?"

"I doubt it. I told Conklin about it, and I expect the deputies added it to their evidence bag."

"Oh, too bad. The aura suggests a spell or enchantment on it. It's best if no one touches it until we can identify what it is." Isolde set my phone on the desk, her disappointment obvious in her frown. At least, she no longer looked anxious.

She thanked me for the coffee and listening, then left. I mulled her words about the paperweight and looked at the photos again. A jagged line or flaw caught my eye, but I couldn't enlarge the image enough on my screen to see it closer. It might only be a speck of dust or corn silk, clinging like memory.

But I didn't have time to examine it more. I had to get over to the mansion to talk to Gary and his crew. I swallowed the last of my coffee, locked my office and the front door, before I trekked across the theatre to the back exit. It was only eleven, but I felt like I'd been up for much longer.

I locked the door behind me and stepped into the misty morning. If Conklin was still chasing suspects, the maze might not be done whispering its secrets.

I CALLED TARA ON the way to the mansion to see if the detective had given us the clearance to open the maze for the afternoon tour.

"Not yet, Isla. The forensic team is still combing the area, so it doesn't look promising. The Alfords, while sympathetic to the tragedy, are also having a cow about the possibility of the maze being shut down over the opening weekend. They put a lot into this."

"Yeah, I can understand that. We've all put a lot into it and the town's been waiting for it. Keep me posted if you hear anything. "

I pulled up in front of the mansion where several cars were parked. Gary's vintage Chevy stood out among the newer vehicles. When I stepped through the front door, the familiar chill air greeted me, sharp as ever. I wasn't sure if it was a ghost or a manifestation from the house.

So far, the two spirits I'd identified were in two separate areas. Fairbourne on the second floor and not going farther than the staircase from the left while his wife haunted the third floor where she died. The third spirit, who I guessed might be Hallie, was sporadic and not tied to the mansion. Since she died in the pond, I considered a connection between it and the mansion might exist.

I found the team at work in the study. A full crew of eight volunteers busied themselves with cleaning, careful not to disturb the authentic cobwebs we'd left in place, and adding more grit to it. In the right corner, Gary and Steve worked to create the ghostly mirror effect where visitors would see a ghost standing behind them when they looked in the mirror.

"How's it going?" I asked.

Gary glanced at me. "It's coming along. You okay?"

"Pretty much. I assume you've all heard about the tragedy."

"It was on the news a short time ago," Steve said, barely looking up from the tiny projector he was positioning. "The reporter from last night had a dramatic report of the drowning."

"Cindy would," I murmured. "Did she give any details?"

"Not really. Sounded like a short sheriff's notice that someone had died in an accident, but the authorities were still investigating, She said they wanted anyone who might have seen or heard anything around the pond area between eight-thirty and nine-thirty to get in touch." Steve paused. "I suppose that might mean us, or at least, me."

"Did you guys hear anything at the landing?" I hadn't thought about them being so close in their corn cubbyhole.

""People were still rollin' through before we closed up," Gary said, brushing dust off his jeans. "I was locking stuff down around nine-thirty, and I saw Andie with this dude. Demon clown costume, mask, fuzzy blue wig. Kinda surreal."

"Did you recognize the man?" A surge of excitement shot through me.

But Gary shook his head. "Nah, full mask, for sure. Dude was maybe five-eleven, six foot tops—but that blue wig made him look taller."

"Were they talking or arguing?" I pressed for more information.

""Nah, didn't seem like it," Gary said with a shrug. "Guy had a bottle of wine; they each had a glass—total mellow vibe."

Steve set his drill down and stood. "I headed outta the corn cubby hole 'round the same time but left my dang keys behind. Had to double back. When I came out again, they were still on the landing, drinkin' quiet-like. So yeah… reckon I'm one of the last folks to see her alive."

"I'd say so. And no signs of a fight?"

"Didn't look like it to me," Steve said. "They were talkin'—real focused—but not raisin' voices or anything."

"You both need to talk to Detective Conklin," I said. "Anything you remember could help. Did Andie seem drunk? Like, enough to stumble into the pond?"

They exchanged glances.

"Nah," Gary said, rubbing the back of his neck. "She had a glass, but it wasn't full. I just passed by—looked chill."

"Same here," Steve added, shifting his weight. "Didn't linger, but it had the feel of a date. Quiet. Focused. Sorry I can't give more."

A masked man, wine, and a quiet conversation. It sounded innocent—but I'd learned not to trust appearances.

Gary frowned. "But we can't go runnin' to the sheriff right now. We've got a ton to finish if we're gonna be ready for the afternoon—"

"It's probably canceled, Gary," I cut in gently. "Tara will let me know, but I wouldn't count on the maze reopening today. Maybe tonight, if we're lucky. But I've got a hunch the landing's off-limits."

Gary's gaze drifted toward the window. "Well, the landing's just fluff anyway. The pooka's the real draw for the night crowd. Not spooky in daylight. If they shut it down, I can rig a timed appearance—every twenty minutes or so."

"That would be great. I'll call Conklin to come by here or get you an appointment to see him later. Oh, incidentally, did either of you see Glenn Harper leave the mansion last night?"

"Yo, me." Tony said. "Da dude cut out 'bout ten minutes after youse," He jerked his thumb toward the hallway like he could still see the guy disappearing.

"That's useful," I answered. So why didn't he go to help Isolde instead of telling her he was at the office? Or maybe he left here to go to his office.

I called Conklin and briefly explained I had three of my crew who saw Andie at the landing. He agreed to come by to talk to them, but it would be around four before he could get here. Since I had him on the phone, I asked, "What's the prospect for opening the maze today?"

"Not good," he replied. "I'll talk to you later." And he ended the call. I relayed the information to the guys and left them to do their job. I wanted to talk to Rob Fenmore.

LOCATED JUST A BLOCK from Commerce Square, Rob's real estate office was a compact space located in a multi-purpose building—Rob's company built it—with shared offices and a couple anchor tenants. The primary building occupant here was Whitmore Home Improvement, a company with a large footprint to display various remodels of bathrooms, kitchens, and dens.

I strolled by the windows displaying some of the options following the hallway to the elevator for the second floor. A spacious kitchen plan caught my eye, making me wish I had the room for a bigger one in my apartment.

Rob's office was the first one out of the elevator, directly across from the door. I pushed the door open and stepped inside, catching Rob digging through the desk on the right-hand side. The name plate on it read: Andie Langley.

"Hi, Rob! I hope I'm not interrupting."

He looked up. "Isla! I wasn't expecting you. Come on in."

A second door stood open on the left side with a slightly larger office within and he pointed that way.

As he shoved a drawer shut, he straightened. "The … uh, tragic death has created a bit of a scramble today. I relied on Andie to keep things filed and handle the office. Unfortunately, I don't know what her filing system was."

He stepped toward his office while I waited a moment. "From what I knew of her, she was efficient, so once you figure it out, you'll be fine." How many ways could people file things? Alphabetical, chaotic, or Andie-style.

"You're right. Did you need something?" He closed the door after I stepped into his office.

I gazed around the sparse space but noticed his real estate licenses on the wall along with a few other credentials. I sat in the lightly padded and curved office chair. "I just wanted to see if you have all the invoices for the purchases my crew have made for the mansion. Work there is going well, and they are right on schedule."

"That's wonderful. Yes, I think we've gotten the invoices with no issues. Andie paid several yesterday." He smiled, a bit of nerves showing in the twitch at the edge of his lips. "This project and the subsequent construction are going to be a boon to the town. Lots of people are going to profit on it."

"I hope so. It's certainly been a bonus for the theatre." I returned his smile, but something felt off. No grief. Just nerves. What was the story here?

"Yes, Glenn has kept me abreast of the progress and your crew's ingenuity. He called me last night to tell me how excited he was. I just hope this tragedy won't affect the plans any."

"I didn't know Glenn had an interest in the mansion project," I said, but my gaze rested on a marbled saucer on his desk. The coloring in it resembled the paperweight I'd found at Andie's booth. Was there a connection? "That's an interesting little plate you have. Do you put business cards on it?"

Rob glanced at the item and shook his head. "No, it's an antique I found in Italy. I thought it was unique. But yes, Glenn is an investor in the mansion project. Andie pulled him onboard a few months ago on a different deal I was running. They were dating at the time, but it fizzled out."

I raised an eyebrow. Dating? Glenn was married. Either Rob didn't know—or didn't care. What an intriguing twist. I didn't press. But I'd be revisiting that detail.

To reinforce my visit pretext, I asked, "Could I get a printout of all the invoices, so I have an idea of how much we've spent so far? It'll help with the planning."

"Of course. I'll get—" He cut off and for the first time, I saw the sadness in his face. "Uh, it may take me some time to locate and print the file. Normally, Andie…" His voice broke.

"Rob, do you know if anyone threatened Andie?" I kept my voice soft to encourage him to trust me.

"No. Not to my knowledge. God knows, she ticked a lot of people off, but enough to harm her? No. I don't think so."

"Not even Glenn?"

"No way. He'd never hurt anyone." I recalled the conversation I overheard. Glenn told me he was talking to Andie, but maybe it had been Rob. He seemed uneasy about the whole thing, turning his wedding ring around on his finger and avoiding eye contact.

"Look, Isla, I need a day or two to process all this and I'll get that report done for you. I'll bring it by, okay?"

"Sure. I'm sorry for your loss. I know you and Andie worked together for quite a while."

He nodded and looked away from me, like he might start sobbing or didn't want me to see he cared.

As I stepped out of his office, my gaze drifted back to the marbled saucer on his desk. It shimmered faintly in the lamplight—too much like the paperweight.

I didn't touch the saucer. But I couldn't shake the feeling that Rob knew more than he was saying.

Chapter Ten
Whispers from the Deep

THE PAPERWEIGHT WOULDN'T LEAVE my mind.

When I returned to the theatre, I transferred the photos to my computer, hoping a bigger screen might reveal something I'd missed.

Tara had texted earlier—Conklin had officially shut down the maze for the day. He hinted we might reopen for Sunday's tours, but the pond would stay off-limits

I shifted forward in my chair to pull up the image where I'd seen the mark. On the larger screen, it was clear: a hair-thin crack in the glass. Not a scratch—an actual break. It didn't mar the beauty, but the flaw was distinct.

Since I had the image up, I asked the search program to look for a similar item to see if it had any history. Within seconds, the program brought up at least three dozen images that resembled it but weren't quite the same. I ran down the images until I came to one that looked exactly like it.

The link under the photo indicated a museum in Istanbul, so I clicked on it. This couldn't be the same object. Andie didn't have a classic art piece in her possession, did she?

A bigger, beautifully photographed image of the paperweight appeared on the screen in detail. The description read: *The Whispering Nautilus -- A spiral-shaped paperweight made from a fossilized nautilus shell, polished to a pearly sheen. Within it, iridescent lavender veins shimmer faintly, but in moonlight are known to glow a deep purple. Embedded in the center is a tiny, cloudy opal that appears to flicker.*

From the image, it certainly looked like the one Andie had, although I couldn't see any flaw in it. The website showed two other photos, including one from almost the same angle I'd taken. No flaw. Either it wasn't the same one or Andie had damaged it. Still, how would she end up with an obviously important artwork?

Intrigued, I keyed in the name listed for the paperweight and three websites provided information on it. I clicked on the first and skimmed through it. While it described the nautilus in more detail, it didn't delve into its history, although it did mention researchers tried to analyze the mysterious veins, but couldn't determine what they were or why they glowed. A final note stopped me cold:

Stolen from the Istanbul Museum. Never recovered.

Stolen? Had Andie taken it—or had someone passed it to her?

The second site leaned mystical. According to legend, the nautilus was recovered from a 19th-century shipwreck in the Bermuda Triangle. The only item found intact was the shell, clutched in the skeletal hand of the ship's navigator.

Locals claimed it whispered to those who held it—offering cryptic warnings or glimpses of the future. Some believed it held the navigator's soul. Others said nautilus shells were used for scrying, especially when paired with opal or moonstone. A few even claimed they could channel memory echoes.

I stared at my photo again. The aura had been real. Not imagined. Isolde might sense more than I could.

I sent her the museum link and the other sites, along with a note: *What do you think of this?*

I stared at the screen, waiting for Isolde's reply.

She'd been helpful. Honest. Nervous, yes—but not evasive. Still…

The Nautilus was stolen. Valuable. Possibly enchanted.

And Isolde had asked to "read" it. Had she known what it was?

I didn't want to believe she'd mislead me. But I'd learned to trust my gut—and question everything.

Maybe she was just curious. Maybe she was trying to protect me.

Or maybe … she'd been searching for it all along.

Just then, Higgins padded into the office and let out a plaintive meow.

It was suppertime and I hadn't fed him yet.

I bookmarked the page and stood. "Sorry, buddy. Let's get dinner."

Not just for him, I was starving too.

I STOOD ON THE LANDING at night, waiting for the pooka to rise from the water. Ribbons of fog drifted across the pond, curling around my ankles like ghost fingers., then the pond bubbled as a prelude to the pooka rising, a special effect to give more substance to the illusion.

The pond bubbled, then stilled. Something rose.

Not the horse's skull I expected—but a woman's face, warped and dripping with algae. The eyes were black rimmed and sunken, seeming to stare right at me. I trembled as the figure rose higher until it levitated above the water and hung there.

A scent of rot emanated from the pond or the figure and I gagged. Something tugged my arm, trying to pull me into the water. I choked as the woman's lips peeled back to speak—

And a squeaky duck quack echoed in my mind.

I woke, gasping for breath and grabbing a tissue to spit. The quack lingered in my mind, leading me to turn on the light and gaze at the rubber duck on the dresser. Enclosed in the plastic bag, it remained on the top ... only Higgins sat on it, tail flicking like he'd claimed it for himself.

I didn't go back to sleep but started another early morning day. Hallie's name lingered on my murder board—and now, maybe, in my dreams. Had Hallie tried to contact me in my sleep? Or was my mind stitching symbols together, desperate for answers?

I needed more information about Hallie Connor, and so far, Conklin hadn't given me anything. With the new investigation, he didn't have time to look at an old case. Unless I could convince him the two were connected, he wouldn't be reviewing Hallie's drowning any time soon.

After I gave Higgins a treat for waking me, I grabbed a cup of coffee and considered my options for the day. As the town historian, Gianni knew everything worth knowing in Arbordale. If Hallie's death left ripples, he'd felt them. We were a small town ... everyone gossiped.

I sent a text message to Gianni asking if he had time to meet with me today, then headed for the shower. By the time I dressed and grabbed a piece of toast, it was about nine. My phone signaled a message while I washed my cup.

I figured it was Gianni, but the message came from Isolde.

I have more information on the paperweight. When can we meet?

I stared at the message. More information? Or another layer of mystery?

If Conklin cleared the maze, it would open at two this afternoon. I replied:

How about noon? At your shop?

She agreed.

About ten minutes later, Gianni called me. "What do you say to meeting for brunch at the Stagedoor Cafe?" his warm baritone suggested. With such a marvelous voice, he should have been an actor.

"I'm meeting someone at noon. Can we go about ten thirty? I need to pick your brain."

"That sounds fine. Anything in particular you need from my brain?" he asked, a chuckle in his voice.

"Whatever you know about Hallie Connors and what you recall about her death. I have some questions about the Fairbourne Mansion." I could probably ask him a dozen questions, but time was limited.

"I shall try to prepare. My brain and I will see you at ten-thirty."

I smiled. Gianni's charm was effortless, even before brunch.

By the time I tended to my daily tasks, checked my email and the mail I hadn't touched the previous day, which included confirmation for a choir's theatre rental in December along with the required fee. I deposited it with the bank's remote option, scanning the check with my phone. That helped the theatre account. I glanced at the time on my computer, grabbed my light sweater, and ran across to the diner.

I ARRIVED ABOUT FIVE minutes late, finding Gianni already seated in a booth, reading a book. He smiled at me and quipped, "Those closest to a destination are always the last to arrive."

"I'm afraid that's often true. I always think I have more time than I do." I settled into the seat across from him. Today, his Hawaiian shirt brought a burst of color to another overcast day.

Betsy, our stage door guard's wife and the chef/owner of the diner greeted us, handing us menus. "Sherie will take your order shortly. Would you like coffee?"

"Might I get a screwdriver?" Gianni asked, looking for more fortification in the morning than I did.

"Of course," Betsy answered.

"Coffee's fine for me," I said. "With cream."

"Have you had any word on the maze for today?" Gianni peeked at me over his menu.

"Not yet. Tara said she'd call if she got the okay."

"Damn shame about the accident on Friday. It's a call back to Hallie Connor's death. Is that why you want more information about her?"

"Yes, it is, and you're the best person to know about anything unusual. Let's order, then we can dive in." I flipped my menu closed, ready to order.

He took the cue and flipped his shut. Sherie soon came to the table along with our drinks and we ordered. I leaned toward Gianni, put my phone on the table, and told him I was going to record so I didn't miss anything.

He chuckled. "You have limited memory?"

"More a case of conflicting memory. I hear something and my mind tries to analyze it so I may miss an important detail."

"Ah, I see. Multi-tasking in the mind. Well, Hallie Connor was the daughter of Ryan and Bridget Connor, who still live on Red Hawk Drive. She graduated from Arbordale High School with honors and was going to the university at Santa Rosa. Quite a pretty and popular girl." He paused to reach in a satchel he'd brought and pulled out a xerox of a young brunette with big eyes and a bigger smile.

"Officially, her death was deemed an accident. Sheriff Bradford couldn't find any evidence to the contrary. Maybe she went for a late-night swim after too much drinking."

"In the pond?" My lips scrunched up with disgust. It was filthy.

"Apparently, Hallie took a dip in it now and then. Chi può spiegare? Who knows why. She drowned and that was the cause of death."

I didn't know the phrase, but his hand flip said enough. "No one questioned it?" I thought it odd that her parents didn't want more answers.

Gianni shrugged. "The whole incident was kinda hushed up. Maybe they wanted more privacy. And you know the gossip circle." He smiled and his brown eyes twinkled. "Some of the rumors suggested she was pushed by some kids, but others said it was an evil spirit. Halloween, you know. But nothing ever came out about it.

Disappointed at the lack of information, I asked, "Was she alone at the maze on the night she died?"

"Ah, that is a splendid question, my dear. A couple of people said they saw her talking to an older man, but they didn't recognize him. And they couldn't say if he went through the maze with her. They started out together, it seems. Later, four or five saw her alone. Inconclusive."

"Did any of them tell the sheriff about it?"

Gianni lifted his hand in a dismissive gesture, waving it sideways a bit. "I don't know about that. Probably, they didn't think about It at the time."

Our food arrived and we paused to attack our respective meals. Mine pancakes with eggs and bacon, while my companion had chosen steak and eggs.

"You said Hallie's parents still live here. Have you ever talked to them?"

"Several times. They are on the library board. Hallie came to see me often. She loved learning about the area's history. Wanted to write historical textbooks like a novel."

I paused to wash down a bite with coffee. "Isn't that what historical novels do?"

Gianni chucked. "Not always. Some writers make up more than a little backstory of the characters. Granted, it's difficult to say what the people were really like, but sometimes they're so far off the mark, you can't believe it. *Perché mai.*"

I looked up at the expression. Gianni frequently sprinkled Italian into his remarks, but I didn't know this one. "What'd that mean?"

"Roughly 'for what reason.' Like why would the writer make up garbage about someone with nothing to back it up?"

"I get it now." I shoved my plate away, eggs and potatoes half-eaten. "What can you tell me about the Fairbourne Mansion? Rumors I've heard are two ghosts haunt it."

He nodded. "That's pretty much it. Jonathan and his wife Abigail. She died in childbirth, but the baby survived—"

"I know that part. Are the ghosts real and are they the only ones?"

"Do you believe in ghosts?" He set his gaze at me, watching for my reaction.

I didn't answer at first, considering how much to tell him before he concluded I was daft. "Well, I kinda do. I mean, every time I walk through the front door of the mansion, a blast of cold air brushes against me. Why is that?"

"Yup." He forked his last piece of steak, holding it up before he continued. "That's the usual reaction. Anyone else in the group feel it?"

"Yeah, pretty much all the crew noticed it."

Gianni chewed, swallowed, then commented. "It's a feature of the house. Not built-in, but a paranormal ward."

"What? How?" I knew about wards although I'd never heard of a house with an active power.

Wiping his lips, Gianni leaned a little closer and lowered his voice. "Part of the myth of the house is that witches passed a protection spell on the house after Abigail's death."

"Did Jonathan believe something evil was responsible for her death?"

"That I don't know. But if you felt the chill upon entering, then you have to think there might be something to it."

Was he kidding me or being serious? I couldn't tell. He was known to be a trickster at times, but usually he was on the up and up when consulted about the town's history. "Have you felt it, Gianni?"

An enigmatic smile settled on his lips and his eyes twinkled. I waited for him to speak. But my phone played a chorus of "Uptown Girl," and I grabbed it up. "Hi, Tara! What's the news?"

She sounded more upbeat when she answered. "Conklin has given us a green light to resume this afternoon at three. I talked to Cindy at the station, and she'll get the news out."

"That's wonderful, Tara. Did Conklin say anything else about the accident?" With Cindy's help, we might get a good crowd tonight.

"Well, there's a bit of bad news there, Isla. He's keeping the lake and the landing cordoned off. Sorry, but no station for the theatre."

"I figured he might need to do that. I'll see you at three."

"Good news?" Gianni asked as I ended the call.

"Yes, the maze is back on. Speaking of the maze, does it have any stories attached to it?"

"Other than the drowning?" he quipped.

While he thought about my question, Missy came into the café and spotted us. Looking fresh and charming in a pale yellow, wildflower-patterned dress, she looked like spring instead of fall.

"Missy, hello. Were you looking for me?" I was surprised to see her since the theatre was idle today.

"Yes and no. I thought I might do some work in the wardrobe this afternoon. I'd like to send some of the older costumes to the high school theater group. But I don't have a key to the door. So, I thought I'd drop in here to see if you'd come over for lunch and it appears you have." She turned a sunny smile on Gianni.

"Right, good thinking. Um, you know Gianni, don't you?"

"I believe we've met." She held out a hand to him and he took it, bending his head down to kiss the back of it. Missy giggled; I rolled my eyes.

"Please join us," Gianni offered. He motioned to the seat next to him and Missy slid into the booth.

"About my question?" I prompted, then added for Missy's benefit. "I asked if he knew any folktales about the maze."

Gianni sipped his drink before answering. "Not so much. Except the land was once part of the Fairbourne estate. You can check the County Recorder to see more about it. Library has a nice section about Arbordale's history and any associated folklore. But how accurate it is, I don't know."

I digested all this information along with my food. In similar fashion, it would take a while to sort through it. But it pointed to the connection with both places. I had more questions, but a glance at the wall clock told me I needed to leave to meet Isolde on time.

"You know so much about the town," Missy said. "I heard the Alford pond may be home to some will 'o' the wisps."

"Ah *ignis fatuus* ... No, I don't recall anything related to the fae." Gianni smiled. "However, I saw something odd once—lights at the pond on a foggy night, but I chalked it up to kids with lanterns. Tell me your fae stories, *bella signora.*"

Before Missy replied, I thanked Gianni, who was eager to talk more, and apologized for having to cut our conversation short.

"Can you let me in the theatre?" Missy asked before I dashed off.

"Sorry. Not right now, and I don't have a spare key with me. Aren't you coming to the maze this afternoon?"

"Oh, it's on again, isn't it? Yeah, I'll wander about it a bit this afternoon. I have the perfect costume to delight the children. "

"Good. See you there." As I walked away, Missy resumed talking to Gianni. I had a feeling those two could chat for a while about anything. And maybe Missy would learn more than she expected.

WHEN I STEPPED INTO Mystic Moon Apothecary, Isolde was busy with a customer, an older woman, who chatted animatedly with her hands. Isolde kept a close watch, so the woman didn't knock any of the potions off the shelf as she waved her arms around like a whirligig.

After a few minutes, Isolde smiled broadly and picked up a bottle and showed it to the woman, who nodded and they strolled to the cash register, the customer talking the whole time. I caught a mention of "low energy remedy" so I guessed the bottle held an herbal energy potion.

Once the customer left, Isolde flipped her Open sign for the Out to Lunch sign. "I'm sorry, Isla. Martha is quite a talker. Come on back to my reading nook."

I followed her to the alcove on the right side where a deep purple velour curtain concealed the door to a pentagon-shaped room. When she called it a "reading nook," Isolde referred to the place she read Tarot cards and palms.

The table, which currently held a closed laptop computer, a teapot and two cups, matched the shape of the room and two comfortable chairs sat at it, with another three pushed against the wall next to a deep shelf that housed several decks of cards, a few velvet bags held other divination objects, and a Ouija board. Another shelf held about a dozen books and the one below it overflowed with candles in holders and incense burners.

"Do you do seances and the board also?" I asked as I sat at the table.

"Whatever the client wants." She poured tea from the pot, the scent of moist lemon and mint drifting from it, and pointed to a sideboard with cream and sugar, then opened the computer and clicked to a page. "I found more information about the Whispering Nautilus. This is mystical and exciting, but also a little alarming. While no one is certain where or when the paperweight originated, a legend says it was recovered from the wreck of a 19th-century ship that vanished in the Bermuda Triangle.

"Yes, I read that also," I said after she' repeated quite a bit of what I'd already learned.

"I have more to say." She turned her gaze at me, blue-gray eyes wide and a flash of power in them. A zing from the intensity scurried along my nerves. I rose to get cream for my tea and quickly returned, shifting forward, eager for more information.

"It gets better," she cooed, almost making me beg to know more.

"Go on," I urged, anxious to hear what else she'd learned.

"Firsthand reports from the locals who held it claim the shell "whispers" to them—offering cryptic warnings or glimpses of the future. Some believed it harbors the soul of the navigator, forever guiding those who dare to listen."

I shivered. "Then I'm glad I didn't touch it and warned Detective Conklin against it." I didn't need any more cryptic warnings; my previous night's dream popped in to say hello for a moment.

Isolde clicked another button. "And I found this article under a website about mystical luck objects. It repeats part of the legend, but adds that the ship called *La Speranza di Mare*—Hope of the Sea— appeared to have sailed from Sicily in 1828. At the time, locals confirmed the ship's departure and that the navigator was Matteo Ferentino, a popular fellow with the local ladies. A few of them also swore he had a paperweight that seemed to whisper.

"But where the luck comes into play is in this paragraph:

'Despite its eerie reputation, it's said to bring uncanny luck to those who respect it. A string of improbable successes such as winning raffles, avoiding accidents, and finding lost things have been attributed to its presence. But the luck always comes with a price: a recurring dream of drowning in a stormy sea.'"

"Holy moly! That sounds like a curse."

"It does. Blessed on one side and tortured on the other. But I bet Andie didn't know what she was getting when she acquired this.

She probably heard the good fortune part and either didn't read or ignored the price." Isolde sipped her tea and waited for my assessment.

"If all she saw was fortune, the rest didn't matter. Could it have contributed to her domineering attitude or was she always like that?"

Isolde shrugged. "Either way, she paid the price. Just not in a stormy sea."

"The next question is how did she get it." The object was stolen in Istanbul, but it could have been sold and resold or stolen many more times since then. Learning all this information didn't make me feel more comfortable with the paperweight, its history, or how it affected Andie. She was dead, but the Whispering Nautilus didn't shove her into the pond. So, who did?

Maybe someone else wanted the object, and Andie wouldn't part with it. I finished my tea and asked, "Did you get the message from Tara? The maze is opening at three today. Are you coming?"

She waved a hand toward the shop. "I'm not doing the afternoons. No one to watch my shop. But I'll be there tonight. Are you sure you wouldn't like a reading?"

I shook my head. "No thanks. I'd rather not be influenced by a prediction."

"But you are, aren't you?" Isolde countered. "You have dreams and visions now and then, I imagine."

How did she know? Could she read my aura or thoughts to know what was in my mind? I squinted at her, half-expecting static. But her aura shimmered—calm blues, crowned with violet, streaked with pink and green. No warning signs. Nothing alarming.

She laughed. "No, I'm not reading your mind … or your aura, which I can see. You have a gift, Isla, but it's not hidden from others who have similar talents."

"Oh, I didn't know that. I've never told anyone about it." Now I could worry how many in Arbordale knew.

"Don't fret over it, dear. I won't tell anyone."

Isolde poured us a second cup of tea and broke out some English biscuits--her lunch snack, she explained.

"Maybe you can tell me something," I ventured while she munched. I didn't need any food and sipped at my tea. "Do you know if the front door at the Fairbourne Mansion is hexed?"

She blinked. "Why do you think that?"

"Because there's a wave of icy cold air when you pass through it."

Her eyes grew bigger. "Really?"

I nodded.

"I'd not heard that before. But it's possible. Not a hex so much, but a warning or protection spell."

"For real?"

"Don't dismiss magic too quickly, Isla. Stranger things happen than can be explained. If it has a spell on it, you will find the components of the spell somewhere near the door."

"What do I look for?" I asked, befuddled by the possibility.

She rose and pulled out a small book. Its tile was *Spells, Hexes, and Chants*. "Here. Take this. It will explain and give you examples."

I took the book and thanked her, tucking it into my backpack.

When we finished tea, she opened her shop again and I thanked her for her hospitality. Before I stepped out the door, Isolde handed me a silver chain with a triangular-shaped black stone in a silver cage. "Wear this," she said softly.

"What is it?" I touched the stone, feeling the cool surface, yet sensing energy within it.

"Black tourmaline—a protective talisman. Keep it with you always."

Stunned and a bit unnerved by the gift, I nodded, and she hugged me before she closed the door. I slipped the long chain over my head, the stone resting just below my collarbone, pulsing in time with my heartbeat.

I stepped out of Mystic Moon, still mulling over the Nautilus paperweight and the strange tingling energy I'd felt when I held it. Isolde's theory that it might've been stolen from a private collection had only deepened the mystery.

The late afternoon breeze stirred the charms hanging from the shop's awning, making them clink and whisper like wind chimes caught mid-gossip. I pulled out my phone and scrolled to Glenn's contact. I typed:

Have you heard the news about the maze? It's reopening. I'd like to stop by and talk to you.

I hit send, then slipped into my car and started the engine. No immediate reply.

Rather than wait, I pulled out onto Main and pointed the nose of my car toward the mansion. I figured if I didn't hear from him by the time I got there, I'd walk the property and check in with the crew.

Halfway down Willow Bend, my phone buzzed in the cup holder.

I'm on-site. South porch rail. Sure, stop by.—GH

That was … brisk. No emojis. No how-are-yous. Not that I expected a warm welcome. The man had been dodging straight answers all week.

I tapped my fingers on the steering wheel as I turned down the road toward the mansion, wondering how best to approach him. Firm but casual? Or jump straight into the late-night timeline and who saw who at the maze?

With Glenn, subtlety was like fishing in the dark—you might catch something, but it probably wasn't what you were aiming for.

Chapter Eleven
An Unexpected Revelation

I PARKED IN FRONT of the mansion, and texted Glenn to let him know I was there. A few minutes later, he stepped out of the front door, a slight limp altering his normal stride. His face was tight, guarded—but it wasn't until he turned his head that I noticed the bruise on his jaw, just turning that sickly green-yellow hue.

"You miss the maze Friday night?" I asked casually, leaning against my car. "Didn't see you there."

Glenn rubbed his chin, fingers grazing the bruise like he wanted me to notice it. "Nah. Figured it was a kid thing. Not really my scene."

My eyes narrowed. The light around him flickered—murky orange wisps rippling outward like smoke caught in a draft. I let my vision shift, calling up the deeper aura sight I rarely used in public. The world shimmered faintly, and Glenn's aura bloomed into full view—a wide halo pulsing with jagged tension, crimson threads slicing through like fresh wounds.

"You get that bruise at the mansion?" I asked lightly, nodding toward it.

He hesitated—just a beat too long. "Yeah. Corner of that antique dresser Rob made us move. Thing's cursed, I swear."

I didn't buy it. The bruise was too clean, too direct. Not furniture. More like a fist.

Before I could press him, heat flared against my chest. The black tourmaline necklace. Not painful, but insistent—like a warning bell.

I let the silence stretch, then pulled the flyer from my bag. "Found this in Andie's booth," I said. "Recognize it?"

His jaw twitched. "No. Should I?"

"There was a paperweight in her display," I said, voice low. "Nautilus shell. Could be antique. Sheriff's office has it now."

His aura flared—red spikes chased by bile-green streaks. He masked it well, but the tourmaline burned hotter.

Glenn swallowed. "Lotta junk in that booth," he muttered. "Don't know why you'd care about some tacky paperweight."

"I tilted my head. "Just seems like Andie cared enough to keep it hidden."

"Crazy woman," he muttered. "She collected weird stuff." He shook his head before saying, "Sheriff has it, eh?"

I nodded, watching him closely. Funny, I thought. He called it a tacky paperweight—but he acted like he'd never seen it.

I paused as I glimpsed Gary exiting the mansion. He scrambled down the front steps and half-ran toward us.

"Hey, Isla!" Gary called out, jogging toward the gate. "Just heading over to rig the auto-pooka."

"That's terrific. Tara cleared it with Conklin?"

"Yeah, she called a bit ago. Said it's a go, but they're sticking a deputy nearby to keep an eye."

"Good. How's the mansion work coming?"

"Pretty solid. We've got a full crew today, so things are moving fast. I'll swing back once the illusion's running." He acknowledged Glenn with a tap at his cap and headed on to his car.

I swung back toward Glenn. "I better head over to the maze now. You coming?"

"Not this afternoon. I have some things to handle. Maybe tonight," he said, already turning away. Like he'd answered enough.

He didn't sound too motivated to go to the maze. Curious. Usually, the committee worked the event several times during the three-week run. He claimed he was there on Friday, but not as a volunteer.

I thanked him for the chat and slid behind the steering wheel of Vee-dub.

ALTHOUGH I ARRIVED AT the maze well before start time, the parking area was already beginning to fill up. I wasn't sure people would come out after the incident on Friday, but it seemed they were always enthused about visiting a place where something terrible occurred. Kind of like the Jack the Ripper tours in London, except this one was more current. One positive was that parents would keep a closer eye on their children if there was the possibility of an accident.

I'd barely gotten into the entry area when I encountered Conklin. He and Tara seemed to exchange words, but neither looked upset or angry, just businesslike.

"Ah, there she is," Conklin said when he saw me. "I was just telling Tara I wanted to talk to some of the vendors today. And your booth is off-limits."

" I expected that. But you cleared Gary to set up the lake illusion to automatic, right?"

"Yes, he's working on it now. You know, the show must go on, right? But we just can't have anyone entering a possible crime scene." He sounded apologetic.

"I get it. So, you're still interviewing people?"

"Right. I have a few more to do. Want to walk with me?"

Tara's eyes popped, surprise evident in her expression. Mine might have looked the same, but I wasn't going to peer down a gift horse's throat. "Sure. Give me a minute to drop off a couple of things."

He looked at me, nothing in my hands, and raised an eyebrow. That quizzical look was kind of cute.

"I have a block of bottled water and some cookies from the superstore for the welcome booth in my car. It won't take long for me to get them." I pointed to the Rabbit.

"I'll give you a hand." He turned from Tara to follow me to the car.

"What's up?" I asked as I leaned in to get the water block.

He edged me aside and hefted it. "You get the cookies. I just want a chance to talk with you."

His statement didn't reassure me. "Am I still a suspect?"

"No. Katie alibied you and you are the same for her. But of course, you'd cover each other, wouldn't you?"

My mouth dropped. "Detective Kevan Conklin! That's an unfair remark."

A quick smile cracked his serious expression. "That's the first time you've called me Kevan, although it was more like my mother shouting at me … if you drop the detective part. But am I wrong? You'd cover for her, wouldn't you?"

I hesitated, asking myself if I would. Would Katie? "No, I wouldn't lie about it. If I couldn't say it was the truth, I wouldn't make the statement."

We walked back to the entrance with our goods. "But you defended her when she was a suspect," he said.

"That's because I knew she didn't do it. Katie had no reason to poison someone, and the evidence was circumstantial."

"Do you even know what that means?"

"Of course, I do. I've watched a lot of mystery and detective shows." I slid the cookie tray on a table behind the booth while Tara had busied herself with setting up the cash box and credit card machine.

"So, detective training by TV shows." He set the water under the table and slid it to the back.

"I've read books as well." I pivoted to Tara. "I'll take the second half of the booth today, okay?"

"Deal." She winked at me. I shook my head as I followed Conklin into the maze.

He set a quick pace, as if he wanted to cover a lot of distance before he slowed to more of a stroll and leaned closer to me. "Thanks for the tip on that paperweight. My deputies and the forensic team always wear gloves to pick up any potential evidence, but once they get to the lab, someone might touch the item. We passed the warning along, but why did you tell me about it? "

Hard-pressed for an answer, I pieced together a rough explanation. "When I saw it, I had a hunch about it, and it seemed to emit an energy field. So, I figured it might have some kind of power source that could shock or hurt someone."

"You felt an energy field," he said again, slower this time. "You just … sensed it?" I nodded, bracing for the eyeroll. "So, we're adding psychic impressions to the evidence log now?" His tone was dry, but there was a flicker—something just shy of intrigue buried behind the sarcasm.

"Some people do have traces of ESP or intuition, and I happen to be one of them. It's not a big thing, but I get certain vibrations from some objects." I couldn't tell him my ghost aunt warned me and sometimes I did detect energy around objects.

He puffed out a breath with a half-hearted smile. "Well, whatever it is, thanks for the warning. Do you know what happens if you touch it?"

"Not for sure. But Isolde and I traced its history to a point. And it's a stolen object." I filled him in on what we'd learned about the nautilus and the legends behind it.

He halted, drew in a deep breath and turned to face me. "Now you're telling me this is a magical or cursed object that has been stolen several times over a few centuries. Do you know—?

I interrupted. "How crazy it sounds? Yes, I do. But there are stranger things …"

"Okay, I can expect this from Isolde Thornewood, but not from you. Does Katie know?"

"Does she know what?" I asked.

"That you're crazy."

I laughed. "Yeah, she knows, but not that I can sometimes get psychic impressions."

We came to a booth and Conklin stepped up to the table to ask the vendor a few questions about Friday's event. It only took a couple of minutes, so we moved along.

"No help there, huh?" I said after a minute of silence.

"Nope."

The silence continued for a few more minutes, so I asked a loaded question. "Did you find anything to indicate Andie's death wasn't an accident?"

Conklin shifted his gaze to me, and he sucked in a breath and coughed. I sniffed the air and detected a musty scent, probably from the corn stalks. But the misty evenings had kept them moist, which might contribute to a mold. I hoped it wouldn't be a problem during our event.

"You okay?" I asked.

He coughed again, then turned away from me to spit. "I think I inhaled a bug or something."

"Ew. Probably a midge. The pond attracts them." I resisted the urge to offer him a tissue. Detective dignity and all.

"Yeah, I know. We found more evidence of them than of a potential killer. What we didn't find was a purse or a wallet or anything Ms. Langley might have taken with her … and one wasn't in her booth."

I connected the dots. "So, she walked out to the landing with no bag of any sort and fell into the pond. Why would she go there unless she was meeting someone? And if a purse or something with her id and money wasn't with her things at her booth, then either she didn't bring it or someone took it."

"That's pretty much the assumption. So far, none of the people I've talked to recall seeing her with anyone or even seeing her at all, except your tech guys."

"Right. Gary, Steve, and Tony. He told me he thought she was with a guy wearing a ghoulish clown costume." I tried to picture it, but it didn't come together. "You'd think we'd notice something like that."

He laughed. "On a night when half the people, including the volunteers, are wearing costumes, it might not stand out as much as you'd expect."

"Could Tony describe the costume?" I figured if a sketch artist could draw it, someone might recall seeing the bizarre costume. Not that it would help identify the person with Andie.

"He tried but couldn't quite piece it together. I asked him to try to describe it to one of our artists on Monday, so we'll see. In the meantime, we don't have much to go on. But if the person wore big clown shoes with the costume, it might explain the oblong prints in the mud near the pond leading away from it and into the cornfield." Conklin flipped his phone out to show me a photo.

I leaned in and studied it for a few moments. Yep, it was exactly as described, and it could have been from a clown shoe. "Where would anybody get shoes like that? A costume rental?"

"I'm checking on that tomorrow. We have two shops in town. There's a chance our possible perp rented them or the costume pieces. It will help if Tony can give us enough pieces for a good sketch."

While I was surprised Conklin told me as much as he did, I welcomed it. He didn't care much for my investigative methods or interference, but so far, they'd panned out. Since he offered me an on-call job as a consultant, I assumed his view was gradually changing. He still didn't trust my methods. But he was listening. And that was new.

We stopped at three more vendors to make inquiries with the same disappointing results. The next booth was Katie's, and she was scrambling to get everything set up before any visitors arrived.

She lifted her head when I strolled up with her boyfriend, and a big smile brightened her face. "Hey. What brings you here?"

The question was addressed to Conklin, not me.

"Looking for leads so I'm talking to all the vendors," he replied.

She came around the table and gave him a hug, saying, "You look tired, honey."

"Long days and nights," he murmured and returned the hug a bit awkwardly, on duty and all the nonprofessional nonsense that went with it. Katie didn't care. He was her guy.

"Have you heard anything from any of the other vendors?" he asked.

"Not really, although I've been chatting with them. A bit of unease with some over the incident, but most are in business-as-usual mode. It feels weird to be celebrating and painting faces when a tragedy is hanging over you." Her mouth dropped at the edge along with her downcast eyes.

To his credit, Conklin pulled her into a gentle hug, running his hand over her hair. "It's okay, sweetie," he whispered. "It's how we sometimes cope."

We left her and moved on, coming to the forks in the path where we encountered Rolf Swensen repairing his signpost. One of the arrows was broken and he was unscrewing it from the post with a replacement ready to go.

"What happened?" I asked after our hellos.

He pointed to the other half lying on the ground. "Hard to say for sure, but I think one of the older boys tried to swing off it.

Probably too heavy to expect it to support a kid using it as a bar and it snapped."

The big guy cast a dazzling grin at Conklin and offered a hand. "I'm Rolf Swensen. I don't think we've met."

Conklin shook his hand. "Detective Kevan Conklin. I'm investigating the drowning."

"Terrible thing." Rolf dropped the other half of the sign's arrow and positioned the new one. "Poor woman. That's a bad way to go."

"Did you have any dealings with Ms. Langley?" Conklin asked.

"Not much, no. I've seen her about three times with the committee, and her inspection of this sign."

"She inspected the sign?" I asked, my voice rising in disbelief.

"Ja. She wanted to make sure it was readable—wasn't too happy with the lettering. Too bad, I thought and didn't change it. She fumed about that for a while."

Conklin took a step back, his gaze running over the cryptic-looking arrow markers. "It looks confusing, but isn't that part of the maze idea?"

"Exactly," the Thor lookalike agreed.

Conklin asked a few more questions and got even fewer clues. Except for a brief remark when Rolf said, "I went for a drink with Glenn Harper and Rob Fenmore after a meeting about the mansion job. They hired me to do some repair work after the haunted house thing. Rob threw out a number for repair costs, and Glenn kinda groaned about it, then said, 'Will Andie control the costs?' Rob assured him it would be fine. But I got the feeling Glenn was pretty anxious about the money."

"Are they partners?" Conklin asked while he made a note in his phone.

Rolf shrugged, muscles rippling under his shirt. "I don't know. I think Glenn is an investor more than a partner, but he seems involved. He said something about a previous deal in Santa Barbara."

Another note scribbled in both my phone and Conklin's.

"Did he suggest what it was?" the detective asked.

"No. He just said that he hoped this deal was more successful than the Santa Barbara one. Rob told him not to worry—'this one's a lock.' His words."

When Conklin thanked him and turned to leave, Rolf moved closer to me and leaned his head down. "Would you like to have dinner with me after the maze closes this afternoon?"

I couldn't hold back the smile that burst through my lips. Although I had a lot to do, I figured I deserved a break, and he was a stunning man. "Sure. I'd like that."

He agreed to meet me at the entry station at six o'clock. Little butterflies danced in my stomach in anticipation, but I tried to control my giddiness.

After we left there, Conklin pointed me to the pond landing. The orange cones and yellow police tape sort of blended with the Halloween theme, although it was clear the area was off limits. The nearest deputy acknowledged Conklin as he led me through the tape, lifting it so we could get under.

I called my aura vision into play and ran my eyes over every inch of the wooden dock. Nothing stood out; no energy signature or a hint of life. Beyond it, I glimpsed flashes of bright blue rising above the water along with the docile golden green tones of the vegetation surrounding it. Fish and plants, like all living things, give off an aura. What I could only describe as pond odor lingered around the edges of the marsh.

When my eyes reached the center of the pond, a streak of red shot above the water line. Anger. Then a puff of gray mixed with brown settled below a sudden ripple on the surface. A breeze fluttered our way, blowing my hair into my face. But it seemed to come after that water disturbance. *Who was trying to get attention?* My subconscious asked. *Hallie or Andie?*

Conklin tapped my arm, and I jerked, startled.

"Sorry. I wanted to show you the prints in the mud." He urged me to follow him, and we backtracked to get down to the embankment around the water. The first one was obvious and right about where we stepped to go down. I noted the size, about fourteen inches long and at least eight wide. The front curved a bit, then vanished completely with just a flat behind it where the front of the shoe might have curved upward. Several footprints later, a deeper rounded shape added to the arch portion of the print. I cast a targeted look at the surrounding ground and pinpointed the culprit.

"The suspect got a stone caught in his shoe," I stated, moving to the next print and seeing the same thing there and in the next beyond it.

"I agree,"Conklin commented. "The small hole shows up in the following prints, leading into the cornstalks."

When I straightened up and looked around, I pointed in the direction the footprints had indicated, "It looks like they were heading to the road."

"Right. It suggests someone came in through the maze, probably from a parked the car on the road's shoulder, and met someone else at the pier, then left the same way." Conklin faced the road's direction and stared as if it would reveal the path.

I caught the hint of a smile on his face. He hadn't brought me here to get any insight. He wanted to see if I could follow the trail and would agree. Maybe he was learning to trust my perceptions.

Before I left the landing to get back to relieve Tara, I gazed out at the pond in time to see the pooka rise from the waters. Only when his noble horse head burst through the water, it wore a pumpkin-patterned design wrapped between its ears.

"Conklin!" I yelled.

He spun toward me, eyes narrowing as the pooka rose from the pond—its head wrapped in Andie's scarf.

For a moment, he simply stared. Then he stepped forward, voice low and tight.

"That scarf wasn't on her body. It wasn't in her booth. If it's real…"

He didn't finish the sentence.

I saw the shift in his posture—the pivot from disbelief to calculation.

"We need to get it," he said. "If it's hers, it could be evidence. Maybe even tell us how she died."

Chapter Twelve
Ripples and Reflections

THE SCENT OF GRILLED lemon and buttered shellfish drifted through the air as I settled into the booth across from Rolf at The Crab Shack on Main. The place was packed, but our corner table gave us a little privacy—just enough for me to decompress without losing the thread of the day.

Rolf leaned back, his broad shoulders relaxed, eyes warm. "You look like you've been chasing ghosts."

"Close," I said, swirling my water glass. "Conklin and one of the deputies took a rowboat out to the pooka illusion. It was sinking fast, but they managed to grab the scarf before it disappeared."

"Wait—the scarf?" His brow furrowed.

"Andie's. Pumpkin-patterned. It wasn't on her body, wasn't in her booth. Just… showed up, wrapped around the pooka's head like a crown." I paused, letting the image settle. "They almost got pulled under with it. Wish I'd thought to video it with my phone."

Rolf whistled softly. "That's wild. You think someone planted it?"

"Maybe. Or maybe it floated up from the pond floor. Either way, Conklin's treating it as evidence now."

He nodded, then glanced toward the kitchen. "Andie could be intense, but she wasn't cruel. She had a sharp eye for detail—wanted everything just so. Even the lettering on my signpost."

I smiled. "But she gave you grief about it."

"Three times. I didn't change it, and she fumed. But she cared. That's something."

"Andie had a booth near Isolde. She heard her berating one of the vendors about his book table, saying he was a phony, and the books just parroted the folktales about Arbordale. She wanted him to leave, but I don't think he did. I don't know if I'd call such an action caring." I had to think about her detail-oriented eye as being a positive thing when she could get so rash with people. She could be harsh when she thought she was protecting something.

But it's not good to think ill of the dead, Daphne often said. *Especially if they can haunt you.* I cast a nervous glance at the front window, half-expecting a flicker of movement.

Our waiter arrived with crab cakes and grilled salmon, and we paused to arrange plates and thank him. As I reached for my fork, Rolf added, "You know, I saw Isolde heading to the restrooms around the time Andie went missing.

I froze mid-bite. "You're sure?"

"Pretty sure. She was wearing that long velvet coat she likes. Hard to miss."

"Could you please tell Detective Conklin you saw her? He has her on his suspect list."

I filed the information away. Isolde had told me she'd gone to the privy, but we hadn't found anyone to verify it. She'd be relieved that Rolf had seen her going that way and not toward the pond.

"Sure, if it will help. It seems quite a few people disliked Andie, but she was having a rough time."

Surprised, I frowned and questioned his statement to Conklin. "I thought you didn't know her."

"I said I'd seen her about three times. One of them was when I installed some shelves at Fenmore's office. She complained about the drilling and dust, but later, she came in … her eyes all red from crying

… and apologized, saying her mom had died in a car accident the previous day."

"Oh, that's terrible. I didn't know. How long ago was that?" Perhaps I had misjudged Andie's attitude, and she'd been stressed.

"About a month. She said something odd… that her 'luck' was sliding downhill, and she needed to change it." He took a sip of water and finished his salmon.

"That is odd," I agreed, but my thoughts ran to the nautilus and its peculiar curse. Had Andie counted on it to change her luck?

Our conversation shifted to movies we liked, comparing notes and favorite scenes, then other things we had in common, plus enough that we didn't to make it interesting. I enjoyed his company and intelligent conversation. Perhaps something was beginning to grow between us. Dare I hope?

Rolf glanced at his watch. "Time to head back. We've got fifteen minutes." He shoved back from the table while I hopped to my feet and grabbed my shawl.

BACK HOME AT NEARLY eleven, I gave thanks the night at the maze had gone smoothly … fewer people than we would have had maybe, but still a decent crowd. I heard lots of comments about the spooky "horse" in the pond, but no mention of it wearing clothing.

After I fed Higgins, I pulled a cold beer from the 'fridge and sat in the chair in front of my murder board. I thought back to what I'd learned and what applied. First, the scarf--freshest in my mind— deserved a card. I wrote *wearing or carrying? How did it get loose?*

Next, I removed Glenn's card and added: *suspicious behavior, questionable jaw bruise, partnership with Fenmore, money issues?*

As I pinned it back on the board, I thought about Rob. I hadn't seen him at the maze or the mansion. What was he doing? Could he have been the ghoulish clown? He'd probably endured as many conflicts with Andie as anyone in town. But why would he kill her when he could just fire her? Unless … she had some blackmail info on him. Maybe a shady deal that blew up? I needed to examine the Santa Barbara venture closer if Rolf's memory was right.

Simply the thought of Rolf softened my heart. He'd been charming and funny over dinner. And I think I convinced him to join the theatre's tech team. We needed a carpenter. I sighed and went back to my board.

Under Hallie, I added a card for an unknown boyfriend and *married* under it with a question mark. I made a note in my phone to contact her parents in the morning to arrange a conversation with them about their daughter.

I'd forgotten Isolde having mentioned the book seller Andie berated, so he might be a suspect also. I wrote Book Seller on another card and stuck it under suspects. I'd check the vendor list in the morning.

And I added a note to the paperweight, *Stolen, good luck/bad luck charm, hexed, and dangerous to touch. Bad juju.*

"Very bad juju," Aunt Daphne's voice said from behind me.

I spun around. "Where have you been? I could have used your help earlier."

"Yes, I heard you. What is that new trinket you're wearing?" Daphne patted her hair back and leaned closer to examine the pendant.

"A gift. From Isolde. She said it would help protect me." I lifted it up so my aunt could see it better. A slight tingle of electricity touched my fingers. Was it reacting to her?

"Isolde, hmm? Don't believe everything that want-to-be witch tells you."

She turned away and settled in the living room, sinking partway through the sofa. That was a new one. Usually, she floated.

"I thought you were friends." I sat on the sofa's arm and leaned against the back. "Are you saying I shouldn't trust her?"

"Not at all. Just that she isn't as strong with magic as she believes she is. I admit, she's quite intuitive, which is why her readings are usually spot on. But when it comes to magical objects, she isn't as adept."

"Well, this one seems to work. It reacts to people's emotions, warning me. In fact, it sparked at your arrival."

"Really? Perhaps someone else enchanted the stone. What did you need, luv?"

"You know about Andie's death, don't you?"

"That loud, obnoxious woman? Yes, I gathered as much when I last saw you at her booth with that paperweight thing. I didn't even want to get near; it sent so many bad vibrations." Her mouth turned down in distaste and she wiped a finger across it. Then, her eyes widened, and her brow lifted. "You didn't touch it, did you?"

"No. And I told Conklin not to touch it either and he passed the word along. But you didn't tell me why." I shifted a little closer.

"I didn't know why, but I detected the evil intent of the thing."

I sighed and went to my question for her. "Were you at the maze on opening night?"

"I was there … for a while. It looked quite nice, and I was proud of the theatre's contribution. The water horse is magnificent and the lighting—"

"Did you see Andie die?" I interrupted.

Daphne's lips slid into a pout as her eyes shifted down as if she was studying her fingernails. "No, I had already left."

"You left?" My whiny voice came out. I'd hoped Daphne had seen what happened.

"Yes, I had things to do."

"Like what?"

She bristled like a porcupine. Even her hair lifted, static crackling in the air. "If you must know, I had a rendezvous with my lovely gentleman caller."

"You had a date? Ghosts date?!"

"Of course we do. Death didn't kill my charm. Do you think we just play a harp all the time?"

"Uh, I didn't think about it. I guess it makes sense, but it's not the same as an Earthly date, is it?" It's not something I had even considered.

She rolled her eyes. "No. It's more of a companionship thing. We need to communicate, even those of us who've chosen to linger on this plane."

"Why did you choose to stay rather than moving on?" I still grappled with this ghost thing. "Isn't it usually a ghost has left something undone, or they can't cut the ties to a place or a person?"

"I think it's obvious, dear. I won't leave until I'm sure you and my theatre are going to be fine. Frankly, that ruckus in the lobby makes me nervous."

"I had to renovate the bathrooms." I straightened to my feet and planted myself in front of her, my arms crossed in defense. "The plumbing is old and needs to be replaced. Don't criticize me for fixing it. And I am taking care of it and myself, thank you."

"I am not criticizing. Just stating it's noisy. As to taking care of yourself, do you not want to bounce theories off me or procure a bit of insider information only I can get? If you want me to abandon you, say it." She flipped her head in a nonchalant pose.

With a sigh, I paced the room. While I resented her wanting to make sure I was okay, I did like having her assistance and advice now and then. Instead of answering her, I diverted to something else. "I think Andie and Hallie Conner are both ghosts now and connected to the pond. Can you communicate with them?"

"Only if they're open to it." Daphne drifted up again. "The Connor girl is too depressed to connect with while the Langley woman is simply angry. But it seems your little rubber duck still has a link to Hallie."

Indicating this was all she had for me, she began to fade.

"Thank you, Auntie. I want you to hang around, okay?"

"Later, luv. I have an engagement. Oh, about a week ago, I saw a short woman wearing a designer tennis skirt and sweater talking to a hooded figure. I think it was your Andie."

She faded a shade more before she added, "One more thing. Don't rely on your supernatural tools too much; they don't perceive the truth as well as your own instincts."

The last wisps of her faded away. What did I learn? Don't trust Isolde but talk to the rubber duck. And what was that last part? Could I be misinterpreting the auras or the signals from my pendant? I rubbed my forehead as Higgins poked his head in, jumped on the couch, and curled up for a nap.

Tired, but still tense, I picked up the book Isolde had given me and started reading while I sipped my beer. The information was interesting, filled with possible enchantments and objects to channel through. When I got to using familiars, I paused to glance at Higgins. Surely, not ... but Aunt Daphne had said he was special.

After a few chapters, my thoughts shifted to the connections between the two deaths. The location, the drowning, the time of year, and both victims accidentally falling into the pond. It seemed too unlikely to be a coincidence. The water wasn't that deep, so unless they were very drunk, they could have waded to shore. But Andie had signs of a head injury. Did Hallie? A flash of my vision with Hallie clinging to the rubber duck played in my mind. I hadn't seen her face, but why was she grasping the duck? Had she been reaching to pull it out of the water when she fell in? Or did someone push her in.

Perhaps her parents could provide a clue or two. I pulled out my laptop and searched for their contact information. Even though several Connors were listed and more than one had the same first name or initial, Gianni had said Ryan Connor lived on Red Hawk Drive and only one address was there. I made a note of the address and phone number, but a glance at the time told me I shouldn't call tonight.

Who was the hooded man Daphne had mentioned? So many sweatshirts and jackets had hoods that it was difficult to see the wearer's face. Without more details, it was impossible to say if it was someone I knew.

Giving up for the night, I shuffled through the kitchen, but before I passed my murder board, the lights flickered for a moment as if signaling me. I paused and studied the tags on it, looking for a pattern within them.

Who might have wanted both dead and why? I leaned forward to where I'd pinned Hallie's copied image at the top, shifting my eyes across to a photograph of Andie. "What really happened to the two of you?" I whispered.

A muffled quack from the bedroom interrupted my contemplation. I turned back toward the living room to confirm Higgins still snoozed on the sofa, which he did, so the noise wasn't cat induced this time. With a touch of trepidation, I opened the door, flipped the overhead light on and looked around. Nothing untoward stood out and the two ducks sat benignly on top of the dresser.

"Hallie?" I called out, thinking the ghost might have triggered the noise, but silence answered. When I turned to go to my bed, I glimpsed something from my eye's corner. A shadowed figure appeared on the bedroom curtains for a few seconds, then vanished. It wasn't my shade, and I could only make out that it was a thin girl with a halo of hair surrounding her head.

Chapter Thirteen
Plumbers, Feathers, and a Journal—Oh My!

AT NINE THE NEXT morning, I called the number for Ryan Connor, hearing a click on the phone as it transferred to a different ringtone. A man's voice answered.

I identified myself, confirmed I was speaking to the right person, then explained I was working with the sheriff's office on the recent drowning at the Alford's pond. A lingering pause grew as I allowed time for him to say something.

Finally, he spoke. "Okay. I see, but what do you need from me?"

"I know this is a lot to ask, but I think the recent incident might be linked to your daughter. I'd like to visit you and your wife to discuss what happened and maybe uncover some clues."

"It was an accident. The sheriff investigated and didn't find anything to indicate otherwise. She fell in." His voice carried the bitterness he felt.

"I know that was the report, but I think someone else may have been with her. Please let me come talk to you about it." The silence lasted so long I thought he was going to hang up on me.

Finally, he responded. "Fine. My wife will be home by noon, and I can come there for a short time. But I really don't think we can tell you anything the sheriff didn't already find."

"Thank you. I'd like to give it a try." I ended the call, aware I'd asked this couple to relive a terrible event in their lives. Yet, I knew Hallie was trying to reach me even though I couldn't tell her parents that their child was a ghost, stuck on this plane until I could learn what really happened.

Noise from the lobby indicated the construction crew had returned. I wandered out to talk to the foreman and find out if the pipes were replaced yet. He knelt next to a section on the floor, running his hand over the eroded steel.

When he heard my footsteps, he looked up. "Morning, Ms. Reed. We just got this big bubba out. From the looks of it, the erosion has been going on for a few years."

He proceeded to tell me all the bad news about the plumbing and concluded with, "You might as well replace them while we're working on it." He saw the frown forming on my face and added, "Cheaper in the long run."

"I'm sure you're right. Can you give me an estimate so I can make sure the bank will approve the extra amount?"

"Of course. I'll get it to you by noon."

"I'll be meeting someone at lunch, but you can slide it under the office door. Thanks." I strolled into the auditorium to find Missy hanging costumes on one of the upstairs racks. "Missy! When did you arrive?"

"About thirty minutes ago. I came in with the workmen. I told you I wanted to sort through the costumes, so here I am."

I climbed up the stairs, the scent of old velvet and dust rising with me, to stand beside her. "You're sure we won't need these for a future production?"

Missy gave a sniff and held up a pair of sequined bell bottoms. "If we ever stage *Disco Macbeth*, I'll eat my wig. Besides, high schoolers love irony."

I laughed. "You know we're not even allowed to say that name in here."

Missy smirked. "Exactly. So my sequins are safe."

From somewhere above the catwalk, a whisper of Daphne's voice drifted down. *"Say it three times and you'll summon a lighting mishap. Or worse—community theater Shakespeare."*

I muttered, "Not helping, Daphne," under my breath.

Missy glanced at me, frowning. "What was that?"

"Nothing," I said quickly. "Just reliving a traumatic dress rehearsal."

I reached into the discard pile and plucked out a pink feather boa, still tangled with gold glitter. "Hey, I wore this in *Blondes with Knives*. It survived three quick changes and a fire drill."

Missy snatched it away with a mock gasp. "And still carries the scent of desperation. If we're bringing this back, we've officially run out of funding *and* dignity."

I arched a brow. "Says the woman who once tap-danced in a gorilla suit to sell cough syrup."

She wagged a finger. "That commercial paid for my first apartment. And it got me a date with the sound guy."

Just as I turned to leave, Higgins poked his head out of the donation bin, looking entirely unrepentant, one paw draped over a velvet bodice like he meant to auction it off.

"Do *not* donate the cat," I said, already turning to leave. "He's moody, eats props, and charges for autographs."

Missy sighed. "Well, he's got more charisma than our last leading man."

I paused at the stairs and glanced back. "By the way, how'd things go with Gianni after I left yesterday?"

Missy lit up, a giggle escaping before she even answered. "Let's just say I now know his favorite gelato flavor, and he knows how I look in stage lighting."

I raised an eyebrow. "That sounds suspiciously flirtatious."

"Isla, please. I'm only guilty of being a little radiant. He's the one who suggested a coffee date—with biscotti and everything. You know, like a gentleman *and* a snack."

I laughed and pointed a finger. "Behave, Broadway."

"No promises," she sang.

I grinned all the way up the stairs.

THE CONNORS' HOME ON Red Hawk Drive nestled in the park-like grounds surrounding it, flaunting the well-to-do status of its residents. I gazed at the two-story, Mediterranean-style mansion and couldn't begin to calculate the millions of dollars it must have cost. Travertine stone tiles accented the arched entry door and the front window against the earth-tone stucco walls, which produced a warm, welcoming vibe.

A riot of colorful flowers, from burgundy chrysanthemums to golden dinner plate dahlias edged the entry flagstone path while a vibrant green lawn was surrounded by tall hedges for privacy. The floral fragrance emanated from the roses planted in front of the windows on each side of the entry.

Simply walking to the door felt like entering a fantasy setting, the scent of roses and warm stone wrapping around me like a spell. and I floated along with the sensation as I rang the doorbell on the polished oak door.

A well-dressed older woman, her dark brown hair pulled into an upsweep, answered the door. Her eyes scanned my jeans-and-sweater look.

"Hello, I'm Isla—"

"Reed! From the theatre," she smiled and motioned me into the house. "Ryan will be here shortly. He got away a little late from the office."

Bridget Connor, I presumed. "Thank you for talking to me, Mrs. Connor. I am from the theatre, but I'm currently doing an independent investigation of the … incident last weekend at the Alford Pond, and I wanted to talk to you and your husband about your daughter's unfortunate experience there. I am so sorry for your loss."

Her smile vanished, replaced by a look of pain at the mention of her child. "Yes, Ryan told me you wanted to know more about it. Let's go into the living room. Can I get you an iced tea or a soda?"

I admired her courtesy in the circumstances. I didn't know how I'd react at being asked to bring up a painful memory. "Iced tea would be wonderful," I replied.

While she disappeared into the kitchen, I settled into the lushly padded, forest green Queen Anne chair and mentally cataloged the expensive furniture in this one room. The chair's twin sat across the room and the sofa matched it. The mahogany coffee and end tables gleamed with polish and the lamps screamed, *I'm from Tiffany*. The walls displayed quality artwork, some originals, but mostly reproductions of classics like Monet's Water Lilies and Japanese Pond.

When Bridget returned with a tray holding three tall glasses of iced tea, she caught me staring at the painting. "Beautiful, isn't it? Ryan and I love it so much, we recreated it in the garden in the back yard. Of course, it doesn't have the same ambiance as the French one, but it is a tranquil place to meditate. We dedicated it to Hallie."

"What a beautiful idea." Although a little odd, I thought, considering Hallie died in a bigger pond.

My hostess set the tray on the low table and handed me the tea glass along with a marble coaster, then sat on the sofa, took one for herself and looked me straight in the eyes. "I don't know if we can tell you anything helpful. While the sheriff found no indications of foul play, our daughter had used drugs and been drinking the night she died. Sheriff Wilson believed those were the primary contributors to her death."

Lips suddenly dry at the calm recital of these facts, I sipped my tea before I spoke. "That's such a tragedy. From what I've learned, she was bright and talented."

"Yes, she was," a man's voice said as an average height, blond-haired man strode into the room from the kitchen. "She'd planned a great future."

Unlike his wife, Ryan Connor spoke with a slight Irish lilt, the kind someone who'd lived in America for a long time retained. I half rose to greet him, but he waved a hand palm down.

"No need to stand, Ms. Reed. No formalities here." He joined his wife on the sofa, and I noticed he held a bag from Harry's Hoagies in his hand. After he handed a wrapped sandwich to his wife, he pulled out another and unwrapped it. "Lunch, you understand. I have another one if you'd like to join us."

Surprised by the offer, I declined politely. "I appreciate you taking the time to speak with me. I don't wish to bring up sad memories, but if you could answer a few questions, it might help me learn what really happened to both Andie Langley and your daughter."

"Of course. If we can help, we will. I just don't think there's much that can connect them." He took a bite of his sandwich, chewing slowly.

"Okay, thanks. Did you know your daughter was taking illegal drugs?"

Bridget fielded that one with a shake of her head. "No, we had no idea. She'd never gotten into any of that here, but I guess when she went to college, someone must have persuaded her to try."

"Do you have any idea who?"

"No," Ryan said flatly. "Since we didn't know about it, we didn't discuss it when she came home for the holiday."

"Did you notice anything different about her? Or did she act strangely?" I tried to recall the signs—anything that might have hinted at drug use.

"Not at all," the mother answered. "She was excited to be home for a few days and had a brilliant costume to wear for the corn maze. But she didn't seem at all out of character, just her usual, bubbly self."

"Had she been seeing anyone?"

"I think she had a friend here in town who she went out with a few times. But I don't know his name." She looked apologetic. "I told the sheriff that also."

"She didn't bring him by, and he met her somewhere most of the time," Ryan added.

"Could he have been giving her drugs?" If she had a local dealer, she could have had an argument with him.

"I don't think so." Bridget's frown told me she hadn't considered it before.

"What about a name?" I asked.

Ryan shook his head. "Nope. She just called him, her guy, and when I pressed her, she simply called him the Poet. She didn't even tell her sister who it was. Kept it her own secret."

Oh, another daughter. That might be another avenue. And the Poet … was that a profession or only someone who spouted poetry to dazzle a girl? "Did she usually confide in her sister?"

"Izzy," Bridget supplied. "Our younger daughter is named Isabelle, but we call her Izzy. And yes, Hallie was quite close to her. But Izzy said she only referred to him as her boyfriend or the Poet."

"I realize this might be an imposition, but might I see Hallie's room?" I entertained the possibility of getting an aura or vibe from the room or something in it might give me a clue.

Bridget shot a questioning look, eyebrows lifted to her husband. He barely tipped his head, but I thought he was agreeing. Then, he replied, "*Yes*, of course, I can show you the room, but we remodeled it two years ago for our granddaughter. So, most of Hallie's things aren't in there anymore."

My heart sank. If it had been transformed, not much of Hallie's essence would remain. Still I could try to find a trace. "I would appreciate it if I could take a look. Do you still have her things stored somewhere?"

"Sorry, no. We donated her clothes, shoes, and other things Izzy didn't want to the Helping Hands charity, but a few of her personal items, like her journal, her favorite figurines, and a book she'd started writing are in the upstairs hall closet." Bridget's voice cracked at the end of that. I'd touched on something painful in asking for this. But it was my best chance of learning something more about the girl.

"You said she kept a journal. May I have a look at it?" The possibility she might have written about her boyfriend could give me a clue.

Bridget looked a little nonplussed by my request and glanced at her husband again for a second vote. He lowered his eyes in a silent signal, which was apparently positive. "Well, I guess it wouldn't do any harm. She's gone, so I don't think she'd object to it."

The Connors might be surprised if her ghost did protest, but I hadn't gotten any suggestion of her spirit in the house so far.

"You go on and take a look in her room if you still want to, while I unpack the journal." Bridget set her sandwich, in its paper, on the tray and we all stood.

I followed Ryan Connor up the curved dark oak staircase to the upper landing. The open design on one side overlooked the living room while six doors lined the other side of the walkway. Four bedrooms and two bathrooms, Ryan pointed out. The master bedroom sat at the end of the hallway to the right where the landing stopped and the bedroom covered the whole front of the upper story over the family room and den.

He opened the first door on the left, leading to a bedroom painted in a soothing pastel yellow with a sunflower motif covering on the wall. A twin bed with an emerald-green canopy pressed against it, while a matching child's loveseat snugged up next to a window with a backyard view. Toys and stuffed animals sat around the room or in a box in the corner.

"Your granddaughter lives with you?" I asked.

"Her father, our older son, and his wife are living here also. He's doing a lot of traveling for his work, so it's easier for Julie and Maura to stay here until they can settle in their own house. Anyway, this was Hallie's room. Not much in here was hers."

I stepped to the middle and partially closed my eyes, letting my aura gift come into play. While I didn't sense any essence of Hallie in the room, one object did show a slight halo around it—-a carousel horse figurine. Drawn to it, I picked it up, the cool ceramic smooth beneath my fingers, and turned to Ryan. "This was Hallie's, wasn't it?"

A fleeting lift of his eyebrows and wide eyes crossed his face. "How did ya know?"

"I have a sort of sixth sense about some things. This one has a strong impression." I set It back down, but I wondered if Isolde might detect anything from it.

"I got it for her when she was eight. She loved horses. We took her to Disneyland to ride the carousel, so I got her a souvenir." His voice wavered some as he spoke and my still narrowed eyes caught the love in his aura along with the sorrow in their colors, a pale blue tinged with pink and a spike of mottled green around his heart. Sorrow never leaves for long.

"I think I've gotten all I can from the room. It's very welcoming though, and I can sense your granddaughter's joy here." With a last look, I turned to leave.

By the time we descended the stairs, Bridget had the journal and a gold chain bearing a cat-on-the-moon pendant sitting on the coffee table. The book was a faux leather volume about the size of a paperback book with the Tree of Life design etched into the cover.

"I found the chain inside the diary," Bridget said. "I don't know where Hallie got it."

"You hadn't opened it before?"

"No," she said with a sad smile. "I wanted to respect her privacy."

"Didn't the sheriff ask to see it?" It should have been part of his investigation.

"He didn't think it would help any, and I admit I was upset about allowing him to look into my daughter's life." Bridget's eyes looked watery.

"May I look at it now?" As she nodded, I picked up the book, my fingers running across the soft leather and noticing a few scratches in it. A musky scent slipped out when I opened it and read the name on the first page. *Hallie Sian Connor's Life Journal* written in a calligraphic hand.

The pages beyond were written in a neat, but still stylistic cursive hand. Easy to read. I flipped to the last page with an entry and read through it. She talked about going to the maze, expecting to see her Poet there. With a capital "P"—so assigning more significance to it.

"Did Hallie ever talk about the Poet?" I asked.

"Not directly, no," her mother answered. "But she sometimes quoted a line or two he'd told her. She enjoyed poetry. Her junior year teacher had opened the door to it for her and encouraged her to try her hand."

"Could she have been the Poet she was seeing?"

"Possibly, but he was a teacher. He wouldn't date a student," she said thoughtfully.

"Once she graduated, she was no longer his student," I pointed out.

Bridget offered a weak smile of acknowledgment.

I closed the journal and looked from one parent to the other. "I'm going to be blunt. I believe your daughter died by foul play. At the very least, someone sold or gave her the drugs, and the police should have pursued it, even if they thought she'd gotten them in Santa Rosa. And she'd been drinking and expecting to meet someone at the maze."

"But the sheriff said it was an accident. He found nothing to suggest otherwise and didn't have enough on the drugs to take it any further. Isn't that right, Ryan?" She shared a glance with her husband, who agreed.

I sucked in a breath before I plunged ahead. "I have a big ask. May I please take this journal and the necklace with me so I can look for more clues?"

"Uh … I don't know," Bridget hedged. "It was personal and maybe …"

Into the pause as Bridget tried to find an excuse, Ryan said, "Let her take it. If anything in there points to someone who might have caused Hallie's death, then we'll have a reason to look for more."

A trail of tears ran down Bridget's cheeks, adding to the guilt I felt at having to stir up memories for this couple. "I promise to take good care of it, and I'll return it as soon as I'm done."

"Will you let us know what you find?" Ryan asked.

"Absolutely."

I stood, hugged the journal to my chest, and thanked them again before I left. I might have found a treasure trove or a waste of time, but I hoped for some clues. and silently promised Hallie I'd listen.

"THE POET DOESN'T TALK much, but I love the way he looks at me when no one else is around, like he's undressing me with his eyes."

I almost gagged when I read that line in Hallie's journal. Settled comfortably on the sofa in my place, I'd begun searching through the pages to look for any mentions of the Poet.

Somewhere I needed to find something to tie Hallie and Andie's deaths together and place the killer at each one. I picked up the necklace, detecting a slight vibration from it. I sent a text to Isolde asking if she could read objects.

"Sometimes" was her one-word reply.

I flipped back in Hallie's journal to the early part of the month, an October 12th entry:

"The Poet says real names bind. I told him mine binds to home. He laughed and wrote my name on a napkin anyway, then folded it into a crane. He keeps doing that. I let him keep this one because he said cranes are for luck and we both need a little."

Interesting comment, I thought and the crane? I'd found a folded crane at Andie's booth, tucked in the money box. I hadn't picked it up, so Conklin might have pulled it in with the evidence they'd gathered. I'd have to ask him about it.

The next few entries weren't so exciting, although she drew a little sailboat on the ocean with a crescent moon above it. No explanation, but she might have been imagining a date night. Or a night she wished had happened. Yet she didn't draw any people.

On October 20th, another entry caught my eye:

Saw the Sage at Coffee Wheel. He thinks I should apply for the docent program at the museum. "You explain like a writer," he said. He wore the tweed jacket again. I told him I'm not a student anymore; he said friendship doesn't have grades. I like the safety of him. I like the gravity of Poet. Is it greedy to want both?

Who was the Sage? Was it the teacher who stoked her interest in poetry? Although Bridget Connor didn't think Hallie had seen him after she graduated, it might be she did. I needed to find his name.

I closed the journal, needing to get to the County Recorder in Santa Rosa to check out the land maps, building permits, and ownership records for the Fairbourne mansion. I paused to give Higgins a treat and a hug.

While I held him, he pawed the tourmaline necklace, pulling it toward him. He licked it once, jerked his head back, then squirmed to be put down. Was that a rejection—or a warning? I cupped my fingers around the stone, feeling a slight warmth from it, but nothing that prompted me to remove it.

The tourmaline held protection magic, Isolde had said. I figured it stoked warmth when I was threatened or perhaps someone lied to me. But what did my cat detect?

Chapter Fourteen
Foundations and Fault Lines

THE COUNTY RECORDER'S OFFICE smelled faintly of dust and toner, the kind of place where secrets slept in manila folders and microfilm reels. I leaned on the counter, watching the clerk flip through a stack of oversized blueprints with the casual efficiency of someone who'd seen every oddity a house could hide.

"I'm looking for original plans and any structural adjustments to the Fairbourne mansion," I said. "And land plots for the surrounding acreage—especially the Alford farm."

She nodded, pulling a binder from the shelf behind her. "No formal submissions back in the 1880s. Building codes weren't a thing yet. But we've got some hand-drawn maps and later updates."

The first sketch was a faded ink drawing on yellowed paper, the mansion's outline simple and symmetrical—until I spotted the den's fireplace. It jutted out past the front wall of the house, a strange protrusion that didn't match the interior layout. I traced the lines with my finger.

"This extension," I said. "It's not reflected inside?"

"Correct. That wall's flush on the inside. But the exterior shows a full bump-out—same depth as the fireplace."

A hidden space? A sealed alcove? My mind ticked through possibilities.

While I took pictures of the mansion plans, the clerk hunted through the land records. "Most of these are scanned now, but these old ones haven't been done."

She pulled out another binder and flipped to a land plot dated 1909. "Here's the transfer record. Fairbourne sold the Alford farm that year. Before that, it was all one property."

I leaned closer. A thin line snaked from the mansion to the farm, a ditch, marked in faded pencil.

"What was this?"

"Drainage, most likely. Or irrigation. It ran from the farm to the house. Might've been covered over later."

A direct link. Physical, historical. I jotted it down in my notebook, heart thudding with quiet excitement. If the ditch still existed underground, it could explain movement between the two sites—or even how someone reached the pond unnoticed.

She called up a record on her computer and turned it so I could see. "This is the building permit Jesse Alford filed in 1935 to cement the ditch and install large irrigation pipes. Would you like a printout?"

From the paperwork, it looked like the pipes ran from the pond to the several irrigation ditches and all the way to the Fairbourne mansion grounds. "Yes, please. This is very helpful."

So, the ditch probably still supplies water to the gardens, unless it was blocked off. I'd need to take a look.

A thought occurred to me. "While I'm here, do you have the building plan for the Playhouse Theatre? My great aunt built it in 1950, I believe."

"In Arbordale, right? I should have it here. Your aunt's name?"

"Yes. Daphne Chase."

"I recall that name. She was an actress, wasn't she? Oh, here it is." She stared at the screen and clicked on a link, then another. "Yes, I have several pages. And I see a new one on file for plumbing work in the bathrooms. I'll print those also."

I left the office with an armful of large printouts and almost fifty dollars poorer. But the idea of looking at the architectural drawings for the theater excited me. I knew Daphne had built in a few hidey holes, not to mention Higgins escape route, so I hoped to spot them in the designs.

As I thought about it, I realized Fairbourne might have built secret rooms or passageways in his house as well. I would really scrutinize the plans this evening.

For now, I needed to get to the mansion to help with some of the work there. Only fair, I do my share of the work.

BEFORE I ENTERED THE MANSION, I walked along the front entrance by the door, looking for anything that might trigger the chilling effect on entry. My time with the hex book gave me ideas of what objects or signs might indicate a spell had been cast. Nothing on the outside, so I knelt at the door's inside threshold, feeling a little foolish and hoping none of the crew saw me. *Nothing to see here. Move along.*

The scuffed runner slid back with a whisper. Under the lip of the oak was a *braided copper wire* tacked into the sill. It looked old, oxidized green where the varnish had worn thin. Four tiny smokey quartz chips sat glued into the corners, the kind of thing you'd only notice if you were the sort of person who crouches on museum stairs. I recalled that smokey quartz was a protective stone, so it could serve as the source of the chill air, but how it manifested it was beyond my knowledge.

Along the inner edge, a small burn-mark ring—a circle about the size of a silver dollar—hid beneath the mat. Not decorative. Purposeful. I pressed my fingers near it. The cold sharpened.

"Okay," I whispered, to the house or to myself. "You're not a draft."

I took photos of each component. When I replaced the runner, the air seemed to soften—not as resistant, as if the house approved of my actions.

"That you, Isla," Missy's voice called from the drawing room.

I hastened to my feet, calling out, "Yes. Just got here."

Her head peeked out into the hallway. "Finally. We were starting to wonder if you'd been lured into a hedge maze by a charming stranger with questionable intentions."

She squinted at the floor. "Or were you blessing the threshold—or just checking for termites?"

"It took me longer in Santa Rosa than I expected. And the traffic," I hedged.

"Santa Rosa? Why did you go there?"

"I had to check on some building paperwork." True statement. "How's it going here?"

"Come see for yourself." Missy waved her hand to summon me into a dark room.

If I thought they'd done wonders with the room before, it was nothing compared to how it looked now. Black lights highlighted features while subtle breezes gently rocked the cobwebs. The jail cell in the corner with the cask looked ominous. A faint scent of mildew and stage fog clung to the air, and the shadows danced just enough to make me question what was real. I stepped inside, half expecting the cask to groan or the jail bars to rattle. The effects here would have the guests jumping every few feet.

The real action now took center stage in the den where the current transformation was underway. This room looked in progress with wooden panels lying on the floor to be painted, jars of paint, various tools, and scraps of dark-colored cloth littered around the room.

Gary sketched a vampire, raised clawed hands and fangs bared, on one of the plywood boards for someone to paint later. Maybe I'd tackle that one. I could visualize a greenish-tan tone for the undead skin. Two more volunteers worked on placing a curtain wall to separate a scene from the room. Music blasted from a boombox to help keep everyone energized and coolers held sodas and snacks. Some of these folks had been here every day, all day, for the past five days.

What I really wanted to check out was the fireplace. I maneuvered through the assorted props, stepping over extension cords, snaking across the cluttered path. It resembled an accelerated load-in when a show set up at the theatre. Chaos, but it would take shape in time.

My first glimpse of the fireplace revealed glistening objects across the mantle. Jars of various spooky items reflected in the broken mirror behind it. I stepped closer to get a good look. One large jar held vampire teeth, a realistic-looking set of teeth with crooked fangs jutting out and the liquid inside cast a slight red glow. Another held eyeballs, painted orbs made to look real, some with white streams like egg whites attached. Creepy. The next displayed worms, gummy or otherwise, crammed together in the jar. Some held various herbs that looked transformed from the common to something wickedly evil simply by the colorful labels… Witches' Wort, Dragons' Bane, Lupin Weed, and Lion's Breath.

"Like my handiwork?" Grace asked, stepping up beside me.

"You did these?" I asked, glancing at her.

"Yep. All my doing, I'm afraid." She looked shy to admit it.

"They're wonderful. I didn't know you were a talented artist. Thanks so much for helping with this project."

Her smile grew across her face. "I'm happy to do it. Everyone was looking forward to the haunted house at the theatre, so we're thrilled to have this venue for it."

"Me, too," I admitted. Even if Rob had shady plans, he'd done all right by us so far.

"Black candles even," I muttered as I noted the two end pieces. "You made those as well?"

She nodded.

"Gracie," someone called. "We're ready for your help."

She glanced away. "Gotta go. I'm painting the gruesome tombstones for the graveyard. It sounds like Bobby has them ready for me to start."

Gruesome tombstones? It sounded like a new addition. I wondered where they would put them.

I turned my attention to the wall next to the fireplace on the left. Although the latter extended out about four feet back, when you included the exterior wall on the other side of the back brick and any insulation included, the room's wall remained consistent with the one on the right side. I peered closely at the seam where the two sections met. A thin line, barely noticeable in the plaster job, showed the cut out for the extended fire box. The fireplace in the drawing room was shallower and sat forward in the room, so the wall there was equal with the back.

If the house exterior wall also sat flush with the box, which the plans indicated, it meant a section of the house – this area from the edge to the end of the room – covered a space about four feet wide by eight feet long. I thumped on the wall, hearing a hollow sound that echoed faintly through it.

"Whacha doin'?"

Tony's voice startled me since I didn't hear him come up.

"I saw the mansion's plan and it appears this part is a false wall. I think there's a fair-sized space behind it." I pointed to the seam between the wall and the fireplace.

He loomed in to get a closer look and nodded. "I tink youse right. I almost got a peek of da open area. I can drill a little hole, so's we can see. Wan-me to do dat?"

I thought for a moment. "Can you patch it easily? I don't want to damage Fenmore's property."

"Yeah, sure." Tony scurried off to get the drill, coming back with it and a small flashlight. "Dis should do it."

I felt like the lookout while he knelt and drilled a one-inch hole about three feet from the floor. He peeked, then handed the light to me and scooted out of the way while I bent down and shined the light into the hole. Although it didn't allow a lot of view, it was enough to see a landing and an entry door across the width.

"Looks like a secret room," I said with a touch of disappointment. I couldn't learn more about it without opening the wall, and it wasn't my property. "Patch it up."

If there were secrets behind the door, they remained safe for now.

"I could drill thru da wall beyond it… see whatz in dere."

I considered it for a moment or two. Another hole in the wall. "Do it."

Tony applied the drill again and another one-inch hole appeared. He peeked through, pulled back, his lips flattening into a disappointed look.

"What?"

"Take a peek." He set the drill down and went to find the spackle.

I peered in, seeing why he looked so down. The new hole revealed a step; the hole cut through right above it and before the next one. A staircase. The mystery deepened. Was it a servants' access to the upper levels? But for now, it remained a puzzle.

I rolled up my sleeves and got to work, helping wherever I was needed. My curiosity about the pipes from the farm to here still nagged, but it would have to wait for another day.

A few hours later, I finished up the paint on the vampire panel and sat back, pleased with the results. He looked scary, and the colors were deliciously grotesque.

"Good job, boss," Gary said as I climbed to my feet and stretched. "I think ya caught the dude's vibe. He'll look frightening once we position him in a dark corner and turn on the blacklights. One glance and people will scream."

"You think so?" I stepped back a few feet and looked at it again. Yeah, it was all right.

"For sure. Hey, someone's waiting for you." Gary tilted his head toward the doorway where a tall, blond hunk leaned against the door frame.

Grinning, I made my way over, seeing fewer obstacles now. "Rolf, I didn't know you were here."

"Got recruited to fix a few things in the solarium before Gary can transform it. I told you I'd help out." His eyes twinkled with amusement. "Can I buy you a burger tonight?"

"I'd love it. Thanks. Let me clean up a little." I glanced at the paint on my hands. I hoped it was water-based.

"Deal. How 'bout I meet you at Burger Busters in an hour? That time enough?"

"Perfect."

He pulled me halfway into his arms, squeezed gently, and murmured "See you there, *fagr*."

I lifted an eyebrow.

"It means beautiful," he supplied, then released me and walked away.

Behind me, I heard whistles and other childish noises from the crew who had a great view of the exchange,

"Just friends," I called out, not even looking back.

I went to the bathroom to wash my hands and Missy tagged along. "He's quite a nice specimen, Isla."

"I only met him recently. He seems like a nice guy. I like him." I rinsed off my hands, happy to see the brown paint departing down the drain.

"He's quite the handyman," Missy quipped, aware of the double entendre.

As I opened the door to Vee-dub, ready to get behind the wheel, I glanced up and not one, but two crows, perched on the eaves above the turret room. They're just crows, I told myself as I drove away. So why did the hair at the back of my neck prickle?

I WANTED TO CHECK some information that Tara might have at the corn maze welcome booth, but I couldn't do it until Wednesday. The maze was dark on Monday and Tuesday to give us all a break and a chance for repairs if anything needed them. So far, Conklin hadn't released our theatre booth, but Gary told me he'd stopped by to shut down the timer on the puca, so it wouldn't be rising every twenty minutes the entire time. Enough that it made fifteen appearances a day—more reliable than Yellowstone's Old Faithful geyser.

So, I went home, fed Higgins, who chatted for about ten minutes about something. He must have had an eventful day. When I went into the bedroom, I felt a chill near the ducks.

"Hallie," I whispered. No response, but then I saw the journal lying on my bed, opened. I hadn't left it there. "Do you mind that I'm reading it, Hallie? I'm trying to help you."

No impression from the ghost, but the rubber duck turned and its beak pointed to the book.

"You want me to read it, right?"

Higgins stood in the doorway and yowled. I shivered at the eerie situation. Believing that was the message, I pulled the journal to me and read the entry marked October 30th:

Red scarf. He liked it. Left hand—tiny crescent scar near the thumb when he reached for me. He said he'd meet me "by the reeds where the path goes dark." I told him no. I left before midnight. I am not a ghost.

I read the entry a second time. Who was she talking about—the Poet or the Sage? "By the reeds where the path goes dark?" Where? If they were at the pond, it would be near the landing. But the path goes dark … what did that mean?

I hurried to change clothes, took my car, and instead of bicycling to Burger Busters, I went to the maze. The evening light was dark enough for the solar ones along the pathways to brighten the way. Hurrying, I followed the route to the pond's landing dock. Lights all the way, each glowing beautifully. I stood on the dock, looking at each light, following their luminescence to the east where the reeds were the thickest. Where I'd found the rubber duck. Water reflected now and then in the light, but it faded about fifteen feet from the dock and only darkness reigned.

Cautious, I stepped off the dock, following the water's edge until I came to the point where the reeds grew too thick and thinned out toward the water, meaning it was deeper here. But no light showed the danger. I pulled out my phone, opened the flashlight app and checked the surrounding area.

A flash of silver caught my eye, and I knelt to examine it, the damp earth cool beneath my fingers. An old light, one that had once been part of a string, now cut free and not replaced when we switched to solar. I took a photo to show the position. I'd talk to Tara about putting a new light in place.

Still, what significance did this have with Hallie and whoever wanted her to meet here?

WITH A QUICK BACKTRACK, I soon made it to my car in time to meet Rolf a few minutes late. The place was jampacked with people and I found him sitting on a bench waiting for a seat.

"Wasn't such a good idea, huh?" he said as I sat down in the narrow space next to him. Our thighs touched, it was so tight.

"I'm sorry, I'm a little late. The parking lot is overflowing."

"It's okay. I got us on the list, so we'll get a table soon." He almost had to yell over the noise.

Within another five minutes, we had a table, but we had to lean close to talk. Once we ordered, I told him I'd gone by the maze to check out a hunch and found a spot that could be dangerous, especially if littles were around the pond unattended.

"It's not a major deal, but if some child fell into the pond there, it would be terrible. Alford should put up a fence across that end of the pondside path." I took a sip of my iced tea and exhaled, still trying to tie my thoughts to Hallie's death.

"You're right. I can talk to Alford tomorrow. It wouldn't take me long to put in a fence or barrier there if he's willing to buy materials." Rolf popped a potato chip into his mouth. They were the snacks while we waited for the burgers.

"You'd do that for free?" I tilted my head a little to gaze into those Nordic blue eyes.

"For a good cause? Absolutely." The eyes twinkled.

The restaurant buzzed with chaos, but we carved out a quiet island of calm between the clatter and chatter. For most of the meal, we were our own island of calm, talking about the haunted house and the mysteries of the mansion.

"What's with the cold waft of air at the entry? Do you want me to check it out?" he asked.

"No, it's part of the house's charm," I said, deciding no one should mess with that spell on it. If Rob wanted to remove it, then he could suffer any consequences.

After we ate, Rolf insisted on escorting me to Vee-dub, which I'd parked two blocks away. I didn't object much, although I'd always felt safe on the town streets.

He ran a practiced eye over my old Rabbit and grinned. "At least, it's an easy car to work on."

"Yeah, no fancy onboard computer or any electronic bells and whistles to go wrong." I defended my ride and patted the side fender like it was a horse.

"No offense meant," Rolf answered, then he leaned forward to give me a gentle kiss. "I'll let you know what Alford says."

Even though he stepped a few feet away, he waited until I pulled away from the curb to head back to his car. What a gentleman. And such a sweet kiss.

AFTER I'D GOTTEN READY for bed, I spread out my copy of the mansion blueprints, looking for any notations or anything else unusual. If this was the original plan, it showed the east wall as even with the back of the fireplace, but not the staircase inside. Even the second floor kept the extension and the concealed space. Odd.

I rolled the copy up and secured it with a rubber band and tucked it into an empty cabinet.

Before I settled in to sleep, I picked up the journal again and turned back from the entry I'd read earlier to see if I could learn who wanted Hallie to meet at the path's end. I found an entry on October 28th, reading:

The Sage warned me about older men who hide inside poems. "Men who love metaphors sometimes mean them," he said. I told him he's not old. He laughed and replied, "Old enough to know better."

I leaned against my pillow. I felt we had two strong suspects, —but neither fit the shape of a killer. Not yet. Both appeared to be literary, one a poet and the other wise, but also a teacher. A visit to the library might help me determine the identity of at least one.

Chapter Fifteen
Secrets in the Study

THE NEXT MORNING, I woke with my mind less muddled after reading the journal entries. While Hallie had mentioned both the Sage and the Poet a few times, it wasn't with a description or anything to point to a specific person. She'd been maddeningly coy about keeping it secret.

I ate a piece of toast smeared with peanut butter and a bit of honey, refilled Higgin's bowl, and descended to my office. The estimate for the new pipes was just the other side of the door where the foreman had slid it. I unfolded it and stared at the numbers, then winced a little. Oh, well, it would come from the reserve account. Thank heavens my aunt had set up the accounts to handle these expenses. I wouldn't have managed it at all. I took a photo of the estimate and sent it in an email to my banker. Check that off the list.

The flyer from Andie's booth sat on my desk and I looked at it again. Simple and to the point:

> **Missing Item. An heirloom paperweight disappeared from my home on September 29th. I am offering a reward of $1000 for the return of the item or information leading to its retrieval. It's a unique object with a nautilus shell embedded in glass.**

Enough information for whoever took it to identify it but not so much the person who placed it couldn't weed out false claims. The phone number to call looked vaguely familiar. I dialed it.

A man answered on the second ring. "Hello, can I help you?"

I knew that voice. "Rob? It's Isla."

A few moments of silence followed, then he said, "Isla, why are you calling on this number?"

Now the silence was on my side while I lined up an excuse but dove in with a version of the truth. "I saw it on a flyer and thought it looked familiar. It's your office, isn't it?"

"My home office to be exact," he admitted. "You saw the flyer? Do you have a lead?"

"I might. Can I come over there and talk to you?"

"Of course. I'd like an update on the mansion, anyway."

"I'll stop by there first. How about one this afternoon? Is that good?"

He agreed and gave me the address for his home on Glenbrook Avenue. For my part, I wanted to know about his connection to the paperweight and how he got it.

But I had Hallie's pendant to check out now. Isolde agreed to take a look, so as soon as I handled my email, I hopped on my bicycle and peddled up the street to Mystic Moon Apothecary again.

Like last time, a few people milled through the assortment of mystic items for sale, some amused and not really believing in the magic while others were excited to buy a potion that promised to revitalize their energy or help with their memory. Isolde said most of them were legitimate tonics, but sometimes they didn't work for some people.

So far as the mystical items, you had to have a certain amount of belief in stones and jewelry conveying special properties and be receptive to it. My pendant tingled, like it was singing with joy to be home.

"I'll be with you in a few minutes," Isolde said and motioned me to her reading nook. She resumed talking to her customers while I followed her instructions and waited at the table where the Ouija board took center stage. I took the necklace out of my sweater pocket and examined it again. Nothing extraordinary about it, although it appeared to be a high-quality necklace with real gold, probably plating. Did the cat have any significance to Hallie or did she just like animals?

On a whim, I held the charm over the board, letting it dangle on the chain. It circled over the top, not pointing in any direction, but just making loops.

"Don't do that." Isolde entered and stated emphatically.

I yanked my hand back, wondering what I shouldn't have done.

"Sometimes an object will lose its vibration if you use it with another charged object, which the board is," she explained. She took her seat, wiped her hands with a packaged clean wipe, then held her hand out for the necklace.

"It may not have anything—"

"Shhh, I am concentrating." She closed her eyes and her hand over the pendant.

I'd wanted to tell her it might not have anything since I didn't know how much of a connection the object might have had with Hallie, and I hoped I hadn't broken it if one had existed.

Isolde hummed a low note, vibrating it to a singsong rhythm for at least five minutes, although it felt longer while I watched. The steady hum settled in my bones, where I could feel the sound, like lying next to a speaker listening to a song.

She inhaled deeply and opened her eyes. "I got a little from it, but not much. Although it seemed to be a newer object in her life, the girl often touched it, rubbing her fingers over the moon shape."

"Could you tell who she associated it with?" I'd hoped it might yield a clue.

"Not clearly. It was a blurry flash of vision. A man, about five-foot ten or eleven, solidly built. I sensed warmth—maybe affection—but no face, no voice."

Disappointed, I let my shoulders slump and sighed. "Too much to hope for, I guess. But at least you got something off it."

"I'm sorry it wasn't more." Isolde handed the chain back, pressing it into my hand. "Perhaps Hallie emotionally blurred her secret lover to emphasize the clandestine part."

"Or I blurred it by playing with it over the board." I might have wiped some of the stored memory. If so, I owed Hallie even more now.

AFTER I LEFT ISOLDE, I cycled back to the theatre to switch to Vee-dub and made the trip out to the mansion to summarize everything for Fenmore. I was sure he'd want an update. Even though I'd been there the previous night, I didn't catalog what was done, so another walk through was needed. Truth to tell, I was gob smacked at how much work they'd completed in such a short time. Most of the tricks were placed and checked out.

Gary demonstrated two of them for me, the first being the magic mirror which worked so well, I turned to look for the ghost standing behind me. The other, a secret closet swung open when a person passed and a skeleton sprang out in front of them. Pretty scary to have it jump in front, even in daylight. At night, in a dark room, it would be spooky. They'd even added fluorescent paint to highlight the bones. And, crowning touch, Missy had made an 1880s coat and top hat to add to the spookiness.

Gary said, "We still have two rooms to spookify, but things are going swimmingly. We had so much of this from our theatre haunted house that it was mostly adapting it for here. We'll be ready to run it by next weekend."

"Fenmore's going to be thrilled," I told him. "I'm still not sure what his real game is with this. I know he plans to renovate the mansion and sell it, but will it bring in enough to recoup his expenditures and turn a profit?"

Gary shrugged. "With the right buyer, maybe. But seriously— who wants to buy a haunted house?"

I turned to him, startled. "What do you mean—haunted?"

"Oh, come on, Isla. You've felt that cold spot in the entryway, right? No vents, no drafts. And we've all heard weird noises. Grace moved a vase from the den table to the shelf, came back a few minutes later—it was back on the table. Happened two or three times. No one else was in the room."

He gave a little shake of his head, like it was just another Tuesday. "This place is absolutely haunted."

The spirits were active. But I knew Fairbourne stayed on the second floor, and his wife on the third. They didn't wander.

"When did this start happening?" I asked.

"The moving vase? Yesterday."

"Weird." I didn't know what else to say. At least the crew hadn't seen the ghosts directly. How many people at the theatre were sensitive to the paranormal?

"Well," I said, half to myself, "our visitors may get more than they bargained for."

ON THE WAY TO my meeting with Rob, I stopped at 35 Cream to grab a to-go container of their uber-delicious pumpkin pecan ice cream, eating it as I mulled over the new development at the mansion. Could the active spirit in the den be Andie? A connection from the maze existed, so it wasn't impossible.

Rob's home was on the western outskirts of town, a well-to-do area, reflecting his success in the real estate development industry. A classic-looking villa nestled comfortably in the green hills. In some ways, it surprised me that Rob hadn't gone for a more modern look, but the style was welcoming and beautifully designed.

He greeted me, opening the door before I barely tapped the knocker. "Saw you through the window," he said, showing me into the open entry. The living room was on the left through a red tiled archway. The open area revealed a dining alcove beyond it with swinging saloon doors leading, I assumed, to the kitchen. The Mediterranean-style furniture suited it perfectly, as did the Renaissance-influenced paintings.

But Rob pointed me to the door on the right, which opened into a roomy office. A big oak desk sat facing the front window and four plush chairs formed a semi-circle around it. But what caught my attention were the display cases lining the north and west walls. They were filled with art or artifacts, depending on how you looked at it. If they were as ancient as I thought they were, they were artifacts. Judging from the flood of warmth radiating from my pendant, it agreed with my assessment.

While I didn't know a lot about antiques or artifact collecting, I did recognize, even without using my aura vision, that a few of the items had a slight energy glow, suggesting they could be magical or memory-charged items. When did this ability beyond my aura scope develop?

"Fascinating, aren't they?" Rob asked, clearly noticing my distracted attention.

"Yes ... absolutely. I didn't know you were into old things." I flashed a quick smile. While fascinated with this aspect, it also unnerved me a bit. Was Rob aware of the magical properties?

He chuckled. "I've always been fascinated by ancient objects and the stories sometimes attached to them. It's the mysterious tales, like Aladdin's Lamp and Charlemagne's Sword, that turn the objects into something valuable.'

"Is that what you're anticipating with the Fairbourne Mansion—that it's past sorrow and ghosts will make it more valuable?"

"I can hope it does. But the haunted house will help expand the myths about it if your crew has done a great job." He winked at me. "Have they?"

"I believe so." I circled to look at the next cabinet. "I just came from there and I was impressed. They'll have it ready to open this coming weekend."

"Excellent. Can I get you a drink?" Rob rubbed his hands together then pointed to the bar with several bottles of alcoholic blends and a few liqueurs.

"Not for me, but I wouldn't mind a glass of water."

"No problem, I'll be right back." He strode out of the office to get it, leaving me the opportunity to snoop a little. I saw a copy of the flyer on his desk and to one side was a photo of the nautilus itself. It looked exactly like the one I'd found.

I heard his footsteps on the hardwood floor as he returned, and I turned to face him. "I just noticed the photo on your desk. Is that the missing paperweight?"

He handed me a large glass of ice water and reached over to pick it up. "It is. I have all my artifacts insured and photos of each one."

"May I ask how you acquired this object? Did you go on a dig or something to get it?" I kept my knowledge of it a surprise—for now.

"Nothing so exotic." He poured a short glass of something that looked like whiskey, added an ice cube, and sipped before he answered. "I found it at an auction in Phoenix a few years ago. The owner had no idea what he had and neither did most of the bidders, so I got it at a reasonable price."

"And you knew what it was?" I asked.

"Well, I knew the shells were rare and to find one well-preserved and encased in glass is a special discovery."

I studied the photo a bit closer. The opal in the middle of the curve looked the same, but I couldn't detect the small crack on the one I'd found. "Is it likely that more than one of these paperweights were made?"

"I doubt it. If there were, each would still be one of a kind. The patterns vary and the opal adds something unique to the value. Why do you ask?" The frown tightening his forehead suggested he was curious about my questions.

"Are you aware it was stolen?" I was thinking of the initial theft.

"Of course, I am," he shot back, an annoyed glare in his eyes. "Someone stole it from me three months ago. I said as much on the flyer."

I pressed my lips together, looking down. "Sorry. I didn't clarify that. I meant it was stolen from a museum in Istanbul about two hundred years ago. They're still looking for it."

Rob's stunned expression told me this was all news to him. He found his voice, some of the cockiness drained from it. "No, I didn't. Is there a finder's fee for it?"

Leave it to Rob to look for a monetary avenue if his paperweight was confiscated.

"I saw a paperweight just like this one on Saturday." I returned the photo.

"You saw it? Where?" His face brightened as he took a step towards me.

"In Andie's booth at the maze." I watched closely for his reaction.

Disbelief was obvious in the sudden drop of his lower lip and his puzzled expression. From my aura vision, I detected a sudden burst of orange cutting though the calm blue of his general positive halo, a clear marker of the shock.

"You're talking about Andie Langley?" his voice came across a bit raspy as if all the moisture had been sucked out of his mouth. "She wouldn't …"

"I'm just telling you what I saw."

"Where is it now? Did you take it with you? There's a reward for its return, you know." His words came out rushed, eager to get the artifact back.

"I'd love to collect that reward, but the sheriff's office has it in their evidence locker. By now, they probably know its history and status." I saw a bubble of dark brown surround his heart.

"You turned it over to the authorities," he muttered and sank into his chair. "I've lost it." His voice faded as he stared at the photo. His concern was for the object, not Andie's guilt or her death, it seemed.

The pendant at my throat warmed, reading his reactions and it pulsed against my skin. I took a sip of water and asked in a gentle voice. "I didn't see you at the maze opening on Friday, Did I just miss you?"

He looked up. "No, I didn't go on Friday or on Sunday."

"Really? I thought you would have wanted to see the result of our work and your contribution to the project."

"Not immediately, no. I was–am—planning for next weekend. Andie was representing me there." His voice sounded shaky while his aura shifted back to a more normal state of blue with a hint of sorrowful gray in it.

"Where were you on Friday night?" I asked, stepping behind the chair near the door and resting my arms on the top.

His head snapped up. "Are you asking if I have an alibi? Do you suspect I might have killed my assistant?"

"I'm not saying that; I just asked where you were."

He jumped to his feet and stepped around the desk. "I did not kill Andie. I was very fond of her, and she was a great asset to my company. Why would I do it?"

Angry flares shot through his aura now, but I couldn't detect if they were a yes or a no to the truth of his rant.

"I didn't say you did. But the sheriff's detective will ask for an alibi if he connects you to the nautilus."

Rob turned to his desk and picked up a slick paper and held it out where I could see it. "This is where I was on Friday and on Saturday."

The lettering on the page read 'California Real Estate Developers Fall Conference' and the dates for the past weekend. Santa Barbara. He'd been in Santa Barbara.

"About two hundred people saw me there, so you can scratch me off your list, amateur sleuth!"

The animosity in his voice encouraged me to take a step back. At my throat, the pendant burned my skin with its reaction to his furious tone.

Rob's shoulders shook with the emotions running through him while his aura colors flowed from one shade to another, confusing me.

I wrapped my hand around my overactive pendant, wanting to relieve the burning sensation from my throat, but inadvertently drawing Rob's attention to it.

"I can't believe you … would think …" His voice broke as his emotions choked him. "I would never … have hurt … her." He swung away from me to lean against his desk. "Your little truth-teller pendant is wrong this time. Get out,"

Stunned at his fury, I stood frozen for about thirty seconds, long enough for Rob to yell, "Get out of here!"

That time, I moved, pivoting to the door and exiting as quickly as I could without breaking into a sprint until I'd hurried through the front door. Then, I raced to my car and left.

I hadn't handled that well. But his aura was shifting so much with his emotions and the pendant signaling an alarm. Now, I didn't know what to think. Outside the villa's walls, the pendant returned to normal. While I drove to the theatre, I tried to sort out what had just happened.

I needed to consult my aura guide, but more than that, I needed a moment to breathe. To stop second-guessing every flicker of color and every pulse of heat. Had I misread everything, and he was just so upset or was Rob behind Andie's death?

Still pondering the reading and the signals from my pendant, I went into my bedroom and dropped to the bed, my stomach aching as the residue of the confrontation with Rob still churned. Why had I been so sure Rob was connected to Andie's death? All the anger and guilty-looking streaks in his aura along with the pendant's fiery warning led me to believe he was guilty.

I slid the pendant over my head and set it on the dresser, next to the plastic duck. I'd come to think of the quacker as Andie's while the rubber version was Hallie's. For a moment, a strange orange light glowed within the dark tourmaline. When I blinked, it was gone. Going into the bathroom, I peered into the mirror and pulled the top of my sweater down enough to see the red mark the pendant had left on my skin. I put a little Vaseline on it, hoping to ease the sting and the damage. From now on, I resolved to wear the pendant on top of my clothing, not against my skin.

I pulled out my book on aura colors and their meanings and looked up the ones I'd seen in Rob's aura. While I had the right idea, some of the combinations could indicate guilt, fear, or anxiety. Reflecting on it, Rob could have been exhibiting all of it. Guilt that he'd somehow involved Andie in something that led to her death. Fear that he would be charged with her murder or the theft of the paperweight. Anxiety over my questions. Did I rely on the stone's interpretation too much when it was simply reacting to Rob's anger?

I heard Higgins growl from the bedroom and walked out to see what upset the cat. He stood on the dresser, back arched up and fur fuzzed out like a Halloween cat, as he sniffed at the pendant. I already knew he didn't like the ducks, but it seemed the tourmaline fell into the same disfavor. To appease him, I stuck all three items into the top drawer. While Higgins calmed down, he still leaned his head over the edge and sniffed distastefully at the drawer.

"They won't bother you," I assured him.

With heaviness weighing on my body, I stretched out on the bed and considered my next move. I probably just torpedoed my business arrangement with Rob, even though I had signed a contract. I could write off any future joint ventures.

Still, Rob did admit he had the Nautilus, whispering or otherwise, but he claimed not to know it was stolen.

Higgins curled up next to me and purred, apparently satisfied I'd slayed the demons. Too bad I wasn't as content. Relaxing to the soothing buzz, I decided the next move needed to be telling Conklin everything. While it would put Rob in the crosshairs, I felt he would end up there anyway.

My eyes felt heavy, and I let them close, thinking a catnap would do wonders for my current negative state. As I drifted off, I heard Daphne's voice. "Trust your instincts, luv. Your gift and the pendant are only magical tools, but it takes a human heart and mind to interpret the truth. Trust your intuition."

Chapter Sixteen
A Question of Ownership

LATER, I SAT ACROSS from Conklin and told him all about my meeting with Rob and how I'd botched it. To his credit, he listened quietly, jotting down notes now and then, but letting me spill the whole sad tale. A cold soda sat next to me, and I sipped it to wet my throat. I'd gotten a bit emotional at my failure, and he'd bought one from the vending machine.

After I stopped, eyes watery after confessing my shame, he pushed a tissue box to me and said nothing for a few minutes. I was ready to crawl out of his office.

"These confrontations with a suspect don't go the way you imagine them, Isla. I've done many role-playing scenarios during training, and the real world seldom follows the script. You couldn't have guessed how Fenmore would react. You never accused him of killing Andie or committing a crime. But he sensed that was where you were heading."

"I didn't make a total mess of it?" I blew my nose.

"Not totally, no. The only fault you made was going alone. If you'd brought this to me, we could have faced him together and done it officially. Now, we need to plan a way to confront him with more facts to get the real story."

I saw a ray of hope. "We? You and me?"

He nodded. "Yep. We'll even take a deputy with us in case things get nasty. Now, let's start with his alibi."

Revitalized, I leaned forward and watched while Conklin made a list of preparatory things to do and questions to ask.

AN **HOUR LATER, I** hunted through the library catalog looking for Arbordale history and folkloric books. I found a surprising number of historical books and even one about the Playhouse Theatre and how Aunt Daphne had brought culture to the town, making it a showplace for the region. I made a note to check that one out, but it wasn't what I wanted right now.

Three books chronicled the tragic lives of the Fairbourne family and one focused on the mansion itself. Yes, I thought with excitement. I wanted to read that one. But it was checked out and the library only had one copy.

Under folklore, I found a dozen books that touched on the tales and myths surrounding our area, from old Native American tales to the latter years of Fort Ross and the Russian attempt to get a foothold in America not too many years before Arbordale was founded only a short distance from the site. One caught my eye because it was a more recent release, within the last three years by a former teacher at Arbordale High School, Eliot Crane. That book was available, so I noted the number and set off to request the books.

The middle-aged woman at the desk, whose name tag read Jubilee, smiled at me as I asked about the books. "Can you tell me anything about the author of *Myths and Mysteries of Arbordale*?

"Oh, yes. That would be Eliot Crane, one of the nicest gentlemen you could meet. He retired from the high school, where he taught English literature, about two years ago and began writing. Of course, he's an amateur historian, so he really focused on the folklore of the area. This is his first book, I believe. It's gotten many good reviews." She practically bubbled over with enthusiasm.

"So, he's still alive and writing?"

"Of course. He's still here in Arbordale. I think there's an email address in his book to contact him. Do you want me to fetch a copy for you, Miss Reed?"

For a moment, it surprised me that she knew my name, but after the last few televised appearances I'd made, not many people in the town didn't know who I was. Somehow, between the theatre and my detective shenanigans, I'd become a local celebrity.

"Yes, please. Um, would you happen to know anything about a person referred to as The Poet?" I stressed the title Hallie had given him to suggest he could be a locally known writer.

She frowned slightly, enough to say she didn't but was trying to make a connection. "No, I don't know anyone specific, but about six years ago, the local poetry society ran a competition to showcase poets in the area. They put out a book with the best entries and the top poems submitted. It was called *The Poetic Voice of the Valley*. The Poet might have a poem in it. Do you want to take a look? We have a copy."

I would love to look at it." I had no idea we even had a poetry society. If it was still functional, they might have some information, and they might be interested in doing a poetry production at the theatre.

I could check out the folklore book, but I had to look at the poetry one in the library, so I settled in to read through a few dozen poems. While some were quite good, they waxed poetic about love, the weather, the crops, and the ocean. And some were downright awful, rambling on with no rhyme—literally—or reason. But one caught my eye with a sense of familiarity in the rhythm. Called *For My Starling*, it spoke of magical love, and the first few lines evoked romantic imagery…

> *You move as moonlight draped in autumn's haze,*
> *A fleeting breath of song the night wind bears.*

The poet's name was G. Byron. I made a note to see if I could find out more about this person. Although most poets had a brief bio included, none was provided for G. Byron. It may have nothing to do with Hallie or Andie's death, but the words were evocative, particularly when it got to the next to the last stanza:

> *Should time unweave the bond that memory makes,*
> *My heart will guard what once you gave to me.*

As I turned the book back in, I asked the chatty Jubilee if she knew who G. Byron was and if any other books were credited to the name.

She checked the book listings and shook her head. "No, not a one. I'm sorry. I don't know who that is. An internet search might turn up something."

"Thanks for checking. I'll try that route." I took my folklore book and headed home, stopping for a coffee in the shop at McKenzie Square where Katie met me, and I told her what I'd learned about Hallie Connor. I asked her if she'd ever heard of someone named G. Byron, but she said she hadn't. However, she vaguely recalled Eliot Crane from high school.

"Gosh, he was about thirty then, Isla, so he'd be in his late forties now. But I recall seeing his photo in our yearbook—a distinguished-looking, but attractive man with a soft smile. I don't think either one of us took a class with him."

"I know I didn't, but now that you described him, I know who you're talking about. He was soft voiced but eloquent when he spoke at assemblies." Could he be The Sage? More than that, was he the vendor Andie bullied the night she died? If so, what had she said to him—and what had he said back? Was it enough to spur him to violence?

Conklin arrived at the theatre to pick me up the next morning at ten. I'd been pacing in front, so I hopped in as soon as he pulled to the curb.

"Does Rob know we're coming?" I asked, curious if Conklin had prewarned him.

"Yes, I gave him a call to let him know I would be by to talk to him about the nautilus thing."

"How'd he respond?"

Conklin glanced at me. "He hesitated to answer, but then said it was fine and when should he expect me. I didn't tell him you were coming."

I swallowed my nerves. Thinking about how this might go today had kept me up half the night. Although I'm pretty self-assured, I was shaken by the altercation and its possible ramifications. I'd been so sure I was on to something. "What about the deputy?" I asked.

"He's going to meet us there. You nervous?"

"Uh huh. I have a business deal with Rob, and this isn't going to sit well."

"Let me guide it. Don't come in off the wall with anything so you can avoid an implosion." Conklin turned toward the hills and glanced in the rearview mirror. "Ah, Wilson has joined us."

I swiveled around to see a sheriff's car tailing us. "I hope we don't need him."

"Did you see any weapons in those artifacts you mentioned?"

"Two swords and a ball on a chain."

He shot a quick look at me. "Decorative swords or useable ones?"

"They looked old and were in a cabinet. The ball looked rusty and kinda crumbly, so maybe medieval." I hadn't looked at them closely, so it was a guess.

We pulled up in front of the house and marched up the walkway. The deputy joined us at the door while we waited for Rob to answer. When he did, the real estate man's smile faltered when he saw two additional people with Conklin—one of them carrying a visible gun.

"I wasn't expecting a group." He frowned at me. "Why'd you bring her?"

Conklin pushed forward a little to maneuver in front of me. "Miss Reed works with the SO now and then and often adds good insight. In this instance, she also has information about the .... uh, nautilus paperweight." He held up the flyer I'd given him. "Did you post this at the library?"

Rob's throat bobbed as he swallowed, but he owned it. "Yes. It's my property and I'm hoping to find it. Ms. Reed indicated yesterday that you have it. Did you bring it?"

A quirk of a smile touched Conklin's lips. "May we come in and discuss this inside?"

Even though Rob held his cordial smile, his eyes told a different story as they slid from Rob to me and then the deputy, and the tale wasn't welcoming. Nonetheless, he stepped aside and motioned for us to come in.

As I strode by him, he whispered, "Traitor," in a harsh voice. I bit my lip and moved forward quickly. Rob took us into his office and offered seats. Conklin and Wilson remained standing, although the deputy moved to the display cases, to examine the artifacts as we talked.

"I have your paperweight in our evidence locker for now. However, its ownership is in question. You may have had a different one." Conklin planted his gaze on Rob's eyes.

Without a word, Rob handed him the photo I'd seen. Conklin studied it and opened his tablet, pulling up closeups of the paperweight from four angles. Not the ones I took, but high-definition ones taken by the sheriff's photographer. Even from where I sat, I could see the crack in the glass. "Is this the same as yours?"

He handed Rob the tablet. Rob's jaw tensed as he looked at each picture, eyes squinting a bit to focus more closely. "Mine doesn't have a crack in it. Otherwise, it looks identical."

Conklin lifted an eyebrow and turned to me. "Is this the object you found in Ms. Langley's booth at the corn maze?"

I took a few moments to peek at each picture. "Yes, it is. I recognize the crack in the glass."

"Are you saying this one isn't yours, Mr. Fenmore?"

He hesitated, looking uncertain, like an animal that didn't know which way to run. "I—no, I'm not saying that. But mine didn't have the crack in it. I really can't imagine two nautilus shells with identical patterns in them, and you can clearly see the bands on the shell are the same."

"I didn't find a case indicating you'd reported the artifact stolen. Why not?" Conklin pressed Rob a little harder.

"I … I …Well, I hoped to get it back without involving law enforcement." Rob's fingers twitched like he wanted to grab something and run.

"Did you suspect someone who knows you took it and would bring it back for the reward?"

Like he's been thrown a lifeline, Rob responded. "Yes. Maybe. I didn't know but I hoped. I just preferred not to report it."

"Is it because you may have purchased it illegally?" Conklin continued.

"No, I got it from an auction house. It wasn't illegal."

"Can you tell me where you got this artifact?" The detective shifted his position, easing back a little.

Rob told him the same thing he'd told me… at an auction in Arizona. Conklin pressed him for more information, the name of the auction company, and if he knew who put it into the auction. Slowly, he dragged out the company was called Ancient Wonders Auctions, but the auction house wouldn't give him the person's name who wanted to sell it.

"From the research I've done on this, it's been missing from the Istanbul Museum for over two hundred years. It was stolen and they'd still like it back. So, if we can track down the person you got it from, we might see how he got it. We won't find the original thief, but we can certainly return it to its proper owner. But now, the question is, who stole it from you?"

"I don't know," Rob insisted. "I don't know how Andie ended up with it. She'd never steal from me. She wasn't that kind of woman."

I'd watched him as he spoke, seeing the medium blue halo around him flicker with yellow and green flashes as his emotions warred with each other. He was beginning to doubt his conviction about Andie while realizing he was in hot water with the object.

"May I ask a question?" I addressed Conklin. His eyes sparked interest, but he nodded. I rose and stepped closer to Rob. "I'm sorry about yesterday. I didn't intend to insinuate anything. But I need to ask you if you ever touched the paperweight without wearing gloves?"

While my weak apology had shown positivity in his aura, the question brought a flash of orange and a puzzled expression. "Yes, several times. Although I know the auctioneer who held it and the person who handed it to me both wore gloves, but that's pretty standard when handling antique objects."

I nodded. "When you held it, did you hear anything like a whisper?"

"What? No. No, I don't think so, but I got a wonderful feeling from it, like luck was on my side."

"And was it?" Had he connected good fortune to the nautilus?

"Maybe. Things went well for quite a while. What are you getting at? Do you think my successful business transactions are connected to a seashell and a hunk of glass?"

Oh, there went a yellow flare in his aura. He was getting annoyed. "Well, you don't know much of the object's history. It's called the Whispering Nautilus and is said to bring good luck to its owner."

"You're kidding." Rob cast a questioning look to Conklin.

"That's part of the story. So, who might have wanted to steal your luck if it wasn't Andie? And how did she end up with it?" Conklin played it cool, voice calm and steady.

Rob sat forward, the whole situation seemed to put him on edge. "Look, all I want is to get my item back. If it's a stolen item, then maybe there's a reward for it. I already told her—" He pointed to me, "that I wasn't involved in Andie's death. I was at a conference."

"Yes, we know," Conklin answered. "We checked out your alibi."

"Good. I'm not answering any more questions without my lawyer." Rob declared.

"Fair enough. I'm not charging you with anything. I'm simply following the object's ownership path to see if it will lead to Ms. Langley's death. Contact your lawyer, and we'll see you at the sheriff's office tomorrow afternoon. Conklin placed his business card on the desk. "Call me with the time you'll be in."

He turned to leave, signaling the deputy and motioning to me to follow. As we left, Conklin thanked Rob for his cooperation and said he looked forward to talking to him again.

Rob's eyes shot laser flares at me. Oh, yeah. That business relationship was shot down.

Chapter Seventeen
The Color of Doubt

ON THE WAY BACK to the theatre, Conklin asked what impressions I got from the conversation. "I need to think about it," I answered. The reactions from the aura surrounding Rob were uneven and confusing but didn't compare with the visual and intuitive signals I received from him.

"No, don't think, just tell me what you picked up while talking to him and reading his body language."

Conklin glanced at me, his eyes encouraging me to use my own intuition to make an evaluation. Did I have one? Was I relying on my aura vision to guide my interpretation. Aunt Daphne had advised me to trust my own impressions more than the magical ones. And I guess, when I got down to it, the aura vision aligned with magical ones.

As for the pendant, it had remained surprisingly silent during our chat with Rob. I'd worn it outside my sweater, not touching my skin, so maybe it needed the contact to react and communicate. But Conklin was waiting for a response.

"Well, for one thing, I think he is sincere about his feelings for Andie. He trusted her and wouldn't do anything to hurt her. I've thought it before—if he had an issue with her bossiness, he would just fire her. Unless she had something on him to keep him from doing it. But, I didn't get that uncertainty from him until we talked about the properties of the nautilus. I think that might be the only doubt I saw in him, the only possible thought that she could have taken it."

"Interesting," Conklin said. "I have similar thoughts. I don't think he lied to us about any of it, not even his lack of knowledge about the object being stolen. With everything he has in that room, I'd say he was a genuine collector, and he just spotted a unique artifact he wanted. But he didn't do any research to determine its value."

"That sounds about right." I agreed with his assessment of Rob's hobby. "He might have gone to the auction looking for something else and spotted the nautilus, at least knowing it was valuable, and saw an opportunity."

"Do you have any other thoughts on who might have stolen it?"

I shrugged. "A random burglar, but why take the paperweight when the shelves were filled with other treasure of equal or more value? Then there's Glenn Harper."

"What about Harper?" Conklin turned onto the side street to park at the theatre's backlot.

"From what I heard, he was involved with a business deal in Santa Barbara with Rob that didn't go as well as he'd hoped. But I don't have any details. Still, if Glenn knew about the nautilus' rumored magic to bring good fortune, he might have risked stealing it from his partner. That's the only quality about the object to make it the sole item of value in the collection." I didn't mention that Rob had at least three other items that displayed active energy, meaning they might be magical or powerful.

"Glenn Harper, huh," Conklin's eyes narrowed a bit as he thought. "He said he wasn't at the maze on Friday night. I recall he said he'd been working at the Fairbourne Mansion that evening."

"I saw him there before I went to the maze." I undid the seat belt and turned to face Conklin. "He was on the phone to someone and made a remark about he hoped this deal—meaning the mansion—worked out better than the last. I got the impression he was talking to

Rob, but when he saw me, he said he was talking to Andie. He was still at the place when I left, but Gary, my lead tech, said he left shortly after I did. So, he wasn't at the mansion."

"Okay, it looks like I need to chat with Harper again to see if I can get more details. What would he have been doing at the mansion?"

"Good question. He wasn't working on any of the tech or decorations and seemed to be running some figures. He was in the den at the desk there. Anything else?" I put my hand on the door handle, ready to open it.

"Not right now. You did good, Isla. We all have some bad days when you're trying to dig up information and suspects aren't exactly cooperative. That Fenmore decided to call in his lawyer suggests that he might have something to hide, or he is just nervous about being a suspect. We'll learn more tomorrow. By the way, good question about the rumored magical properties of the object. I think that rattled him a bit, but it also told us he didn't know much about its history." He nodded toward the door. "Go ahead. See you tomorrow at the station for round two?"

I hesitated, "You want me to sit in on the interview?"

"Actually, I want you to watch and listen from the other side of the glass. I think Fenmore will be more forthcoming without you there."

"Okay, I can do that." I hopped out and waved a quick goodbye before going into the theatre's back door.

I felt a little queasy. That wasn't the most pleasant experience for me when I realized what I had at stake in the conversation with Rob. He wouldn't forgive me for bringing the law into this and suggesting he was involved in Andie's death. Even though I didn't say it. The nautilus was the link, but I felt we needed to find who stole it. If it wasn't Andie, then it was the person who killed her.

It was in Conklin's hands now. I felt like I couldn't rely on my aura vision for answers, and I'd become too confident in my reading ability. I went upstairs to grab a soda to calm my nerves while I consulted my aura book again. What did those mixed colors really mean?

A half hour later, I sat on the sofa, book open by my side and considered my misread of Rob some more. I had interpreted his emotions in the wrong way, not judging how the colors worked together and taking them individually. I sniffed, the threat of tears imminent. If I couldn't use my gift to help people or learn the truth, what was the use of it? All my life I'd thought I understood how it worked and how certain colors meant something. How many times have I gotten the meaning wrong?

"Don't beat yourself up, dear," Aunt Daphne's voice sounded like it came from a distance.

I turned my head toward the patio door. "I screwed up, Auntie. It turns out I'm not as clever as I think I am." Tears welled up and overflowed, like a trickle down a stone dam. "I didn't just almost accuse Rob of being involved in Andie's death, I also ruined the deal the theatre made with him for the haunted house."

Daphne drifted down to sit beside me. "It's not as bad as all that, dear. You have a strong gift, and you've mostly encountered straight-forward situations in your aura observations. But under stress, auras become more volatile and nuanced. A mood can shift in an instant, emotions turning them into a minefield of little explosions. You hadn't tried reading them when someone may have many thoughts and triggers going off."

Despite her words, the tearful flow ran down my face, and I reached for a tissue, finding the box almost empty.

"Better get more," Daphne said sagely, then added, "Your detective didn't find you lacking, did he?"

My aunt's kindly look and open arms told me she wanted to hug me like she did when I was fifteen and just discovered the boy I liked didn't feel the same about me. I shook my head. "No, he didn't. He said I did good. But he didn't just blow a big financial deal."

"Isla, Fenmore still needs the theatre to do that haunted house. He'll pay you. You might have screwed up any future deals, but the solution to the theft and the murder could change his mind."

Grateful for her consoling words, I still wished we could hug, giving me the comfort of her touch. As I gazed at her, my watery eyes so grateful to have her spirit with me, something landed in my lap. I looked down at the same time, Higgins extended his forearms and gave me a kitty hug, paws on my neck, head resting on my shoulder, and a purr offering comfort. "Thank you," I said softly.

Daphne smiled. "You're never alone, luv. Now, dry your eyes and we'll tackle the ghosts at the mansion tomorrow."

My eyes snapped to her, seeing she was beginning to fade. "What?! Why tomorrow? And what are we going to do?"

"Help them, of course. Toodle-oo."

She was gone before I could ask anymore. Higgins batted the pendant, trying to pull it off me.

I held it close, wondering what tomorrow would ask of me—and what the ghosts might answer.

Chapter Eighteen
Through the Glass

SEATED IN THE SMALL room off the interview room, I settled in to observe Conklin grill Rob through the one-way glass. My nerves were still taut, influenced by the guilt nestled within me, yet thrilled to have this opportunity to watch the interrogation. Still, I thought I pulled Rob into this mess, but then I corrected myself. No, he got himself into it. I just discovered it.

The door opened on the other side and Conklin escorted Rob and his lawyer, a short, stocky man with round glasses and a shock of orange hair in a patch on the middle of his head. Rob seemed nervous, his gaze going around the room, taking in the camera, the table, and the microphone. His surveillance stopped when he looked directly at the window and pointed.

My heart thumped and I jerked in my seat, reminding myself that he couldn't see me. While they got seated, Deputy Wilson opened the door to the viewing room, and I lurched again.

"You all set?" he asked.

I nodded. He came in and took the seat next to me. "Conklin asked me to watch this with you. It's okay to talk softly. They can't hear or see."

I nodded again, not wanting to say anything even if they couldn't hear.

Once Conklin and the other two were settled in their seats with Rob and his lawyer facing the window, the detective switched on the recorder and the mic at the same time and started speaking. "Detective Kevan Conklin interviewing Robert Fenmore in the presence of his lawyer, Albert Swift. Time is 1315 on Tuesday..."

Rob coughed and I didn't hear the rest, but presumably it was the date. Conklin repeated Rob's rights and acknowledged the lawyer who stated he and his clients understood their rights. After he explained this was a follow-up interview to the one on the previous day at Mr. Fenmore's home, Conklin launched into the new business.

"First, I'd like to confirm the information you gave me about the nautilus paperweight is correct as to where you acquired it and that it was stolen from you but not reported at the time. "

"That's correct," Rob said.

"Now, can you tell me if you suspect anyone who was at the corn maze on Friday, the18th, might have stolen it from you?"

Rob glanced at his lawyer, then leaned toward the mic. "Since I wasn't at the event on Friday, I couldn't say if anyone there was likely to have taken it. I was out of town."

"To confirm, you don't believe Andrea Langly stole it from you even though it was found in her booth?"

"That's correct," Rob replied.

After a few more questions that repeated some of the ground we'd covered the day before I could see Rob relaxing a bit as the tension eased out of his shoulders, and he settled back in his chair. His lawyer made notes as we went along.

"Was Andie aware of your plans for the mansion?'"

Despite my resolve, I narrowed my eyes when Conklin asked the question.

"Yes, of course. She was my assistant, so she handled a lot of details for me." Rob sounded solid when he said it, but I noticed a flash of deep red shooting out from his stomach followed by a streak of yellow. Someone wasn't telling the whole truth.

"Did she ever object or try to warn the historical board?" Conklin shifted in his seat and reached for the water bottle.

Ron looked befuddled. "No, I don't believe so. Why would she do it? The place was for sale and—

The lawyer tapped his arm before he said anything more.

"Just asking. It's a historical building, so I wondered if you cleared the remodeling plan with the society."

"Oh, I'm sure she took care of that."

Then, out of the blue, or so it seemed, Conklin asked, "Tell me about your business partnership with Glenn Harper."

"Glenn? He's an investor in some of my business ventures." Rob replied, looking at a piece of paper Swift slid in front of him. He bobbed his head once to acknowledge. I couldn't see what was written, but my guess was the lawyer was reminding him to only answer the question in the shortest reply possible.

"Was he involved in a deal with you in Santa Barbara about four years ago?" Conklin checked something off his list.

"Yes."

"What was that investment?"

"A hotel. Straightforward."

"Yet, you lost some money on it." Conklin didn't frame it as a question. He'd done his homework.

"There were problems with the construction, and it overran on the budget."

"And is Harper investing in the Fairbourne Mansion remodel?"

"Yes."

"Do you think he might harbor any animosity about the earlier deal?"

Rob's eyebrow shot up. "No, I don't think so. Glenn's a good guy and he understands the development business isn't always a success."

Conklin nodded. "So, you don't think Harper might have taken the paperweight with the intent to sell it?"

"Absolutely not." Rob's face turned a little red. "Glenn's not a thief. He wouldn't do something like that—especially not to Andie."

I perked up. Did Glenn have a thing going with Andie? I hoped Conklin followed up … and he did.

"What do you mean? 'To Andie'?"

Flustered, Rob mumbled, "They went out … a few times. It wasn't serious."

I leaned forward, surprised by this revelation. I hadn't suspected this kind of connection, not the way Harper had acted around her. If they'd had anything going, it must have imploded at least a few weeks ago. He was married and fooling around with another woman? That song was familiar. Hallie had been seeing a married man also. A little more fuel to connect the earlier victim to Glenn. Not enough to make an accusation though.

Swift tensed up, slapped a hand on Rob's arm and glared. "That's not relevant to this situation, Detective."

Rob nodded, realizing he'd said something that might cause a problem for Glenn.

Conklin asked a few more questions, but nothing more useful tumbled out of Rob's mouth, and he pretty much stuck to short answers.

"Is my client being charged with anything?" Swift asked.

"Not at this time." Conklin gathered his papers back into the folder he'd brought in.

"Can I have the nautilus back?" Rob asked. I almost choked. He knew it was a stolen object and a piece of evidence, and he had the audacity to ask for its return.

Swift put his hand over his eyes and looked at the table, like he couldn't believe he heard his client say that.

Conklin stayed cool. "I'm sorry, but no. If it's the same artifact from the Istanbul Museum, it will be returned to them. For now, it is locked up as part of this case. It may or may not have a relevant part in it, but until the case is solved, it's in our possession.

"But I didn't know—"

Swift cut Rob off. "My client purchased the object in good faith from a known auction house. He didn't know it was a stolen item."

"And I am not charging him with anything at this time," Conklin repeated. "But the nautilus won't be returned to him."

Rob's face turned to a mask of disappointment and a bit of anger as I caught him clenching his hands into fists before his lawyer touched him again.

"Is that all, detective?" Swift asked.

"For now, yes. You're free to leave."

Rob and his attorney hopped up and vacated the room as soon as Swift picked up his papers and briefcase. Conklin took a minute or two more to turn off the recording devices before he came out.

Deputy Wilson urged me out of the observation room, where we met Conklin just outside. The layout of the office was open with the conference/interrogation rooms along the side. The detective pointed toward his office cube, and I followed him over.

"What do you think?" he asked.

I sank into the chair. "Rob was nervous, but for the most part sincere in everything he said. The revelation about Glenn Harper and Andie was accidental. I didn't have any idea. Most of the interactions I've witnessed were more abrasive than friendly."

An eyebrow lifted and Conklin said, "How so?"

"Andie was a … domineering woman," I answered. "She wanted things to suit her vision and expected people to yield to her demands. In general, she rubbed anyone who had to work with her the wrong way. Although it seems Rob wanted a woman like that in his office."

Conklin nodded. "I imagine she was efficient and thorough at getting things done. Let's say she learned about the nautilus paperweight's background and found the same information you did. Maybe she told Harper about it, and he took it. If it brought luck, then he needed it. "

I picked up on his thread. "Then he and Andie stopped seeing each other and Andie took the artifact from him for some reason. She might have held it ransom and wanted Glenn to pay her for its return."

"Pure speculation," Conklin said. "We don't have anything to tie it together. Let me check into Harper's background to see if there's anything there that looks hinky."

Hinky? Who uses that word these days?

I thought, for a moment about telling Conklin my suspicions concerning Hallie Connor's death, but I hadn't actually tied Harper to it, and the clues were so cold. It didn't contribute anything to this case.

For now, I'd continue to look for clues to lead to Hallie's murderer on my own. Or maybe with my ace helper.

I noticed a folder on the detective's desk labeled Nogales Pedro, a name I'd first heard in connection with a migrant worker's death a couple of months earlier.

"Any movement on the Nogales Pedro situation?" I asked. It had been quiet on that front, but I hadn't forgotten the whispers.

Conklin shook his head, his expression unreadable. "Not much. Since we pulled in Reynaldo and George, things have gone cold. He's careful—smart enough to keep his hands clean and let others do his dirty work."

"Still operating on Tribal land?"

"Far as we can tell. That makes it tricky. Not our jurisdiction unless they invite us in." He rubbed the back of his neck. "I've got feelers out, but Pedro's a ghost for now"

`I nodded. "Well, if he surfaces again, I have a feeling Arbordale will be on his itinerary."

Conklin's mouth tightened into a half-smile. "Wouldn't surprise me. And if he does, I'll be ready."

I glanced at the time on my phone and realized I should have been at the mansion already. I'd told Gary I'd be there to check out the last few tricks they'd set up.

HURRYING BACK TO THE theatre to switch from my bike to the car, I also took the time to dash in and check in with the construction foreman.

"Good news," he said as I looked around the almost cleaned up lobby. "We should be finished by tomorrow afternoon."

"That is great news! Can I take a peek?" I hadn't seen either bathroom since they first started work on it at the beginning of the month.

He showed me into the men's room, explaining they still needed to finish the sinks in the ladies. Stunned, I stood in the middle, appreciating the new sinks and stalls. The colors reflected the theatre with light off-gold paint trimmed with burgundy finishes to mimic the spotlights and curtains. Even the air carried a fresh scent.

The foreman pointed to a unit in the wall near the entrance. "Odor neutralizer. Both restrooms have one of these. It's the latest trend for public businesses to install them."

"It sounds like a fabulous improvement," I answered, although I had questions about it. At least, the construction would be done, and I could solidify some dates and plan the winter holiday programs.

Before I left again, I went upstairs and scooped up Higgins, wanting to take him with me to the Fairbourne Mansion. I wrestled him into the cat carrier while he objected with sounds of disapproval and a fierce will not to be confined. For all his resistance, he was a good cat for not scratching or biting me. But he could kick hard, and he was not a small feline.

As I loaded Higgins into the car, I glanced back at the theatre's glowing lobby. One mystery might be unraveling, but another was just beginning—and this time, I wasn't going alone.

A DROWNING AT THE MAZE

Chapter Nineteen
Passages and Treasures

AS I TRUDGED UP the stairs at the mansion entry, lugging Higgin's carrier, I stepped through the usual flash of cold air. Gary greeted me with a grin wide enough to rival a jack-o'-lantern and shut the door behind me so I could release my captive.

Higgins darted out, hissed at the staircase like it owed him treats, and veered toward the den.

Gary raised an eyebrow. "Still beefin' with the upstairs, huh?"

"No, he doesn't like it," I agreed, glancing up at the ghostly haze lingering near the top. "Must be picking up something foul. So—show me the latest additions."

"Sure thing. Let's start with the dining room. It's got a vibe today." He swept an arm toward it like a game show host revealing a prize.

I stepped forward, half expecting cobwebs to swing down like an Indiana Jones trap. But as soon as I put a foot toward the archway, I hit a wall of cold, unrelenting air.

I stepped back, scanning for a sensor or hidden effect. Nothing. I tried again, bracing myself—and failed. The air didn't budge.

"What the heck?" I muttered, staring at the invisible blockade.

Gary chuckled. "Feels like walking into a fridge door, right? It's been like that all morning."

My mouth dropped open. "You mean you guys didn't rig this?"

He shook his head. "Nope. Whatever's in there ain't takin' visitors."

I narrowed my eyes and summoned my aura vision. A faint shimmer of gold hovered in the doorway, but no ghostly signature. "Is this the only room acting up?"

"Far as I can tell, yeah. Everything else is normal. Well—except the back bathroom. Got a soap dish doing its best David Blaine impression. Wanna see?"

Apparently, the ghosts are restless, I thought. Something's shifted.

We headed to the bathroom tucked under the stairs. It was narrow but roomy enough to avoid claustrophobia. I peeked in—and sure enough, a soap dish hovered midair like it was waiting for applause.

My lips felt dry. "This isn't one of your tricks?"

Gary crossed his arms, a wry smile creeping in. "Wish it was. I'd take credit. But nah—this place is officially off the rails."

"Good observation, Watson," I muttered.

Higgins peeked in, fur puffed like he'd licked a socket. He growled and bolted, claws tapping a frantic rhythm on the wood floor.

Gary snorted. "You gonna break it to Fenmore that he bought a fixer-upper with ghosts?"

"At least you're not spooked." After the last couple of days, it might be gratifying to tell Rob.

Gary shrugged. "Hey, I think it's kinda cool. Adds character. You wanna check out the den?"

"Yep. I'll be there in a couple minutes."

While I still stared at the soap dish, I needed to be alone to try to summon Daphne. I had a hunch about these odd happenings, and I hoped my aunt could confirm it.

As soon as Gary left, I whispered loudly. "Aunt Daphne, where are you? I need your help." I held my breath, fearing she wouldn't respond. A yowl behind me brought my head around to see my aunt's ghost materializing in front of Higgins.

"Isla, dear, what is the problem?" Her hair was pulled up and a large towel covered her body.

"Were you having a spa day?" I asked, amazed to see her in this state.

"As a matter of fact, yes. Now what—?"

I pointed at the soap dish and Daphne giggled like a schoolgirl. "Lovely, someone is having a tantrum."

"That's not all. Follow me." I took her back to the dining room archway and showed her I couldn't get into the room.

"Oh dear. This might be an ectoplasmic lock." She tried to poke her arm through it and failed. "Even stops spirits. Interesting." Undaunted, Daphne stepped to the wall a few feet away and blithely floated through it.

I blinked and waited. And waited. Then Gary called from down the hall.

"Isla, are you coming?'

Since it appeared my aunt wasn't coming back soon, I turned to go that way. Then it hit.

The mansion shook with a series of rolling jerks, sending loose objects jiggling across the room. I grabbed onto the stair's banister to keep my balance while I heard Missy scream, "Earthquake!"

It lasted for less than a minute, but it felt like much longer as the whole house shuddered. Fall and spring were what I referred to as earthquake seasons, the time when the earth had warm days and cold nights in the higher extreme. Sure, there's no proof of my conclusion, but I'd been on the west coast all my life and endured enough of them in those two seasons to have an opinion.

When it settled, I looked around the entryway, and everything seemed fine, crooked wall paintings and a pot that shook off a stand and broke. Minor damage. I heard Tony yell, "Holy Crap!" from the den and ran that way. Pushing through the door, I came to a halt and stared at the end of the room where Tony, Gary, and Louise grouped, pointing at the wall next to the fireplace.

What had happened and where was Higgins? I fast footed it to push between them, seeing the gap where the wall had opened, pulling away from the bricks. Through the opening, the door Tony and I had spotted through the peephole stood out in the light streaming in from the opening. Higgins sniffed at the bottom, running his nose back and forth like he was hunting.

"Looks like weese gotta closer peek," Tony commented.

"Can we open it any wider?" Not my property, but I wanted to see what was behind the door, and I needed a few more inches to get into it. Gary and Tony went to work to clear the opening more, tossing a few loose bricks into the room.

"What a jolt that was," Missy said as she came into the room and wandered back to see what we were doing. "We have decorations down in the drawing room, looks like the witches rode broomsticks through. Oh, what have you got here?"

"A secret passageway," I said, moving another brick out of the way.

Missy, dressed in country overalls with a scarecrow-design shirt, clapped her hands and butted her head in closer. "Oh, good! I always wanted to explore one."

Once the passage was cleared enough, I slipped in and crouched beside Higgins to inspect the lock. I jiggled the handle, tried again, shook it like I could rattle it loose. No luck.

"It's locked," I announced, stepping back.

Tony weaseled his way in, shoulder-first. "Yo, lemme take a crack at it."

I slid aside, cramped in the tight space.

Tony fiddled with the lock, gave it a twist, and it popped open like it owed him money.

"Cool, dude," I said.

He snorted. "Please. Child's play. I grew up in an apartment that ate keys for breakfast."

He pushed the door open just as Higgins perked up, ears twitching. The cat bolted into the stairwell, tail high, disappearing into the dark.

"Higgins! Come back here," I called, but he was already gone—his footfalls echoing, sliding side to side like he was chasing something invisible.

Just then, Aunt Daphne whispered in my ear, like she was standing right behind me. "The frozen wall to the dining room is a new ghost."

"Great," I muttered. "Now I need to find out if this stair is safe."

"I'll go up," Missy offered, peeking over my shoulder.

"Not until I check it out." I wasn't about to risk anyone on a staircase that might collapse under them.

And Daphne disappeared again.

Using the flashlight option on my phone, I started up the stairs, hearing a creak in the wood on the very first step. I looked up at the steps ahead.

"Higgins is up there somewhere," I whispered, hoping the confined space wouldn't amplify my voice.

I pressed on, testing each step before putting my weight on it. I passed the second floor where a door to the left probably led into the hallway, although Fairbourne might have blocked it off when he closed the downstairs entrance. I tried the knob, but it was locked or stuck. Continuing, I made it safely to the third floor with only three steps complaining as I stepped on them.

"You okay, Isla?" Missy called from the bottom of the stairs.

"It's fine so far," I yelled back. "But don't come up. Some of the stairs may be a little loose."

About two minutes later, I heard footsteps climbing behind me. Probably Missy. Sometimes, she just does what she has a mind to do. I continued up the last flight, which I hoped had an unlocked door. I didn't fancy going back down three flights and having to pass Missy.

I reached the fourth-floor door and tried to open it. The door didn't appear locked, but something on the other side blocked it. I pushed again, and got it open about two inches, but I couldn't see what rested against it. Well, that was it. I ran the light around the small landing and saw another flight of stairs going up. Where did those lead?

Ahead of me, Higgins let out a predator meow. It sounded muffled and his claws scraped on the wood. Encouraged, I mounted this set, hoping it was the last flight in the house, and I could get inside wherever it ended. A frail step gave way, breaking when I stepped on it, and I caught my breath, pressing both hands against the walls to give me support if I fell, but it caught on the one below it, so I could easily get my foot onto the next one up.

"Broken step, Missy," I called so she'd know if she continued to follow.

When I reached the top, I found Higgins huddling down with a mouse between his paws.

On my left, another door, but this one wasn't locked. "What's behind this?" I whispered, hoping for an answer. Nothing. My aunt had left me alone on this escapade.

With no warning, an aftershock shook the house again causing me to grab the knob and lean into the door for support, It gave way, and I stumbled into a hexagonal room with Higgins shooting through my legs to get to safety.

The air shimmered. Just for a second. A flare of violet and silver pulsed across the ceiling beams—like moonlight caught in a prism, then vanished. I froze, heart thudding, unsure if it was aura vision or something older, deeper.

Higgins crouched near the far wall, tail twitching, eyes locked on something I couldn't see.

"Hallie?" I whispered, not knowing why I said it. But the room felt different—not haunted, exactly. Guarded

I caught my breath as the house settled and took in the beautifully furnished girl's bedroom before me. A giant stuffed giraffe sprawled on the floor. A dresser with three drawers faced me and two comfortable velvet covered chairs squatted facing the room, where a lavender canopied baby crib sat on the far wall with an infant-sized doll lying in it.

"A child never born," Aunt Daphne's voice whispered in my head.

What?" I asked, but no voice answered.

Something was in the room, I could sense energy, but I couldn't see anything, not even a mist. A waft of cold air brushed past me, causing me to jump back. "Hello," I said to whatever spirit was there. "I'm here to help you. Who are you?"

A moment later, the ornate mirror on the west wall fogged over, like something cold touched it. Then a line formed on one side, followed by another and another until it formed an H. Little by little, the name showed on the now frozen glass. H ... A ... L ... L ... I... E.

Although I'd figured it out from the first three letters, a chill touched my spine when the spirit finished writing. "Hallie, I know who you are. You've been trying to reach me, haven't you?"

For a few heartbeats, the spirit appeared, mostly transparent but visible. Holding her appearance at her death, she looked like a drowned rat, hair dripping water that never hit the floor, clothes soaked, and her face bore a bluish pallor. Then she faded, yet a mist remained and I sensed her presence.

"I've read your journal, Hallie." I focused my eyes on her, letting her know I could see her.

Read it? A raspy voice asked in my head.

"Yes, your mother let me take it for a few days. I know you drowned in the pond."

I could feel the spirit compress. *Pushed ... pushed. Drinking with him ...*

"Who?" I prompted. "Who were you with?" Were you seeing The Sage?"

Sage? Her voice shifted to a sad, dreamy tone. "*Poet... no one can know.*"

Confused by her answer as to which man she was with, I tried again. "Did you see The Poet the night you died?"

Secret. I promised him to not tell...

"Hallie, he murdered you. You can break that promise." I pleaded with her. What did he say that night?"

He called me Persephone... I told him I preferred Maeve... Star crossed lovers... We stood among the reeds, hand in hand. He whispered, 'Beneath the golden moon, our hearts beat in tune, But come the light of day, the bliss will fly away.'

Even in my mind, her voice hitched with sorrow. He was saying goodbye to her. The Poet. Her killer had to be the Poet. I tried again. "Who did you meet? His name, give me his name."

The Poet hides behind names... Her voice sounded like a sigh, but still not an answer.

"*My room ...*" She shifted the conversation, evading my question.

"You've claimed this space?" I played along, finding it sad yet hopeful that she'd moved into the mansion. It confirmed the connection between the house and the pond.

Mine, yes...

At that moment, Missy stepped through the door. "What is this? Ohhh... a baby's room. How cute? Why would they put it up here? What is this place?" She waved a hand to indicate the odd shape.

"I think we're in the turret. Are you okay?"

"Yes, I got knocked down with that roller, but I didn't tumble down the stairs. You're okay also?"

"Yeah, I stumbled in here."

"Lookie! There's a chest at the foot of the crib," Missy said, excited by it.

I had seen it, but not really registered it, but now I stepped closer to get a better look. It was more like a travel chest, probably one the Fairbournes had used when they traveled across the country to settle here. A padlock secured the chest, but it looked old and rusty.

Private ... Hallie's voice cautioned. *Don't open it.*

"Why?" I replied, my voice soft but Missy still heard.

"Why what?"

Not yours, Hallie answered. *You don't open.*

Then the spirit dissipated, no hint left of her presence.

I sensed the sorrow in this room, perhaps seeing why Hallie was drawn to it.

"Aren't you going to open the chest? I can't wait to see what's in it." Missy practically danced with anticipation.

Why did Hallie tell me not to open it? It wasn't mine, but it wasn't hers either. But it might give some insight into Abigail Fairbourne and what her husband chose to store in it.

I knelt and jiggled the lock. Although Rusty, it still held. "Look for the key," I told Missy. We both searched the room, opening drawers—one held baby clothes, and the others were empty—and searching under crocheted runners and behind the mirror. I even picked up the baby doll, turning it upside down and looking under the crib pad. Nothing.

Missy studied the lock, then plucked a hairpin from her bun and inserted it into the key opening.

"Are you kidding? You think you can—?"

The lock clicked open along with my mouth. For the second time today, I discovered I had potential thieves in my theatre circle.

Raising her eyes, she said, "Turns out hairpins are good for more than keeping my bun from falling apart."

She motioned to me to open the lid, and I almost felt Hallie breathing down my neck, even though she was no longer there. Her words bothered me. Even seeing and hearing her spooked me a little.

My fingers fumbling with excitement, I lifted the heavy top, and my eyes grew bigger. Three tiaras, covered in jewels, shimmered among four bundles of evening gowns in jewel colors. A dozen or more velvet-covered jewelry boxes formed a row behind them. I picked one up and opened it to reveal a stunning emerald necklace with diamond accents.

"OMG," Missy gushed as she held up a rose-colored velvet gown. "This is gorgeous." Then she saw the necklace. "Did we just stumble into Cinderella's dressing room? This is… wow. Are these real?"

"Your guess is as good as mine, but I believe they are. I'm guessing this is a treasure trove of Mrs. Fairbourne's best items." I opened another and lifted a sapphire necklace with matching earrings.

Each box revealed more lavish jewelry pieces, Missy picked up one of the tiaras, went to the mirror, and placed it on her head, comparing herself to a princess. "Admit it, Isla. This town is ready for Queen Missy the First."

Still chuckling, I replaced all the boxes in the chest and sat back on my knees. "Now I know why Fenmore wanted this house. He must have learned a treasure in jewels was stored somewhere in it. I'll need to call the sheriff on this."

"We can't keep it?" Missy's joy wilted.

"Nope. It belongs to the descendants of Mr. Fairbourne, if the authorities can locate them." I moved to a corner, although all of them were angled, and dialed Conklin to tell him about my find. Keeping my voice low, I added that I thought it might tie-in to Hallie's death and Andie's. I didn't know anything for sure about it, but it gave the detective an excuse to be involved.

I closed the chest and sat on the floor, thinking about the revelation and how it impacted what I knew about Fenmore, Harper, and their business dealings. Yet, I needed more to connect all this to Hallie and Andie. And I needed to find the Poet. Who was G. Byron? Was Crane the Sage or the Poet?

Chapter Twenty
Paper Cranes and Paper Trails

THE NEXT DAY, I called Gianni to see if we could meet again. I had more questions. Around ten, we stopped to get a cappuccino from a street vendor at McKenzie Green and sat on a park bench to chat.

"I think I have a pretty good lead to Hallie's killer, but I need to tie it up with Andie's death. I think it's the same person," I stated.

"That might be a big leap," he said, savoring a sip of his frothy coffee.

"I know. Hallie's journal only referred to her two lovers—if they both were—as the Sage and the Poet. I found a poem in a book released by the Arbordale Poetry Society, written by G. Byron. The poetry sounds like a snippet Hallie put in her journal. You wouldn't happen to know this person, would you?"

Gianni thought for a few moments. "Nope. The name doesn't ring a bell. Sounds like it could be a pseudonym or the person wanted to be likened to Lord Byron."

"So, you don't think it was their actual name? Why would they use one?"

"Several reasons, but the most likely in this case is that they didn't want anyone to know who they really are. Often, it's related to business notoriety or the need to hide their identity for professional reasons, much like actors and authors do."

"Oh." My mouth turned down in disappointment. I'd hoped for more. So, I went to my next question. "Do you happen to know Eliot Crane?"

Gianni perked up and grinned, "Of course, I do. He's a fine man and an author. I had a drink with him a few nights ago at the Vine."

"Wonderful. I'd love to talk to him. Could you give me a contact number?" I had the email address in his book, but it was through the publisher. A more direct contact would be quicker.

"Hold on." He pulled out his phone and sent a text message. "I never give out a phone number without asking the person first."

"That's fair. Or he can call me." I appreciated that courtesy.

"I thought of another instance regarding your Byron poet. Perhaps he's using a first name initial and a middle name or vice versa. Chi può spiegare?"

Who knows, again. But it was a possibility. When Gianni didn't get an answer to his text, he shrugged. "He's probably busy or driving. I'll tell him to call you when he replies."

"Thanks for that. I appreciate your help." I finished my coffee and rose to leave.

He got up at the same time, caught my hand, and kissed the back of it in a charming gesture. Old school and polished. I couldn't suppress the smile forming on my lips.

My next stop was the corn maze, and I made it there in fifteen minutes, catching Tara as she started up the path to the committee's booth. I waved.

"Isla! I wasn't expecting you this early," she called out, pushing her sunhat back a bit.

"I wanted to check something with a vendor, and I figured you'd be here getting ready for this evening."

"You know me too well." She resumed walking and I fell into step. "Which vendor?"

"Do we have Eliot Crane on the list?"

"Eliot... I believe we do. His booth was under Crane Books."

Crane... it occurred to me then that Hallie had mentioned the Poet folding a paper crane for her. Could that be the connection? "Did you handle the maze six years ago when Hallie died?"

"No, I didn't start until the next year. Why?"

"I'm curious if Crane had a booth that year." If he did, then I would have a positive connection.

We came to the booth, and she motioned me in. "We can check the previous year's records. I have the file with me, and it goes back ten years."

Tara pulled out the binder from a plastic carrier while I settled on the edge of the big ice chest. She handed me the folder from that year, and I opened it. Inside were the check-in sheets for each night of the attraction. I ran my finger down the side where the vendors were listed, each signed off by those who attended that night.

I didn't find Crane or a book seller on the list, so I went to the next page, and the next. I jumped to the one for Halloween night and scanned it. No bookseller and no EC initials anywhere on it. I sighed. "It doesn't look like he was here."

Tara's expression reflected puzzlement. "Well, not as a vendor, but it doesn't mean he didn't come as a paying guest."

"True, but no way to prove it."

"You're right. But you can ask him. He'll be here tonight."

"Good point." Why hadn't I thought of that. "By the way, did you get the pond light at the end of the reeds replaced?"

"Yep, brand new solar light there. And Andie had made a note a few days ago about the lack of a fence at the end of the bank. Rolf took care of it yesterday. He's right on top of this stuff."

Andie made a note? Interesting.

As I rose to go, I gazed at the entrance path to the maze and a scene popped into my mind. Glenn standing there as I walked into the maze, and he muttered, "*Come the light of day, the ghosts will fly away...*"

A shudder ran through my body. Almost the same words Hallie had said. When I chided him about it, he'd simply replied, "Byron."

I hadn't thought much of it then. Now, it felt like a crouton—soggy, half-submerged, and not nearly as charming as it pretended to be.

BACK AT THE THEATRE, I picked up the mail and retreated to my office. With the renovations, the place had seemed unusually quiet, not even Eamon on the stage door or Barb coming in to do tickets. With the work completed, we'd be getting back into routine after Halloween. I was eager to fill the space with voices, noises, and music—to bring the creative life back into its home. More and more, I understood Aunt Daphne's devotion to the theatre.

Sliding into the desk chair, I thumbed through the mail, not finding anything urgent. So, I set the letters and bills aside, turning to my computer. What might have Glenn Harper's full name on it? Birth certificate? No, too hard to access, even if I knew where and when he was born. Driver's license? A possibility, but I'd need Conklin's help for that one. He owned a construction company, so he had to have a business license. That might have it.

I searched the county office and found the business license link online. Next, I located the inquiry option to verify a license. I entered the company name, Harper Renovations and Repair, sucked in a breath and waited.

In just a few seconds, it returned the information on Glenn's business.

        License: 9864002519463
        Business Type: LLC
        Owner: Glynn B. Harper
        Address: 8036 Shady Hill Lane, Arbordale, CA

I exhaled. "Got you." Not conclusive, but B. could stand for Byron. It was enough to solidify my suspicions he might be the Poet, but not enough to nail him for two deaths. I printed the information, including the filing date and put it in my desk.

Now, to find out if Eliot Crane was the Sage and where he was on the night Andie died.

THE THEATRE'S BOOTH AND the pond were still off-limits, and Conklin couldn't tell us how much longer it would be. But the pooka still worked, so at least that bit of awe entertained the visitors.

I made my way through the clusters of people, checking out the booths to check that each vendor had everything they needed, and their displays conformed to our rules. Most of the time, nothing changed from night to night, but a few vendors shared their space and alternated nights.

I paused to talk to Katie for a few minutes, promising to stop by the shop the next day, before moving on to chat with Isolde.

"You're not wearing the pendant," Isolde noted quietly.

"No, I'm not. I find it interferes with my readings, so I left it at home." The assortment of colorful potion bottles caught my eye as I scanned the mystical objects she offered.

"Interferes? That's unusual. In what way?"

"The auras appear chaotic, and my mind is muddled when trying to read them. I never had the problem before. And it burns my skin. But I appreciate that you wanted to help protect me."

"Perhaps it's a clash of magic. Your source is a natural birthright, not cultivated over time. I probably can adjust the tuning on it."

"Not necessary. My intuition is enough, unless you have one that's an actual shield," I joked. "And thanks for the book of hexes and charms. It came in handy."

A smile blossomed. "Ah, did you fix the door?"

"I found the spell, but I didn't try to remove it. That will be Rob Fenmore's problem."

As I strolled away, I heard Isolde's chuckle.

Crane's book booth was three stations from Mystic Moon's and faced Andie's now-covered booth, which was cordoned off with yellow police tape. I wondered about the folded paper I'd seen when I found the nautilus and if the deputies had taken it with whatever else they removed from the booth.

I glanced around, seeing only a couple of people on the path now, then slipped behind the stall. As I expected, the back wasn't as snug as the front, and I crept inside to see what was left.

My phone light revealed the brochures and flyers still on the table, but all personal effects had been taken into evidence. I lowered the light to the ground and glimpsed the shine of white paper. Squatting, I reached in my pocket and pulled out a tissue, using it to pick up the folded paper, resembling a crane. After I carefully folded it into the tissue, I slid it into my pocket to take it to Conklin.

I continued to Crane's booth and paused for a few moments to study the attractive, fiftyish man who wore an Elizabethan costume, replete with a black and gold-trimmed helmet. On a stand, his new book *Echoes of the Golden Hind*, displayed a cover with Sir Francis Drake in the same garb.

He smiled at me when he saw my interest in his book. I returned it. "Mr. Crane, I'm Isla Reed. I wanted to talk to you—"

"Yes, yes. Gianni sent me a text, and I didn't have a chance to call you today. New book and all. How can I help you?"

"I have a couple of questions, if you'd be so kind to answer. I see you have a good view of Andie Langley's booth."

His cheek tightened, pulling his lips a little thinner. No love lost here.

"Did you have an altercation with her over your booth?" I asked bluntly.

He huffed. "I wouldn't call it an altercation. She insulted my book …" He paused to point to the book about Arbordale's legends and myths. "…and my integrity. She had a vicious tongue, that woman. She threatened to have my booth removed from the event until I pointed out that she, alone, did not have the authority to do it." He lifted his chin, showing his defiance and pride.

"So I heard by the local gossip chain." I sympathized with him. "Did you see Andie leave her booth around nine on opening night?"

"No, I didn't see her leave. I was helping my customers with sales, but when I glanced over about ten minutes after nine, she wasn't there. I didn't see her return that evening. Why are you asking?"

I glanced down at the spread of books and artifacts decorating the table. Fair question. "I'm assisting the sheriff's office with the investigation of Andie's death, but I'm also looking into Hallie Connor's. She was a student of yours, wasn't she?"

His look softened. "She was indeed. A brilliant student and a joy to teach."

"After she graduated, you remained friends, didn't you?"

"Correction. We *became* friends. In school, I mentored her, but it was always professional. After, we often met for tea and conversation. I was heartbroken when she died."

"I am so sorry." My mouth felt dry, so I ran my tongue across my lower lip. "Did she ever call you the Sage?"

A chuckle prefaced a tender smile. "Yes, she did. And I bore it proudly."

"She mentioned you in her journal. I'm sorry, but I have to ask, where were you on the night she died?" I squinted at him, ready for his response.

His face sobered and he swallowed hard. "I … I was in Canada at a college friend's wedding. Do you suspect me of contributing to that poor girl's death?"

Grief, sorrow, but truth. I shook my head. "Not really. But I think she was murdered, and I'm narrowing the suspects."

I paused to peer at Andie's booth, which was located at the top of the curved path. Crane had a good view of it. "Back to the night Andie died. Did you happen to notice if anyone might have confronted her that—"

"I did notice a clown stopping by who seemed to be having an intense discussion with her. But I couldn't tell you who was in the costume. But after he left, Ms. Langley's face looked like a tornado about to hit town."

Another vote for the clown. I thanked Crane, took a bookmark, and continued my rounds. The maze was full of shadows. But I had the map now—and the last pin was falling into place.

Chapter Twenty-One
The Bait Beneath the Bonbons

AS PROMISED, I STOPPED by Beldon's Sweet Shoppe to see Katie. "Hi-ya." I said when she looked up from the counter where she was rearranging a display platter of Halloween candies.

"Hey, Isla! I was just thinking about you." Katie grinned.

"You were? In what context?" I took the truffle she offered and popped it in my mouth. Yum, chocolate caramel, one of my favorites.

"I want to do a demo of the Glitz Lady products, and I hoped you'd be my model."

I almost choked on the candy. Ever since she'd started selling the cosmetics, she'd been after me to help her with it, and I had said I might do a demo with her. But now? Not a good time. "Not until after the end of the month. I am swamped until then."

"I figured as much," she said, her mouth downturned.

"I promise I will … after Halloween."

She lifted her eyes, giving me a doubtful look. Now I felt like a jerk asking for her help. "Well, bestie, I'd like to bounce a few things off you."

Her mood lifted again, and her lips curved into a shallow smile. "I hope it's juicy gossip."

"Not quite. I've had a couple of bad days, but I think I see the light."

"I'm due for a break. We can go into the back to talk. Should I bring truffles or rum?"

"Both," I answered as Katie called her mom to take over the counter.

Roseann Beldon came out, spotted me, and came to give me a hug. "How are you doing, Isla? I haven't seen you in a few weeks."

"I'm doing okay. Just crazy busy with the maze and a haunted house while workmen are tearing up the theatre bathrooms." I tried to make light of it, but I realized all this was getting to me.

"I'm taking a break to talk to Isla, okay?" Katie informed her. Her mom nodded and the two of us retreated behind the door to the chocolate factory.

"Keep an eye on that batch of chocolate," Roseann yelled as the door closed.

Katie put a saucer of candies on the bistro table in the room and pulled out a bottle of rosé

. "No rum, but will this do?"

"Perfectly." I didn't drink often, but the past couple of days warranted a little fortification. When Katie sat down, I began telling her about the events since Saturday when I discovered the whispering nautilus.

I took a long sip, then exhaled. "I didn't tell you about the artifact. Not all of it. The thing Andie had—it's called the Whispering Nautilus. It's enchanted. When touched, people say it whispers to them."

"Really? Did you touch it?" Katie raised a brow.

"No, Aunt Daphne warned me before I picked it up."

"You're still seeing your aunt?"

I detected a shade of worry in Katie's eyes.

"I do. On a regular basis. Anyway, she told me not to touch it with my bare hands. Isolde and I both researched it, and the reports claim it brings luck to people who own it, but it can turn on them also and possibly harm them."

"Do you believe that?' Clearly Katie didn't, if the tone of her voice was an indication.

"I know some things can carry magical properties. I held up my pendant. Isolde gave me this for protection and it reacts when it feels I'm being threatened. Higgins doesn't like it."

"I think you've been hanging around with Isolde too much. Really, Isla?" She sipped her wine and grabbed a candy, taking a bite.

I ignored her and told her about Glenn and his involvement with Andie. "I don't know if it was an actual affair or if they were just good friends, but the way Rob clammed up after letting it slip, I think it must have been the former."

"No way! How did you get him to say that much?" Katie asked.

"Well, I didn't. Conklin did,"

"Kevan? You were with Kevan?" Her eyes gleamed with a stab of anger.

"We're working the case together, Katie. He was in the interview room, and I was in the observation one so I could hear what Rob had to say."

She relaxed a little and the fire left her eyes. She could be a bit sensitive when it came to her boyfriend. But I had to give her more details than I originally had planned.

"Now that I think about it, I remember Glenn came into the shop two—no, three times to buy boxes of candy. I thought he was getting them for his wife, but one time he wanted a box delivered."

"Do you remember where?"

"Uh, no. It was a while back. But it might have been the real estate office. I didn't think about it much." Katie shifted her position and shrugged.

"It's all right. Now here's the core of this. Rob was the owner of the nautilus, and it was stolen. I think, but I can't prove, that Glenn might have taken it.

"I was thinking," I concluded and leaned forward, lowering my voice. "If we could get him to talk—say too much—maybe at the maze …"

Katie's eyes lit up. "I could bait him. Pretend to be curious or clueless. Play up my airhead side."

"You don't have an airhead side."

"I can fake one for justice," Katie said, grinning. "What's our angle?"

"We talk to him about the maze. You can say you've heard I'm reopening the landing for Halloween weekend. Hint that Conklin has closed his investigation into Andie's death. Really play it up. Then drop a line about the nautilus—see how he reacts."

Katie nodded slowly. "We'll need Kevan in on it. Quietly."

I reached for my phone. "Then let's set this trap." I tapped the speaker once I had Conklin on the line.

"Hi, honey," Katie said, setting the tone for this conversation.

I cringed a bit, but we explained what we'd come up with. Our goal focused on getting Glenn to confess to killing Andie, but in the back of my mind, I still thought he murdered Hallie. I was almost positive the Poet was Harper, and he killed Hallie even though she hadn't spoken his name. The final question was why?

CONKLIN WASN'T ENTHUSED ABOUT the two of us doing it although he admitted it was a viable plan. "But you'll have to be careful how you approach this. Let's work on it together so we look at all possibilities."

We agreed and made an appointment to talk to him the next morning over breakfast at the Stage Door Café.

After we hung up, Katie and I began tossing more ideas around.

"How do I approach Harper on this?" Katie asked. "It's not like he comes in here often and since Andie's dead, he won't be sending more candy to her."

"Well, he is in renovation, maybe you could talk to him about remodeling the shop or the house?" I suggested.

"That's more your area than mine. That whole theatre is ripe for renovation. But … Mom has been wishing we could remodel the bathroom. It wouldn't hurt to get some ideas and an estimate." Katie wrote a note on a piece of wrapping paper. "I'll have to clear it with her."

"It'll work. We need to have him come to me, so we'll need a good hook to get him to the landing. Contrary to some stories, the killer doesn't always return to the scene of the crime." Although, I reflected, if Glenn killed Hallie there, he already had returned.

The stage was set. All we needed was the right line—and the man who'd already played his part.

Chapter Twenty-Two
Pumpkin Pie and Pressure Points

I SLID INTO THE corner booth at the Stage Door Café just before Katie arrived for our eight-thirty a.m. appointment with Conklin. He was due in a few minutes, and she'd insisted on coming to explain her part in our plan, forcing her mother to handle the shop alone.

I signaled the waitress and asked her to bring coffee for three. "I'm a little nervous," I confessed. "This whole thing haunted me all night." Actually, it was Hallie or the rubber duck who did the haunting. I kept hearing her words and her warning not to open the chest.

Conklin and a deputy came to the mansion after I'd called them about the discovery. They'd taken possession of the chest and I'd begged Conklin not to tell anyone about it except the sheriff. I didn't want word getting out about the find. I needed to maintain the status quo with Fenmore and Harper.

But I questioned all my actions now. Should I have heeded Hallie's words, not opened the chest, and left it where it was until this whole incident was settled? Was I right in connecting Glenn with the Poet? Hallie didn't exactly say that it was him. If he killed her, what was the motive? Was it just a scandal with his wife or was there more to it?

Conklin arrived, walking in with the confidence the uniform afforded him and casting a quick smile at the waitress who pointed to our booth. He strode over, slipped into the booth next to Katie, and added a bit of cream to the coffee before he said hello.

Katie shifted a little closer like she was on a date, and I looked away. I knew they didn't see each other as often as she liked, but this was awkward.

"Did you learn anything from the trunk?" I asked. I didn't know what he might find, but I knew he and Deputy Wilson were going to go through and catalog everything.

"Mrs. Fairbourne was a size seven," he replied drily. "And the jewelry appears to be authentic. It's quite a find. For now, we're keeping it under wraps like you requested. Will you tell me why?"

I took a deep breath, which was when the waitress came to see what we'd like. I ordered French toast with pumpkin sauce. Katie just wanted a bagel and Conklin ordered a slice of pumpkin pie with whipped cream. Katie's eyebrows shot skyward.

"For breakfast, Kevan?" Her voice rose a note or two.

"It's good for you," he answered. "Eggs, cream, a vegetable—what's not to like?"

"But—it's dessert!" She looked to me for support.

"I don't know, Katie. He's got a good argument."

Conklin's expression turned into a smug look, half-smiling lips and a hint of a laugh in his eyes. He was pretty cute around Katie, I admitted.

"Back to the reason we wanted to meet," I said to get his attention. "I believe Glenn Harper was involved with both Andie Langley and Hallie Connor. I know the evidence isn't really strong, but here's what I've learned."

I told him about the journal and Hallie's references to the Poet. "Her parents said she was dating an older man, but she wouldn't tell anyone who it was. That suggests to me that the man was cheating on his wife."

"It's kind of weak, Isla." Conklin sipped his coffee.

"I know, but I have a strong feeling about it. The question there is motive. Why would he kill her instead of just ending the affair?"

Conklin gazed at the wall behind me for a moment or two, then pulled out his tablet and keyed something into it. "Hold that thought." He scrolled through a couple of pages then smiled. "Well, this might be a reason. Harper's wife is the wealthy one in the family. Ten years older than Harper and worth a lot of money. If he was seeing a young woman and it got back to his wife, he might have stood to lose a lot in a divorce. Infidelity could void a lot of marriage agreements. Possibly, Hallie threatened to tell his wife about it, and he reacted on impulse."

"So," I speculated. "They met at the maze, shared drinks and he dropped a bombshell on her, telling her he was ending their affair. Hallie didn't take it well and threatened to tell his wife, and, drunk and angry, he shoved her. She hit her head and drowned."

"It's a possible scenario," Conklin agreed. "And you think something similar happened with Andie Langley?"

"I do. And I think that paperweight has something to do with it. Remember? Rob let it slip that Andie and Glenn had a thing going."

"He came into the shop a few times to get candy and one time he asked me to deliver it to Fenmore's office, where Andie worked," Katie interjected.

"Did it include a card suggesting anything? That could be a clue," he replied dryly.

"Oh, piffle, I don't remember a card," Katie mumbled, ducking her head.

Conklin looked at me. "What else you got?"

I sipped my coffee, tapped the spoon on the edge, and dropped my theory. "I believe Glenn needed money and learned about the nautilus Rob had acquired. He looked it up and found it wasn't only valuable but was rumored to bring good fortune to those who listened." I paused for a breath, really into the story now.

"It sounded like the Santa Barbara deal with Rob didn't go so well, so Glenn took the paperweight, believing it might bring fortune to him. He had opportunity with access to Rob's office. When Andie found out Glenn had stolen it, she took it and attempted to get a payment from him to get it back or she would go to Rob." I concluded only moments before our orders arrived.

Conklin studied me through narrowed eyes until the waitress left. He didn't smile, just peered at me. I squirmed a little, feeling like a bug under a microscope.

Katie touched his arm. "It's just a theory, Kevan." She looked a bit nervous.

Finally, he spoke. "I … like the way your brain works, Isla. I can dig into Harper's background more to see if something jumps out to suggest Langley had a reason to blackmail him."

"That would help," I answered. "But what Katie and I really want to talk about is—"

"We have a plan to force Glenn's hand," she blurted out.

Conklin almost choked on the bite of pie he'd taken and had to cough it out into a napkin. "What?!" he gasped out after he drank some water.

This wasn't going to be an easy sell, but Katie jumped in anyway. "Isla and I figured out a way to lure him to the pond where she will pretend to sell the paperweight back to him, while trying to cajole an admission that he killed Andie."

Conklin's eyes turned to steel as he shifted them to me. "You think it's that easy? It's downright dangerous." He switched his glare to Katie. "And what part do you plan to play in this?"

"Let us explain." I wiped my mouth and leaned toward them, so I could speak softer. Even though only a few people were in the diner, I didn't want anyone to overhear. I explained, with Katie tossing in an embellishment or two, what our plan was. To his credit, Conklin listened without interrupting us.

"We'll want you to back us up," I concluded. "And be there ready to arrest Harper."

He didn't say anything for over two minutes, although he seemed to be considering the plan. He turned his eyes to Katie. "I don't like that you're involved in it."

"It's just a few little hints when he comes to look at the bathroom. I won't be involved in the actual sting." Katie's eyes reflected the love she had for Kevan's concern for her. "Isla's got the hard part, but she's a good actress, and she can sell it."

Conklin swallowed hard. "I'll have to clear it with the sheriff. I don't like the risks you're taking, but it could work. We can work out the details after I get it cleared."

Relieved, but more nervous now, I leaned back and finally addressed my now almost cold French toast. Getting only the first step. I had to make sure I knew my part and could manipulate Glenn. We also needed one major prop, and I thought I knew where to get it.

Chapter Twenty-Three
A Haunted House Opening to Remember

EVERYTHING WAS IN PLACE by Friday afternoon, every detail worked out. Katie had done her part, calling our suspect out for an estimate to remodel her mother's bathroom. Roseann hadn't been crazy about the idea, but admitted she'd like to know how much it would cost and had even contributed suggestions to Glenn. Then casually, Katie told him about the landing opening again and how I'd be there, hinting about a rumor concerning an unusual paperweight. Did he know anything about that? She said he ate it up, asking questions and trying to learn more about how I'd gotten it.

But for now, the haunted house officially opened at dusk, and I needed to be there. While I wore the Missy-designed Elvira costume for the mansion, black wig included, I brought a change of clothes to slip into before going to the maze.

Rob Fenmore promised to stop by for the opening; he didn't want to miss a publicity opportunity. When I arrived, he was already chatting to the people lining up to get in. He'd promoted the heck out of this with ads on radio, TV, and a billboard. When he spotted me, he grinned and pointed to the six-foot-wide sign set in the garden. Presented by the Playhouse Theatre Company and sponsored by Fenmore Realty, along with his charming business logo.

I smiled back, hoping he had forgiven me for bringing the sheriff into the situation with the Whispering Nautilus. I narrowed my eyes for a moment. If he harbored any animosity, it didn't show in his aura. The man appeared genuinely happy.

With a wave of my hand to the crowd, I yelled, "Another five minutes!" and slipped past Rob to join the cast at the haunted mansion. Eerie sounds flowed out to the street, drawing people toward it. Luckily, the Fairbourne estate encompassed a lot of land, so no nearby neighbors could complain. A scarecrow with glowing eyes welcomed visitors while an assortment of little animated goblins with red eyes guided them up the steps to the entrance.

On the veranda, a volunteer in a reaper costume scanned entry codes for those who purchased in advance while Barb, in a Merryweather costume, sold tickets to those who waited to buy.

Dressed like Sally from *A Nightmare Before Christmas,* Missy swept by me in a rush. "Time to let the victims in!" She continued down the steps to the black and orange rope tied across the entrance. With a wicked-looking grin, she announced as loudly as she could, "Come along, pumpkins. The dead are getting restless."

Rob did the honors of unhooking the rope entry as soon as she finished. Anticipation rolled through the crowd. A few kids squealed in delight, and even the teens shuffled forward with nervous excitement.

The cold sweep of air still greeted everyone who stepped across the threshold. Many people commented on it and a few ladies shrieked when it hit them. I overheard as one woman turned to her husband and said, "That felt possessed." The kids really loved it, running in and out a few times to experience it over and over.

I waited inside, ready to direct them to the first room, the drawing room. After that, they were free to wander downstairs as they wished. We had signs upstairs to point to the two additional haunted venues. I tried to space the groups, so the rooms didn't get overcrowded. Inside the bigger rooms, curtains provided separation so people could move through easily.

While the dining room entry was somewhat free of the ectoplasmic wall, it felt sticky when anyone walked through it. I heard yells and shrieks as people made their way around the rooms and the set-ups. Gary had turned the split wall in the den into a frightening closet with a vampire, played by Carter Hamilton, the most handsome vampire since Frank Langella—Aunt Daphne had adored him, so we saw the video a few times—jumping out to frighten them and even suggesting they could share some blood.

I beamed, enjoying the success of the attraction as the visitors, laughing and excited, entered in a steady stream. But I was a little distracted with thoughts of what was to come.

Sauntering up, Missy snapped her fingers in my face. "You look like you're auditioning for the role of Guilty Conscience, and honey—you're nailing it."

I smiled lamely. "Just have a lot of thoughts buzzing right now."

Missy grinned. "It's going great—"

A crash like breaking glass resounded from the dining room. I swiveled my head toward the entry and automatically ducked as a large serving bowl flew in my direction. It hit the newly restored, apparently, ectoplasmic wall and bounced back crashing onto the floor. More objects swirled in a strange dance around the room, pivoting one direction, then another.

In the room, a trio of visitors crawled under the dining table to avoid being blasted by the animated objects. At the front archway, more people peered in, thinking this was part of the show. I motioned to Missy, who stood nearby, her eyes like saucers and mouth hanging open.

"Keep an eye on this and reassure anyone who gets panicky. I'm going to get help." I turned to run toward the back where it was quieter, and I could summon Daphne.

"Help? It's a crazy poltergeist rebellion in there. What are you going to do?" Her face was even whiter than the makeup she'd smeared on for her costume.

"Find a ghost buster," I replied, turning to find Gary, dressed in an appropriate costume, coming toward me.

"What happened?"

"Our shield is up again, and a spirit is having a tantrum." I sprinted to a quiet place. I wouldn't be able to cover this ghostly activity up, and by now, Gary and Missy had put two and two together and come up with ghosts in the house.

"Aunt Daphne," I hissed loudly. "Help. I need your help."

I prayed she was lingering in the vicinity and could hear me. She'd said she would be close by tonight, certainly for the maze operation, and I hoped she was here now.

A few heartbeats later, she appeared, fading in like a special effect. "What is it, dearie?"

"Andie's having a tantrum!"

While Daphne's eyebrows reached a new height, she stayed calm. "I'm on it. Meet me at the arch."

"It's solid again."

She rolled her eyes and blinked out like a light. Nonetheless, I ran back to the arch where the aerial display continued. Broken glass covered the floor and one of the fake ravens was triggered, cawing loudly from the front corner. Missy and Gary talked to people, telling them it was a technical issue, and we'd get it fixed shortly. When Missy saw me, her eyes sent a message: *Fix this ... now!*

I pushed to the front, standing in the middle of the archway and yelled, "Please, everyone. We have a technical issue here and will have it fixed soon. Please go to one of the other rooms now and enjoy the scares there. Thank you." I waved my hands to shoo them away. Most went, some just stepped back a few feet to see what happened next.

I spun toward the room and tested the arch. Yep, still solid. Through what seemed like a mist, I could see Daphne flying around the room, her hand outstretched. She moved it like a tap on the shoulder … and Andie's spirit popped into my view.

Somewhat like Hallie had appeared, Andie, too, looked like a drowned rat. But her face wore a mask of fury as she flung her arms around, not exactly directing the pots and dishes, but flinging them in various directions. Daphne got her attention and pointed at the archway, yelling something. If she'd been able to shake Andie's spirit body, she would have been whipped back and forth like a palm tree in a hurricane, but a moment later, Daphne waved her free hand at me, and I put my palm to the arch again.

Sticky, but I could get through, even though I left quite a few strands of my black-haired wig behind. I moved as close as I dared without getting slammed by one of the pots, which were now whirling around in a more or less stable pattern.

I leaned down to the people under the table and waved toward the arch. "Keep low and go now. We'll get this machine under control soon. Thank you."

I didn't have to tell them twice. Wide-eyed and frightened, the parents led the way, bending low and hurrying, with the mom pulling a boy about ten along with her. Unlike his parents, his eyes lit up with joy and wonder at what he saw. "Best haunted house ever," he shouted to me.

I managed a weak smile, praying they wouldn't sue.

When I finally got close to Andie and she'd quit doing an aerial ballet, I said, "Please, Andie, calm down. I know you're angry and—"

"Damn straight, I am. Where is that weasel? I am going to haunt him the rest of his pathetic life."

"It's Glenn Harper, right?" I asked. "That's who pushed you into the water, isn't it?"

"Ha! You figured out that clown, didn't you? Everyone says you're clever." A sneer crossed her face.

Jeez, did she resent me that much?

"Just confirm it's Glenn, and I'll get him for you, Andie."

She pulled her head back in a *huh?* jerk and peered at me. "You'd do that? For me?"

"Yes, I will. Just tell me what happened."

"Well, the clown showed up and told me to meet him at the landing to talk. He knew I had the paperweight." She told me the whole story, much like what I'd imagined, but enough details of the meeting for me to nail Glenn Harper.

"Thanks, Andie," I said. "Be at the pond at nine tonight if you want to see the real show."

A rustle of a breeze flowed through the room, carrying Andie's scarf that I had retrieved.

I smiled, 'We'll get him, Andie."

At ease now, she nodded and floated off to the kitchen, vanishing as she did.

Daphne winked at me. "Good job, luv."

Right. I looked at the mess and went to find a broom. I had about an hour before I had to be at the corn maze. I heard footsteps and Missy came up beside me. "I'll help you with this." I glanced back and Gary was already picking up the unbroken crockery. A smile emerged from my gloom. Darn, I had a super good team.

But the toughest part of the night was yet to come.

Chapter Twenty-Four
The Night of Reckoning

DRESSED IN JEANS AND a light jacket and wearing a simple masquerade mask, I strode out onto the landing by the pond. As promised, all traces of the crime scene tape and orange cones were removed. Solar lights edged the landing where dirt supported it and gave off a gentle, candle-like illumination to the serene setting. A light mist from the ocean enhanced the water's hazy look, similar to the night Andie died. Underwater fairy lights added an eerie glow as they reflected on the water.

Perfect for a lovers' rendezvous. Or an illicit business deal.

The musty scent of mud and the reeds filled the air. A slight rustle to my right alerted me to Conklin's presence. He and his deputies chose to use the "concealed in the corn-stalks-hidey-hole" trick the tech team used. Not exactly roomy, but enough for the four of them to crouch down out of sight.

I took a deep breath and strolled along the edge of the landing, glancing toward the path like I was waiting for someone. I was, but the target of this trap wasn't aware. I had the lure—a phony duplicate of the Whispering Nautilus that Dennis, a model-maker friend, whipped up for me from the photos I had. Until you inspected it closely, you couldn't tell the difference. In the dark, it would be enough to fool Glenn.

My nerves tingled, on edge and eager to get this done. At this point, I questioned my sanity. On paper, it seemed simple: lure the suspect, cleverly get the confession, and Conklin takes over.

Now, my mind conjured the other scenario. I liked Glenn, so it was hard for me to see him as a killer, but nice people can have an evil side. He'd killed two women already. What if he tried to make it three? Nerves tightening, I nudged a pebble off the landing, and a splash told me about where it hit the pond.

Footsteps followed the sound, coming closer and approaching me. A thud resounded as they stepped onto the wood. I turned to see if my mark had arrived.

No clown costume this time, Glenn wore an Indiana Jones costume, minus the whip but didn't look as dashing as the actor. But he had a wooden truncheon strapped to his thigh. I smiled. "Hey, Glenn, fancy meeting you here."

His return grin was a bit too wide. "Expecting someone else, Isla."

"As a matter of fact." I looked around him like I expected another visitor and dropped a name for his reaction. "You looking for Persephone?"

His smile faded and he gazed around the area, looking for any other people, probably. "Don't know what you mean. But this fine full moon on a clear night wouldst make the meeting more bright. But since we have it not, we must find our very own spot."

"What an observation, Lord Byron." Not really impressed with the couplet but waiting for his reaction to *this* name.

For a split second, his eyes widened, and his mouth twisted, but he recovered quickly. "What's that?"

"You know, Lord Byron, the *poet*. That was a bit of poetry, wasn't it?"

"Yes. I like to dabble. But, to the point, you do know someone else, like me, could be interested in that artifact you acquired." He was playing it coy, calm-voiced and persuasive.

"Really?" I lifted my eyebrows in question. "How much is your reward offer?"

"Five hundred."

"That's a bit low. The person who posted a flyer is offering more."

He frowned, his mouth turning down. "It's a big reward for returning something stolen from me."

"Stolen? I found it in Andie's booth the day after she died. I'd say it was hers."

"She stole it from me," he growled. "Now I want it back."

I took a step away as I felt his charming demeanor slipping. "As I understand it, the artifact belonged to Rob Fenmore. At least, that's his story."

"I borrowed it. Another reason I need it back, so I can return it to him." His voice shifted to a degree lower. I hoped the wire was picking this up.

"Hmm, borrowing without asking is theft, Glenn. You swiped it, and you're self-righteous because Andie took it from you. Is that why you killed her?"

His shoulders shot back, and he feigned surprise and an innocuous face." What are you suggesting? I didn't kill anyone. I just asked her to give it back to me. Do you have it? I need it."

Curiosity rising, I responded, "You *need* it? It's an old glass paperweight." I pulled it out of my jacket pocket and held it up.

"You don't understand, Isla. I lost a lot of money on a Santa Barbara deal with Rob. He *owed* me. That object's supposed to bring good fortune. I *need* it."

"Enough to kill?" I called in my aura vision, knowing it wouldn't pick up as well in the dim lighting.

"She took a swing at me. Hit me with her purse right in the face. I thought it was in the purse and grabbed it. She … she fell."

A half-truth, I didn't need to see; I felt it in the vibrations from his words. "What about Hallie Connor?" I asked. "Did she have something you wanted?"

His right hand dropped to the truncheon as his face contorted into an angry mask. "Don't go there, lady. Just give me the damn artifact and this will be over."

"You are the Poet, aren't you? The one Hallie wrote about in her diary. I've seen the poetry collection. That rhyme was in her diary."

"I took her out a few times, but she was needy. Too young for me, really. I ended our relationship." He sounded almost sincere, but I detected the break in his story.

"Did it have anything to do with the prenup you had with your wife about affairs. You'd lose a lot if she divorced you, wouldn't you?"

"That's none of your business. I broke off—"

"Did Hallie threaten to tell your wife or someone who knew her?

His jaw tightened and he slid the truncheon out of its harness. "Hallie's death was a mistake," he said sharply. "She got drunk. Fell in. I tried to grab her. I—I panicked."

"And left without a word. Just like you did with Andie."

He lunged so quickly, I barely escaped a full-on hit, but the baton caught my hand, knocking the duplicate nautilus out into the reeds surrounding the dock.

"*Merde!*" I gasped, my hand pulsing with pain, and I tried to put distance between us.

Fury blazed in Glenn's eyes as he lunged for me again, swinging the weapon like a baseball bat. It caught my knee and as a blast of pain shot up my leg, I crashed to the edge of the dock. A scream rose in the air. I was sure it was me. Where the hell was the rescue squad?!

I tried to push up, but my leg gave out as another jolt of pain came from my knee. Before I completely registered it, a boot kicked me in the side … once, then twice. The third time resulted in a shove off the edge of the pier.

Desperate, I grabbed for the edge on the way down, but missed the dock. As I hit the water, I heard the scramble of the deputies coming onto the wooden platform. Conklin's voice rang out. "Isla!"

My head banged into something hard—one of the support posts—on the way down, and everything went lights out. When I opened my eyes a short time later, I almost inhaled a lungful of water before I realized I was underwater. I tried to orient myself, with no clue which way was up.

Everything was dark as I floated by pond scum and some drowned reeds. If they were anchored, the other way was up, I reasoned and pushed upward. While my hand and knee ached, the pain wasn't as severe as it had been. The cold water helped, but the rest of my body didn't appreciate it. My jacket tugged me down, yet I didn't want to shrug it off.

After a minute or two, I realized I was swimming down as the reeds floated away, untethered. Double *merde*, I thought, wondering why I channeled my mother's favorite expression. Turning, I spotted the underwater lights, dim but at least a direction to the surface. My lungs burned as I forced myself to swim, shoving against a current. The surface shimmered above me—just out of reach. But I wasn't done yet.

Not that way, a voice said in my head. It sounded like Andie. Since when did I hear her ghostly voice? *Get out of the current.*

The pond didn't have a current, did it? But the water did seem to pull me in a certain direction. Wind, maybe? Feeling like my lungs would burst any moment, I shoved hard to the side at an upward angle and broke the surface. I gasped for air, drawing in two shallow breaths before I felt myself slipping under again.

Taking a deep breath, I looked around for the shore but spotted the head of the pooka about to break the surface. Had the illusion tech triggered? Or was it something else, something older, pulling it toward the surface? Did my eyes deceive me or was Hallie perched on its head? Hair soggy and coated with scum and some rushes, she motioned for me to swim to the horse figure.

A wave overtook me, pushing me under. After a blink or two, I saw the pooka and dog paddled to it, pulling myself onto the upper foreleg of the rearing beast. I hoped it was sturdy enough to hold my weight. Five heartbeats later, it broke the pond's surface, hauling me up with it. The puca glowed with an ethereal light, making me question if I was among the dead now.

I gazed toward the head where Hallie still sat, waving at me. Then I tuned my head toward the dock where bright lights now lit the platform. Three officers had Glenn face down on the pier while they handcuffed him. The capture had taken a while if they were just getting him. How long had I been under? And where was Conklin?

The second question was answered a couple of minutes later as Conklin swam up close to the horse. "Isla, are you okay?"

"Hell, no! I'm not. I almost drowned!"

He grinned and tossed a hook attached to a line up to me. Of course, I missed catching it and nearly slid off my slippery perch. He shook his head, got closer, and tossed it up again. "Catch it and hold on to it. Wrap the rope around your waist and I'll pull you back to shore."

"Not with the pooka," I replied, fearing he would ruin our display.

"No. Not with the pooka. Once you're secure, slide back into the water and leave the rest to me."

I followed instructions although it felt like my right hand was all thumbs and it ached, By the time I managed it, the pooka started descending again. I waited until I was waist deep before letting go.

Conklin pulled on the line and the tug toward the dock started. He held onto the strong rope, but I soon realized they had a portable wench on the dock and two officers pulled both of us back to it.

He stayed in the water until I made it to the dock, then he undid the rope and hauled me out of the water onto the mud and grass shore. I rolled over and spit up water as my stomach heaved it out. Not my finest hour.

"Isla!" I heard Katie scream and raised my hand, unable to speak.

"She's okay," Conklin said, breathing hard. "EMTs are on the way.

I wanted to say I was fine, but I didn't feel it. I couldn't even speak without more water pouring out of my mouth. Icky pond water at that. I was lying in the mud, coughing up dirty water. Ugh.

I heard a commotion above, a shout and a bit later, Rolf was leaning over me. He lifted me like a kid in his arms and carried me up onto the landing. "It's okay, baby. You're safe now. Help will be here in a bit, and you'll be fine," he murmured.

He took off his jacket and laid it over me, mumbling something about needing to get the wet clothes off. I laid my hands on top of his. I liked him but he wasn't undressing me in public.

Conklin dragged up beside me, Katie at his side. "You scared me, girl."

Fair enough, I conceded. I scared me. I croaked at him. "We got ... him! Right?"

He looked over at a deputy, Walsh—the only woman on the force, and she nodded. She bore blankets in her arms and handed them to Katie who dutifully covered me with one and wrapped the other around her man.

"Yeah, we did. My team took care of it, and he's on his way to jail."

The pond water clung to me like a memory. Hallie was gone. Andie was gone. But Glenn wasn't getting away with it this time.

Katie had a thermos full of coffee and poured cups for Conklin and me. By this time, I was lying with my head in Rolf's lap, and he helped steady my hand to drink. After a grateful swallow, I muttered, "Next time, I'm using a stunt double."

Everyone around me chuckled. Then the EMTs arrived, and the fun really began with the high-speed ride to the hospital.

The ghosts had spoken. The living had answered. But the story wasn't done—not yet.

Chapter Twenty-Five
The Last Light

I OVERSLEPT THE NEXT day, not moving until noon, and even then, I struggled to get up. I ached all over and a glance in the mirror showed I'd acquired a few bruises in the scuffle with Glenn. The hospital had released me after x-rays, bandages on my hand, one knee, and a check up to be sure I was okay. Conklin went through the same ordeal just for jumping in to pull me out. I had a bottle of antibiotics since I'd swallowed pond water, but I declined to spend the night under observation.

Even after a cup of coffee, I felt like a limp noodle, dragging myself from the kitchen to the living room where I could elevate my leg on the ottoman. But we'd gotten Glenn Harper. I poured a second cup and picked up my phone. Three voicemail messages from Katie and four text messages, checking on me. Conklin had called once. Sensible man.

I leaned back against the sofa, put my feet on the coffee table, and reflected on the confrontation. I'd been careful but hadn't been prepared for Glenn to come after me with a weapon. I'd underestimated his physical fighting ability. But my time in the water was foggy. Did I actually hear Andie's ghost or see Hallie on the puca or was I hallucinating it? I wanted to believe the former.

The ring tone for Katie drew my attention and I picked up my phone. "Hi, Katie," I croaked out, my voice sounding rough.

"How are you feeling?" she inquired.

"Stiff and sore. I just got up. How's Conklin?"

"He's fine. I had brunch with him this morning, and he's in a great mood after catching Harper last night. We did it!"

"Yeah, we did. Did he hear the bit about Hallie?" I wanted to verify the confession had implicated Harper in her death as well. My voice lacked the enthusiasm of hers, but it felt anti-climatic at this point. Still, our plan had worked and that deserved a celebration. But not today.

Katie detected my tone. "I think so. You need to ask him. You're not fully rested, are you?"

"No," I agreed. "I slept late and I'm ready to crawl back to bed. But I want to know what happened."

"Call Kevan before you go back to sleep. He'll fill you in."

"I will." I took another sip of coffee.

"You scared me last night." Katie's voice sounded unusually somber.

"I scared me, too. That pond is an eerie place at night. I need to thank your boyfriend for pulling me out."

"He didn't hesitate. Listen, Isla, you rest today and tomorrow. No maze or haunted house. You got that?"

"No challenge from here. Thanks, Katie." After I ended the connection, I dragged myself to the kitchen for the third cup, then stretched my arms and legs, feeling more muscles registering their complaint. And I was hungry. I threw two pieces of bread in the toaster and reached for the peanut butter, pulling a shoulder muscle in the process.

How many muscles does it take to evade a man, duck, and get kicked into a pond big enough to be a lake, then panic and try to get out? More than I would have thought.

I took my toast and strolled onto the patio. With my robe on, I was warm enough in the cool mid-day sun and it felt good against my face. After I ate, I called Conklin.

"How do you feel?" he asked.

I told him. "Sore, aching, and groggy. And tired, really tired."

"That sounds about right. It isn't just the physical effects but also the emotional and psychological impact."

"All that?"

He made sense, I conceded. It all felt like too much had happened.

"Yeah. Especially when you know someone you're setting up for the fall. It's less emotional when the person is a stranger or a slight acquaintance. But someone you've been working with. That's a hard one."

I countered his evaluation with what Glenn had done. "Did he confess?"

"Oh, boy, did he ever. And we have the recording of the conversation on the landing."

"To both murders?" I pressed. I wanted to get him for Hallie as well.

"Yes, even though he tried to claim it was an accident but eventually broke down. He said the girl was trying to blackmail him, threatening to tell his wife. How did you know he did it, Isla?"

"Her journal held a lot of clues, my intuition, and a little rubber duck." Which I needed to return to the Alford's pond. I'd take both toys back tomorrow. I wasn't doing another thing today except resting.

"What happens with the Whispering Nautilus?" I'd pondered its fate, along with the danger of anyone owning it.

"Well … the SO's attorney has contacted the Istanbul museum that still has a finder's fee posted. They want it back, but the only question is who gets the fee. Fenmore has a receipt for his winning bid although the object was stolen. Our attorney explained we couldn't return it until the trial was complete and the evidence released. I suspect there could be a couple of claims filed for its possession, but ultimately, it belongs to Istanbul."

"It's too dangerous for a single individual to own," I said, feeling the curse on it was too powerful.

"I agree. The museum says they're aware of its power and have a special display for it. Much safer now than when it was stolen." His chuckle sounded genuine, and I suspected his influence would guide the artifact home when the courts were done with it.

I headed for my bed to continue with my rest.

THREE HOURS LATER, AUNT Daphne shouted into my ear. "Wake up, Isla. We still have some business to conclude."

My eyes popped open, and I stared into my aunt's ghostly face peering down at me.

"Go away," I murmured and closed my eyes.

"Get up or I will go away and never come back." She sounded annoyed.

"Is that supposed to be a threat?" Nonetheless, I raised my head, and my eyes met the frown on her face.

"And here I was … worried about you. Those two girls worked hard to save you."

I sat up, still unwilling to go anywhere. "I wasn't that close to death, and those nurses were helpful, but—"

"Not the nurses! I'm talking about Hallie and Andie. It wasn't easy for them to go into the pond. Bad memories, you know. Yet they did. Andie helped you get oriented and pointed in the right direction while Hallie … Well, Hallie was brilliant. She rode that fake pooka to the surface and scared Harper so much he froze."

That got my attention. "He saw her?"

"He saw something ,.. the same thing everyone else watching did … a sea witch riding a pooka … and the thing looked real. "

"The witch?"

"The pooka. It may have been the mockup the tech boys made, but Hallie … and you … made it look real and otherworldly. And that's not all. Harper kept babbling that she'd spoken to him, saying, "Your punishment is coming … I won't forget.""

"For real?" My jaw dropped to a new low.

"By the time the deputies reached him, he was ready to confess everything." Daphne's eyes twinkled as she laughed. Then she sobered. "Now let's go get those spirits to their next destination."

How could I say no even if I thought it could wait a day?

My aunt was determined we had to do it now, saying, "We must help. Jonathan hasn't seen or held his wife in almost two hundred years. Poor Abigail has been crying on the third floor as long without feeling her husband's lips on hers. Jon has been hoping this will release them."

I got dressed, threw some food in the bowl for Higgins, who seemed standoffish today, not even coming over for a chin scratch.

"Cats are sensitive to magic," Daphne said when I commented on his behavior. "He probably detects a scent of the wild magic thrown around last night."

"Or the icky pond," I muttered. I still smelled of It despite showering last night and again a few minutes earlier.

On the way down in the elevator, I thought about how we would free the spirits. "Do you know how to do this, Auntie?" I asked, leaning on the cane I'd borrowed from the hospital.

"Not entirely," she admitted. "I know a few ways to release a spirit, but I know whatever is holding them here must be satisfied for them to move on."

"Any idea what that might be?" I led the way to the car in the back lot.

"Well, with Andie and Hallie, I believe it was bringing their killer to justice. But I think Jonathan and Abigail may have any number of triggers."

Well, that narrowed it down.

We arrived at the mansion two hours before the first visitors invaded. I hoped we had enough time. Gary and Tony were in the dining room, patching up damage and sweeping debris like it was just another Tuesday.

Gary spotted me and strolled over, wiping his hands on a rag.

"Dudette, what happened to you? You look like you wrestled a banshee."

"It's a long story. Thanks for coming in to clean. It was a mess." I hesitated. "Was that a real ghost last night?"

He scratched his head. "Eh… I'm leaning poltergeist. But I think it's gone now. Or at least groovin' on a coffee break."

He absorbed the moment, then tilted his head. "Isla, how long've you been seeing ghosts?"

It was a fair question, but I hedged. "I don't actually see them. More like… I see what they do. Like throwing things around."

Gary blinked, then gave a slow nod, like he was recalibrating. "Cool. That came in handy last night. Let's hope tonight's show doesn't come with bonus effects."

I moved on, cautiously going to the second floor where Daphne chatted with Jonathan. When she touched his arm, I could see and hear him. Subtly motioning to move to the end of the hall, I herded the two ghosts out of visual range of the lower floor. I didn't need any of the crew to see me talking to myself. My secrets were slipping out and soon half the town would be whispering that I could see dead people.

Once in the less visible area, I asked, "Is there something your wife needed or wanted done before her death that might be keeping her here?"

Jonathan, looking dapper for a two-hundred-year-old ghost, concentrated, thinking back probably. "Not anything specific that I can recall. She planned for the baby, made a quilt for his crib, but that was completed. Perhaps the only thing I can think of is that she didn't get to even hold our son for more than a minute before she died."

Well, that was traumatic, but not something we could help her complete. Besides, their son was also dead now and wouldn't that have released her?

"What about the baby she lost?" Daphne asked.

"Abigail planned for her also. She already had a name picked out, Celeste Marie. Her grave is on the hill in the backyard." His eyes grew cloudy as he remembered the details.

"Did she have a special item, something she might have connected with?" I asked.

A sad smile touched his lips. "She had a baby doll; one she'd had for years. When she was expecting Celeste, she cradled it a lot. She was devastated when she miscarried and hid the doll away, not wanting to see it to remind her of the loss."

The doll in the crib, I thought. "Did she get it out again when she was pregnant with your son?"

"No. She said it was bad luck. I'd set up the turret room with everything for Celeste, so I moved the doll into the crib there after her death."

I shot a look at Daphne. "That might be it." Turning back to Jonathan, I asked, "Can I reach the turret room from here?"

"Of course. The stairs go all the way to the top, but the door is locked. Abigail is on the third floor, the fourth is the servants' quarters and the narrower stairs go to the turret. The key is in the closet on the left just before the room. It's hanging on a key rack."

"I'll meet you there," Daphne said and blinked out, leaving me to make the climb with my achy body and contused knee. But she blinked back before I made it to the steps.

"I can't enter the room. Same as when you found it. Someone put a protective spell on it to keep spirits out. It's the only explanation." She crossed her arms, a dour look tightening her face.

"But Hallie was in it," I countered. "How did she get in? Unless she was the one who set the spell." Was it possible?

I turned and climbed the stairs, Daphne floating along beside me.

By the time I made it to the turret level, I was huffing and puffing. How could it seem worse than the climb from the den? I leaned against the wall, then checked the closet. There was an old-fashioned key on a rack, just as Jonathan had said.

When I unlocked and stepped inside, Daphne tried to follow and couldn't. "Take a look at the doll, luv. Can you sense any vibrations from it?"

I narrowed my eyes and moved closer to the doll. Cute, wearing a darling dress, and a masterpiece of 19th century dollmaking, but nothing to indicate it carried either memories or magic. "That's not it."

I kept my eyes squinted, moving from one location to the next, focusing on small objects and things Abigail might have made. Nothing. I turned to the pretty dresser, about to dismiss it when I noticed a thin haze of gold and blue light coming from the top drawer.

Crossing quickly, I opened it and my vision lit up on a baby bonnet. The embroidered initials of C and M clenched it. "This is it. It glows. Abigail poured her love into making this."

Daphne hovered at the door, trying to get a peek. "I believe you are correct."

We wasted no time, taking the bonnet to the third floor where Daphne hunted for Abigail. Since I couldn't see her, I just waited, my fingers touching the fine threads and sniffing the rosemary and lavender scents from the sachet placed in the drawer.

At last, Daphne pulled a reluctant, petite, brown-haired woman from the middle bedroom. She looked shy and sadness filled her whole demeanor. Lord, had she spent almost two hundred years in mourning?

"Abigail, this is my great-great grandniece, Isla."

Smiling, I said, "Hello. I've been wanting to meet you. I've brought you something." I held out the bonnet.

She flung a hand over her mouth and her eyes lit up like candles. "My little girl's," she whispered, and reached her hand to touch it. Of course, it went through the fabric and tears formed in Abigail's eyes.

I cast a concerned glance at Daphne. Now what? The ghost couldn't hold the material.

Her lips pulled tight, frowning at the edges, my aunt said, "I don't know, dear. Do you have any feelings about it?"

"Me? You're the ghost. Haven't you encountered it before?"

"Where would I have?" She pulled her shoulders back and stared me down.

I didn't think wiggling my nose like Samantha Stevens would work, so I resorted to the Halliwell sisters instead, although there was only one of me, I wasn't a witch, and I didn't have a Grimmoire. I thought for a minute, rehearsing possible incantations in my mind. Here goes, I thought, and using a chant-like voice, said,

> *"By stitch and sigh, by mother's thread,*
> *Return the lost to love once shed."*

For a few moments, nothing happened, and I searched my mind for other ideas, then the bonnet's glow increased, and the light rose from it to encompass Abigail. She smiled and her eyes softened with the memories that returned to her.

"I am free," she whispered. "Thank you."

"Now, we need to free Jonathan," Daphne said, lifting her dress as if she would be walking downstairs.

"Maybe he can tell us what will set him free," I handed the bonnet to Abigail, and she managed to hold it.

I turned toward the door back to the stairs when Jonathan zoomed into the room. "Abigail!" he shouted and swooped his wife into his arms. "My love," he murmured. I've waited so long for this reunion."

It was a joyous moment, and somehow, I could see the ghosts. "Had my gift changed—or was it the bonnet's magic?

Abigail flung her arms around his neck, and I stepped back waving at Daphne to leave. We should give them this private time.

But Jonathan released his wife enough to turn to me. "Thank you, dear girl. You've done the impossible. It was a fortuitous day when you entered this house. We can only offer our gratitude."

A shriek came from the bottom floor, and I knew the haunted house would be active soon. "You've offered me more than that ,.. a very special Halloween and soon a bunch of visitors."

"Then we shall be away now. Our children await us." He pulled Abigail close to him, ready to depart.

"Before you go, do you know where Hallie and Andie are?"

"The other two ghosts? They've gone already. Last night. Farewell to you both." He made a half bow to me and then to Daphne. My last view was the couple as they strolled down the hallway and vanished before they got to the end.

"Well done, Isla." Aunt Daphne wiped a tear from her eye. "That was lovely, dear."

"We did it," I replied. "All of them have moved on now."

Daphne turned a thoughtful look to me. "Perhaps it's time for me also. I might go soon."

Caught off guard. I spun to her. "Leave? Forever? Aunt Daphne, what would I do without you? How will I manage the theatre?"

She huffed a small laugh. "Why do you think I stay?"

I wanted so badly to hug her, but the best I could do was the open-armed-COVID hug. She floated into me in a ghostly embrace, and a sense of warmth and love filled my soul.

AS I PULLED INTO the parking lot, my phone chimed, telling me I had a text message. It wasn't Katie or Conklin—I had special ring tones for them. I turned off Vee-dub and read the message. It was from Rolf, asking if I'd like to go to dinner tonight.

I pocketed my phone and went upstairs. I wanted to see him—but going out, bruises and all? Too many questions I didn't want to answer.

After I gave Higgins a treat, I settled in the living room and read Rolf's message again. Instead of replying, I called him. "Hi, I got your message. I'd really love to see you, but I feel kind of anti-social right now."

"Does that mean you don't want to go to dinner, or you don't want to see me?"

"No, I want to see you. Don't get the wrong idea. But you saw me last night and I look worse today." I tried to play it down some.

"I know you look a little battered," he said gently, but I think you could use a little TLC. I have another idea. I can pick up some food to go and bring it to your place. Do you like Chinese?"

God, that sounded good, and I was getting hungry. "Make it Thai from Thai Pepper and you've got a deal."

"Even better. What would my lady want?"

"I love curry with pumpkin and pot stickers. Oh, and shrimp Rangoon, Is that too much?"

"Not at all." His voice sounded like he was smiling. "I will see you in about an hour and a half."

"Can't wait." I reflected on those words as I ended the call. Did he interpret them differently than I'm hungry and eager to eat. With the raspiness of my voice, it could have sounded like I was hinting at something else.

I was definitely not up to that tonight. I tidied up the apartment a little, sprayed some air freshener, and set up the patio table with placemats, plates, silverware, and glasses. I had a couple of beers in the 'fridge. When I bought a six pack, it could last for weeks. I also had a few sparkling waters in mixed flavors.

With the patio fireplace, one of the kettle types, to keep the area warm and four solar tiki lights, we would be fine dining out there. At one hour and thirty-five minutes, I got a phone call and saw Rolf's number.

"Hi, almost exactly on time," I said.

"Yeah, well, I am standing here outside of Fort Knox. How do I get in?" His voice carried a bit of sharpness.

"Sorry, I forgot to tell you to text me when you got here. I'll come down. Are you in the front?"

"I am."

"Do me a favor and come to the back where the loading dock is? There's a small door to the right side when you're facing it."

"Sure, I can do that."

"Meet you there."

Higgins accompanied me to the elevator then darted down the stairs. He was waiting for me when I arrived. I flipped on the backstage lights and opened the door for Rolf.

He looked fantastic in tight jeans and a blue sweatshirt, holding two bags of food and a drink carrier. I reached to take the carrier out of his hands and stepped back to welcome him in. After he stepped through, he turned to look at my face. "A couple of bruises on that beautiful face, but you still look great."

A warmth rushed through me along with a flush of joy at seeing him. He brings food, he flatters, and he gazes at me like I'm the only girl in the world.

I showed him to the elevator and across to my apartment, limping all the way.

"This is amazing," he said. "Really rad. And you own this?"

"My great aunt left the theatre and the apartment to me. So, yeah, it's mine." I pointed to the sliding glass doors. "Let's go out on the patio."

In a few minutes we settled and opened the boxes of food. "What are the drinks?" I asked, adding, "I have a couple of beers in the 'fridge."

"No, thanks. This is Thai tea, and it's perfect with the food." His bright smile challenged the tiki light.

Higgins watched us from his cozy spot near the planter. "You haven't introduced me to your cat," Rolf said.

"Sorry. That's Henry Higgins, and he's an exceptional feline. He belonged to my aunt, so I inherited him. But I've known him for a long time. Higgins, this is Rolf, my new ..." I hesitated to define Rolf's status. "... friend."

Higgins looked up, stared at Rolf for about a minute before he blinked and went to sleep. I grinned. "I think you passed the Higgins test."

He laughed. "Glad to hear it. I'm also glad you're doing okay today. That was quite a kerfuffle last night."

I thought for a moment. "Yeah. But it helped me remember what matters. I can't always fix everything. But I can listen. I can help. And maybe, once in a while, I can have a normal night out."

"Define normal." He popped a shrimp puff in my mouth, delaying my answer.

"Dinner, no corpses, no cursed objects, and—if we're lucky— a cat that doesn't land in the middle of the table."

Simultaneously, we turned our heads to look at Higgins, who gave us a slow, deliberate blink.

"Well, three out of four's not bad," Rolf said, lifting his tea glass to clink against mine.

We ate and talked our way through a feast. I enjoyed Rolf a lot, liked his views, his ideas, and his sense of humor. After we ate, we cleaned up, shut down the fireplace and retreated to the living room where we watched a movie. I didn't mind his arm around my shoulder, pulling me close so I could rest my head against him. It felt natural, comfortable.

By the time the movie finished, I was ready to sleep and almost drifted off on his shoulder. He noticed.

"I better get going." He leaned into me, placing his lips on mine with a sweet touch, "You are a beautiful girl, sugar. Let's do this again. What do you say?"

"Uh hmm, when I recover more. Yeah, let's." I mumbled, then he planted another kiss, longer this time. A zing touched my heart, a jolt of something I hadn't felt in a long time—warmth, want, possibility. I leaned in, just for a second more, not ready to let it fade. It took extraordinary will power for us to separate, but he stood. 'Now, my princess in your ivory tower, will you let me out?"

Moving like a zombie, I escorted Rolf to the back door. He kissed me again and I waited in the doorway as he got into his—my eyes popped when I saw it–vintage Jaguar. He'd brought the treats, but he had some tricks of his own.

I locked up, switched on the ghost light, and shut down the backstage array, then took the elevator up. As I came to the murder board, I paused, studying all the threads of this case. Picking up a black marker, I drew an exclamation point down the middle of Glenn Harper's card. "Got 'ya!" I muttered.

The dead had found their peace. Now, it was my turn to enjoy the living.

The End ... for now.

Isla, Daphne, Higgins, and the crew return in'

A Masque of Shadows

From the Author: Thank you for reading *A Drowning at the Maze.* I hope you loved it as much as I did writing it. If you enjoyed it, please consider leaving a review at <u>Amazon</u>. Be well and avoid any stray quacks.

Read on for a Bonus Scene and an Epilog.

Bonus Chapter
A Ball for the Ages

Halloween Night

THE SECOND-FLOOR CONSERVATORY sparkled with fairy lights amid bats, black cats, and pumpkins. The tech team hadn't used the space for the haunted house, so we'd decorated it for the Halloween Ball. An oblong room, with a glass dome roof, it had once supported plants and miniature trees. Now, the shiny marble floor glistened and welcomed our guests.

Although I hadn't been sure, we'd manage to pull it off and delayed selling any tickets, we'd still sold out the fifty couples' tickets we allocated.

"It's fantastic, isn't it?" Missy asked, her eyes glowing with light glittery rose makeup surrounding them. Her gown sparkled with silver and pink shades as she'd come as Glinda, the good witch. I wasn't surprised to see her escort for the event. Gianni had dressed as the Wizard of Oz to compliment her costume. "We could have sold more tickets. Everybody is buzzing about it."

"We're doing good to get a hundred people in this space," I said as the Green Frog Band—two guitars, a bass, drums, and keyboard—a group assembled just for this occasion, started their first song of the night.

We'd closed the haunted house at eight-thirty and the ball opened at ten and would run until one a.m. Strictly for eighteen and older guests, some of the teens who just missed out grumbled quite a bit. One made me promise we'd hold a ball the next year.

In costume as Thor—what a surprise—Rolf strolled over with a cup of hot cider for me. I was not a Valkyrie but had chosen to come as a warrior princess. My braid was rolled into a knot on top of my head, and I felt the weight of the long hair pressing down. A dainty little tiara crown perched on top.

Katie looked resplendent as Belle from Beauty and the Beast, while Conklin looked like … a sheriff's deputy. She'd conquered a major hurdle in convincing him to come. Many of the attendees wore masks, so I wasn't sure who some were, but everyone was smiling and laughing, having a great time.

Then the band started playing "The Monster Mash" and soon everyone was bobbing and dancing to the beat. Rolf claimed he had two left feet, but he handled it just fine." When the band segued into "I Put a Spell on You," we shifted into a slow shuffle, mostly swaying back and forth, but he put his hand on my waist and held me like a doll, pulling me close. I dropped my head on his shoulder, enjoying the evening. It had been a while since I'd danced with someone.

The spicy sent of cinnamon and clove grew stronger as the night wore on and the cider continued to cook in the three crockpots we'd set up. A ghost light in the corner winked now and then, a short or it was sending Morse code. When we finished our fifth dance, I tugged Rolf toward the refreshment table where I switched to a cold drink and picked up a pumpkin doughnut. He took the cue, and grabbed two, then we found a couple of empty chairs.

"Reminds me of my high school prom." I bit into the doughnut.

"You decorated it for Halloween?" He gave me a "you're weird" look.

"No, not that. Just everyone dressed up and having a good time. I was thinking more about the ambiance."

"Yeah, it's nice. But we could use cozier chairs."

"Hey! We were lucky to find these." I patted the metal folding chair, like it might have been offended by the remark.

He gazed into my eyes and leaned a little closer, his face moving in for the kiss …

"It's a great party, Isla," Katie said, coming in for a landing on the chair next to me. Conklin followed slightly behind her and sat.

Rolf pulled back and took a quick sip of his drink. Moment gone.

I summoned a smile and said, "Yeah, it is. Somehow, we need to figure a way to do one next year. But we'll be at the theatre. No room to dance there."

"Don't you have rehearsal space upstairs?" Katie asked.

"You know, I think we do. On the second floor. I never go that direction when I stop there. I'll have to check it out. Maybe we'll have a Christmas Ball."

"Just don't do it after a play." Katie peeked around me and grinned at Rolf. "You look authentic in that Thor costume. Are you having a good time?"

"Absolutely. Good music, a colorful location, and refreshments. It's all good." He lifted his drink as he smiled.

"What about you, Conklin?" I asked, leaning forward to see Katie's date. He looked a bit bored. "Great costume, by the way."

He cast a challenging glance at me. "Very funny."

"No. I'm glad you came tonight. But you could have come as Sherlock Holmes."

He rolled his eyes. "At least this way everyone thinks I'm on duty so there'll be no shenanigans tonight."

On cue, the lights blinked and went out, leaving us with only candles and the ghost light in the corner.

"Don't panic!" Gary said from the stage. "It's part of the plan. This next song is really romantic, so it's time to take your partner and dance to "Love Song to a Vampire.""

Rolf reached out his hand, and we moved into the dance space, ready to do our slow shuffle. I recognized Grace's voice singing the Annie Lennox song; she poured her heart into it. As I pressed my head against Rolf's shoulder, I noticed the ghost light winked—going off then back on a few seconds later. What caused that? I tensed a little, causing Rolf to run his hand over my back.

"What's the matter? I can feel your tension?"

"Nothing, really. Except the ghost light flick …" My voice faltered as I got a glimpse—a fleeting few moments—of an unexpected gatecrashing ghost couple. Elegantly clad in masquerade costumes, Jonathan and Abigail Fairbourne waltzed across the end of the room, their bodies almost translucent. They'd come for a last dance in their home. And I could see them!

All legends say the veil between worlds is the thinnest on All Hallows Eve. How could I say otherwise after this?

"Never mind," I whispered to Rolf. "Everything is perfect."

Rolf guided us another direction and another non-paid pair of dancers flashed into view. I missed a step, almost tripped, and Rolf quickly caught me.

"Are you falling for me?" he quipped.

Recovering, I replied, "It would seem so." I smiled at him, but my eyes tracked back to the new arrivals, who were more solid-looking than the Fairbourne couple.

Across the way, the strikingly beautiful cinnamon-haired woman in a radiant golden gown twirled in the arms of a dashing Civil War soldier who looked like Clark Gable. Stunned, I couldn't believe Daphne Chase had brought her ghostly beau to the ball. Tears of joy and love slid into the corners of my eyes.

Daphne wore a remarkable black velvet necklace with an ivory carved pendant showing a profile image of a woman that looked, at least from this distance, like her. I urged Rolf to dance more toward them, so I could get a closer look.

He resisted. "What's up?"

"I just thought we could move closer to the refreshments." I pointed toward the tables that were only a few feet from my dancing spirits. "I'm getting thirsty."

"We can just walk over," Rolf slowed his steps, turning that direction."

"No, it's better if we dance over to it. I don't want to draw attention."

He chuckled but obliged, bringing me close enough to confirm the image on the pendent looked almost exactly like Daphne, but I'd never seen it before, and it wasn't in any of the things I'd inherited from her.

My aunt cast her eyes at me, then rolled them toward her partner. In my head, I heard her voice. "My beau, luv. Isn't he a stunner?"

We reached the refreshments, and Rolf handed me a glass of lemonade punch, then picked up one for himself. He raised it. "To a successful haunted house, a smashing ball, and the most bewitching woman I've ever seen."

I think I blushed if the heat rushing to my cheeks was an indication. I took a sip, then held the glass up again. "And cheers to my very handsome and charming Nordic god. Skål,"

We drank again, then we both laughed. It felt so dramatic, but also heartwarming. I glanced around, seeing my aunt and her date half a room away, waltzing through the crowd as the band changed to "Black Magic Woman."

By half-past midnight, the people were beginning to thin out as they called it an evening and headed for home. The ghosts disappeared around that time as well, leaving about half the number to party on until almost one.

I collapsed into one of the chairs while Rolf had to excuse himself for a bit. Too much lemonade punch for him; too much dancing for me. I was knackered.

Katie found me in my quiet corner. "We're leaving now. It was a fantastic ball! I had a wonderful time, and I think Kevan enjoyed himself."

I glanced past her where Conklin, waiting a few feet away, saw me and waved his hand a couple of times. He looked anxious to go.

"Glad you both came. We'll talk later." I stood to give her a hug and watched as she walked out with her man, his arm around her waist. They seemed happy.

Could I find that kind of relationship with Rolf? I sank back into the chair, wondering if it would endure.

The thought drifted away as the image of the pendant on a velvet band drifted into my mind again. I was sure my aunt had a story behind it and maybe I could pry it out of her.

For their last song of the night, the Green Frogs played "Bad Moon Rising". Nobody was dancing now, but maybe next Halloween, we'd do it all again.

The End

Epilogue

London, Present Day

THE DUST DANCED IN golden shafts of morning light as Nigel Wetherell, senior curator of the London Theatre Museum, climbed the creaking stairs to the attic of Madame Bellina's former flat.

He stepped into the musty, dimly lit room with the scent of faded patchouli, wormwood and something he couldn't identify making him sneeze. He pulled out his handkerchief and wiped his nose. Then he cast his watery eyes around and sighed at the disordered mess of ... things scattered around the space.

The old mystic had passed away two weeks ago, and her will listed the museum as guardian of her "theatrical curiosities." Most of what he spotted so far looked to be parlor trick junk: fading tarot cards, palmistry pamphlets, a crystal ball that might once have doubled as a fishbowl. Trinkets dangled on chains, none of the stones in them real, but cheap knockoffs she'd sold to unsuspecting marks.

One shelf held three decades worth of playbills from London shows. "Hmm," he mumbled. Sorting through the first few. "Maybe the old bat might have a few of the ones we're missing."

Near the top of an older stack, he found three playbills in a row that were signed by Daphne Chase from three different plays. His old lips tightened in a fond smile. She'd been quite the darling of the London theatre scene.

Then he found the trunk, large enough for a whole traveling wardrobe.

Black lacquer. Bronze fittings. A broken wax seal still clinging to the lid. And a handwritten tag in looping script:

For Lady Daphne Chase — care of the Playhouse Theatre, Arbordale, California, U.S.A.

Nigel ran his gloved fingers across the brass inlay. The design shimmered faintly in the dim light — a theater mask flanked by thistles and lilies. A stylized sun crowned it all.

Curious, he pried the lid open, pieces of the wax seal drifting to the floor.

A three-foot mirror lay face down over a handmade, worn quilt. With practiced ease, he lifted it, seeing a thin black silk hanging off the front and placed it, face first against the wall. A mirror in mourning was a bad sign, something he didn't wish to disturb. Lifting the quilt, he found a trio of lovely gowns from period plays and a large wooden, ebony box with a simple clasp and a scarlet scarf holding it closed. When he lifted the box, a light shaking emanated from within it. He almost set it back down, undisturbed, but his curiosity got the better of him. Sliding the scarf off, he opened the container.

Inside, swaddled in faded blue velvet, lay a single item: an elaborately carved masque. Ivory and gold. The eye sockets seemed... too deep. Almost alive.

His stomach tightened, like someone walked on his grave.

Fingers shaky, he lowered the lid with caution and replaced the scarf. Every instinct told him to never touch it again. He replaced the quilt and the mirror, exactly as he'd found them, and closed the trunk.

He reached for the clipboard he'd tucked under his arm and scribbled, flipped it and read the notes from the will. Yes, it was as he thought. He made a note on the top sheet:

To be shipped via express courier to: Playhouse Theatre –Arbordale, California. Return to sender: Not applicable.

He hesitated, casting a forlorn look at the trunk. "A pity about the dresses," he whispered. "But best they all remain together."

Then he added:

Contents: Personal artifacts belonging to Lady Daphne Chase. Do not open.

As he walked away, the shadows lengthened, and a soft sigh followed him out.

A Masque of

Shadows

A Spotlight Sleuth Mystery

Book Four

Rene Averett

Coming in Summer 2026

Chapter One
A Trunk Full of Trouble

NEVER IN MY TIME with the Playhouse Theatre did the cast, crew, and media show so much interest in an upcoming play. Ben Pellet, the director, pulled his cast around him like a football coach prepping his team for the winning touchdown.

"Now, Adrian Hale will be here any minute. Remember, he's only another actor and let's keep this professional," he admonished.

"Does that mean we can't ask for his autograph?" Grace inquired, a worried crease breaking the smooth finish of her forehead.

"Not right off," Ben snapped. "After we've worked with him for a bit, then you can ask. We want to present ourselves as a top-rated, dedicated, and experienced company."

Ha! I thought. We were all bundles of nerves with the Academy Award nominated actor gracing our stage for the upcoming five nights of charitable performances to benefit the Arbordale Children's Network's annual fundraising drive.

Katie, my BFF, paced the back of the stage, trying to calm herself before the man arrived. She had signed up for a bit part in the production just to get a chance to see Adrian Hale up close. During the two weeks prior to Father's Day, she wouldn't normally take any time away from the candy shop she owned with her mother. She must have pestered Roseann to death to get her to agree.

I noticed Missy Evans, our wardrobe mistress lingering by the curtains at stage right. Although she wasn't flustered by clothing anyone, she seemed unusually anxious about costuming a Hollywood star for our Victorian play, *An Unquiet Woman*. She'd even taken a small role to make her stage debut.

So far, our crew had been rehearsing for a few days, but this would be the first run through with Hale. I glanced at the clock on the back wall to check the time—almost three. He should arrive at any moment. On the thought, a commotion of several voices, one of them being the Irish brogue of Eamon—our guard, a decidedly English voice, and the clunk of something being pushed through the stage door echoed up the hallway to the stage. What the heck?

With a glance at Ben, I shrugged and trotted toward the stage door. When I came nearer, I saw our guest actor just inside, leaning back against the wall while a man in brown delivery clothing wheeled an aged-looking trunk toward the stage. Eamon had an arm out of the exit, seemingly pushing people back. "No, you cannot come in. This is a rehearsal, no press allowed," he declared with enough volume for me to hear.

"Come on, fella. Just one photo. Gimme a break, okay?" A man's voice asked. I assumed he was a news photographer.

"Sorry. No. Get a press pass for the open rehearsal on Wednesday." With that, Eamon shoved the door closed and secured the lock.

I came up to the trunk rolling down the hall. "Hello. What's this?"

The man halted and let the dolly settle. "Special delivery for the theatre. You Daphne Chase?"

I eyed the trunk, taking in the battered exterior and dark coloring of the leather. "No, Daphne was my great-great aunt."

The guy nodded and picked up a clipboard that was hanging off the dolly. "Can she sign for this?" He held the board with the paperwork out to me.

"Uh, no. Not in her current state. She passed away five years ago. I own the theatre now." Who on earth would be sending this to my aunt?

He took a minute to absorb what I'd said, then replied, "Can you sign it then?"

"Who's it from?" I wasn't sure if I should accept this. No one told me it was coming, so who would send it without at least notifying the theatre?

After a glance at the paperwork, he said, "Came from the London Theatre Trust, it looks like. Don't know nothin' else about it." He paused and pushed a pen toward me. "You gonna sign or what?"

I spared a glance at Adrian Hale, who was trapped behind the delivery. An amused expression covered his marquee handsome face, and I detected a twinkle in his periwinkle blue eyes. "I'm so sorry, Mr. Hale. I wasn't expecting this." I motioned to the trunk but reached for the clipboard to sign the paper. "Do I get a copy of that?" I asked, pointing to the delivery slip. I would need to contact the shipper to find out any more information.

The man nodded, took the clipboard back, and tore off the bottom sheet of the triplicate shipping form. Old school, I thought. Whoever shipped it adhered to paper. Following up the thought, he held up a tablet and pointed to the line at the bottom of the digital form. "An initial will do, ma'am."

My jaw tensed. I hated it when people addressed me with it, like I was an old biddy. Not even thirty yet. But I scribbled my initials and pointed toward the stage. "Now, can you take it to the backstage area? It's just a little beyond the end of this hallway?"

Then, it was my turn to lean against the wall, so the trunk could get past me. I turned my head to speak to Adrian again and he laughed. "Most entertaining reception I've encountered at a theatre." His rich, velvety voice coated me like a layer of warm caramel. Delicious.

I might have blushed; at least, my face felt warm. "I'm Isla Reed, the owner of the theatre. Welcome to Arbordale."

"Delighted to be here," Adrian answered graciously, resuming a proper walking position now that the trunk had passed.

"I'm sorry, Miss Isla," Eamon said. "I tried ta get the lad in safely before those poppy-rot-zies stormed the door, then the fella with the trunk pushed through."

"No harm done, sir," Adrian answered before I could reply. "Thank you for dealing with them."

I motioned to the actor, adding my two cents. "What he said, Eamon. You handled it fine."

I swung around to walk back to the stage. "Come this way, Mr. Hale, the—"

"Adrian, please. Mr. Hale is too formal."

My smile was tiny, almost shy. "As you wish, Adrian. The cast and director are waiting for you."

And—they were. The entire cast, principals, minor roles, director, and stage crew had gathered. Katie stood to one side with a GoPro video in her hand, filming as we walked in. She offered to help with publicity for the show, but I was concerned she might go a little overboard. I introduced Adrian to Ben, and the director took over after that, identifying each of the principals by their character names.

As I watched, I thought Ben might be more nervous than any of the rest. Made sense. He was the one who would tell the star what to do. While the director briefly ran through the first few scenes, his new lead actor listened attentively and politely, nodding his head now and then.

Katie sank into the seat next to me and released a deep sigh. "Isn't he gorgeous? In person, he is even more dishy than on the screen." Her eyes remained locked on Adrian like he was some sort of god. I admitted he stunned with those magnetic eyes, lightly tanned skin, and, well, just about everything about him.

"Better than Conklin?" I queried, reminding Katie she had a pretty good-looking boyfriend.

She blinked and turned her eyes to me. "Well … no. I mean Adrian Hale's a dream-like actor, but Kevan's my real deal. That guy probably has an ego as big as his fan base."

With a wry smile, I let my thoughts drift to the mysterious trunk sent to the theatre. I pulled the delivery receipt out of my pocket and peered at the sender's address:

London Theatre Trust

12 Marlowe House, Penbury Lane,

Southbank, London SE1 9QJ

On the stage, Adrian suggested they might do a read through, so he could identify who each actor was playing and their interpretations. Ben agreed, a look of relief flashing across his face as he suggested they could sit on the floor. After an eyeroll, I interrupted before everyone sat. "We have at least a dozen folding chairs in storage. Gary, can you and a couple of your team bring them in?"

"Sure, Isla. I'm on it." Our lead set designer motioned to a couple of his guys to follow. Before they went out, Danny Marino, my former husband—until the annulment— caught up with them to help.

While the actors chatted a bit, Grace easing closer to Adrian with a charming smile covering her face, I gave in to my curiosity about the trunk, mounted the stairs, and strode to the back of the theatre's right wing, where the delivery man had deposited the awkwardly large box. More like a steamer trunk than a smaller storage one, it was about the size of a desk. If it was Aunt Daphne's, why didn't she bring it with her when she moved to America? Why send it now? Since it was addressed to her, the sender didn't know she was deceased.

Two straps held the box closed and although it had a keyhole in the lock, it didn't seem to be engaged since it bulged out a little, making a shallow opening behind it. Maybe the person who sent it put a note inside to explain more. Kneeling, I undid the straps on each side, pausing to admire the beautiful bronze plate, and pushing them away, then moved to the lock. I sensed Katie and Missy coming up behind me, their curiosity aroused.

"Are you sure it's safe?" Katie asked, her voice a low whisper.

"It's a trunk, not a bomb," I muttered. But it was a fair question. Something about it felt off, like it might be booby trapped or something. "Maybe you'd better stand back," I told them. By now a few more people arrived, including someone I'd never seen before—a thirtyish fellow a little taller than Katie with dark brown hair and gray eyes. Then I recalled Ben had brought on a new actor for a bit role. Even Adrian wandered over with Ben right at his elbow.

"It's just an old trunk, evidently my aunt's," I told them. I flipped the lock back and slid my fingers under the lid.

"Ah, old theatre ghosts, no doubt," Adrian quipped as I raised the lid. He wasn't wrong … if you considered a trunk filled with stage props from a cloth covered mirror to an ebony box with a red scarf around it, several gowns, a veil, and a few Spanish fans to be ghosts of another era. But I didn't see an envelope or note to tell me anything more about the contents. Were all these old stage props my aunt had used? Why would anyone send them here?

As if summoned by the trunk, a black and white streak crossed the stage, howling all the way. Higgins skidded to a halt, his hair standing on end, then arched his back and hissed at the trunk. "What is it, Higgins?" I asked, concerned enough with the cat's reaction that little chill bumps rose on my arms. Narrowing my eyes, I examined the trunk again, seeing a weird green aura emanating from two objects within it. The ebony box leaked a muddy green halo, looking malevolent enough to deter opening it, and the mirror seemed to hold an image within it.

"Get back—" I said, rising and urging everyone to get away from it.

But the new guy had darted forward and grabbed the box. "What's in this?" he asked, opening it before I could speak. His eyes grew wide, as he lifted an ivory mask with intricate carvings on it. His mouth widened with excitement as he lifted it to his face.

"Stop!" I said, but he'd already pressed it to his skin.

"Behold! I am king of the fairies, and I control everyone at this—"

His voice broke off as he collapsed to the floor like a dropped bag of sand. His legs twitched twice, then he stilled on the floor.

A few feet away, the mask rested in its ominous glow. Caught in the shock of the now unconscious–I hoped not dead—man, I knelt to feel for a heartbeat and didn't see Adrian pick up the mask.

"This is an unusual object," he commented. "I think it's reminiscent of an early nineteenth century masquerade ball style—" His voice broke off, and as I looked toward him, he dropped the relic, stumbling back.

He'd gone pale, his eyes huge with surprise or alarm. Before I moved, Missy hurried to his side, guiding him to the set's lounge chair. He leaned forward, catching his breath, then demanded, "What the hell was that?!"

"A little too much of haunts from the past," Missy told him.

Meanwhile, I'd verified the new actor wasn't dead, but he wasn't good either. "He's alive, but—"

Katie interrupted me. "I've called 911, Isla."

I nodded, turning my narrowed eyes to the green-shrouded mask laying so innocently on the floor, begging someone else to pick it up.

"No one touches that mask—until we know what it is."

A Masque of Shadows coming in the summer of 2026.

ACKNOWLEDGMENTS

AS WITH ANY BOOK, I have people to thank for their help and encouragement while I worked on it. A huge thanks to my beta readers, who helped me fine-tune this story and pointed out little plot holes. To my dear friend Patricia, who has always been my first reader and supporter. To Michael and Aaron, who encourage me and profess to love my books. Thank you all for keeping me going when it gets rough.

A special thanks to Diana and Russell, who provide many answers about working in both community and professional theater. With my limited experience in working in volunteer theater, I turn to them often.

Thank you to everyone who has read or will read my books. I appreciate all of you and hope you are entertained by my "Spotlight Sleuth." More books will be coming. The best way to let me know how you liked it is a review and/or a note to me at: RPAverett@gmail.com

Please check out my website at www.RPAverett.online.

ABOUT THE AUTHOR
Rene Averett

When I was a child, I used to dream mystery stories. But I always woke up before I got to the end! Later, I fell in love with fantasy, science fiction, and spy books. (Curse you, Ian Fleming!) But I always enjoyed a good mystery in my books. Over time, I finally wrote stories with the elusive endings.

Although my Isla Reed books are my first foray into a paranormal cozy mystery, I've written books under two of my pen names in both fantasy and romantic suspense that include mystery elements. So, I've never ventured far from the mystery aspects.

I was born in West Texas and migrated farther west after graduating from high school, living in California before backtracking to Nevada. I've lived in the Reno area for enough years to almost be considered a native. I share my home with my longtime companion, a whirly-gig poodle, and three affectionate felines.

Where to find me:
Substack: https://reneaverett.substack.com/
Facebook: https://shorturl.at/gtyDH
Amazon Author Page: https://shorturl.at/8eHDZ
Website: www.RPAverett.online

Also by Rene Averett

Cookbooks

Meals for Two – Low Carb Magic

Sweets By the Season – Low Carb Magic

Magic Muffins for a Low Carb Lifestyle (eBook only)

Breakfast Choices for a Low Carb Lifestyle (eBook only)

Mexican Food for a Low Carb Lifestyle (eBook only)

***

Spotlight Sleuth Paranormal Mystery Series

A Fatal Sweetness (Book 1)

A Harvest Moon Murder (Book 2)

A Drowning at the Maze (Book 3)

A Masque of Shadows (Book 4) – Summer 2026

A Trapdoor Tragedy (Prequel via website)

A Phantom Reunion (Christmas 2024 Short Story – website)

FROM PYNHAVYN PRESS:

You might enjoy some of these books from our authors:
Angelina Fasano
Urban Fantasy
Vampires Suck!

YA Urban Fantasy
Alpha's Song (Les Loupes Garou*)*
Beta Rising (Les Loups Garou)

***

Riona Kelly
Romantic Suspense Fantasy
Cat Whisperer

Romantic Suspense
Bitter Vintage
Echoes of the Past – American Rose Abroad
Signature of a Soul – American Rose Abroad

***

Russell D. Jones
Science Fiction
Orbital Strain
Gearforged: Undercity Scars Book 1

***

Nicole Frens
URBAN FANTASY
CryoShift (Cryoverse Book 1)
Flight To Tomorrow: The CryoShift prequel (Cryoverse)

Mary Weatherington
POLICE DETECTIVE MYSTERY

For Eleven Million Reasons	(Book 1)
$ide $wiped	(Book 2)
The Gentle Giant Returns	(Book 3)
Sometimes Love's Just Murder	(Book 4)

Lillian I. Wolfe
URBAN FANTASY/ MAGICAL REALISM
Funeral Singer Series

A Song for Marielle	(Book 1)
A Song for Menafee	(Book 2)
A Song of Betrayal	(Book 3)
A Song of Forgiveness	(Book 4)
A Song of Redemption	(Book 5)

Sci-Fi Fantasy
O'Ceagan Saga

O'Ceagan's Legacy	(Book 1)
In Strange Waters	(Book 1.5)
Outer Rim	(Book 2)

The Heliotian Cycle

Novice Mageistra: Empty Promises (Book 1) (Coming 2025)

Rising Mageistra: Recalibration (Book 2) (Coming 2026)

TIME TRAVEL
Time Threads

Time Walker (Book 1)

Splintered Time (Book 2)

Time Reversed (Book 3) (Spring 2026)

***

CHILDREN'S BOOKS
By Rene Averett

Connie and the Missing Ladle – Connie Cooks (K to 3rd)

Storm Squad Rising - *(Mid-grade)*

***

By Arlene Llewellyn (Illustrated by James Gayles)

Holly's Happy Heart *(K to 3rd)*

***

For updates on any books released through **Pynhavyn Press**, please visit our website and sign up on our mailing list. We only use this to notify you of any upcoming and imminent book releases.

www.pynhavynpress.com